SPIES LIKE ME
MITHOS
BOOK ONE

LEXIE WINSTON

NEIGHPALM
PUBLISHING

About the Author

Lexie Winston has been an astronaut, rock star, princess and time traveller. In her dreams. But none of the dreams have lived up to what becoming an author has been like. She gets to live in a world of pure imagination, and her heroines get to do the things she's always wished she could.

When not writing books, Lexie is a mother of two gorgeous teenagers and the wife to a patient and understanding man. They live in Western Australia and are lorded over by a black toy poodle. She loves camping, reading and if her iPad was stolen, her world would explode. (It has the kindle app on it.)

And check out my website at lexiewinston.com

And you can find all my links at
https://linktr.ee/LexieWinston

Also by Lexie Winston

The Collectors Division

(Paranormal Reverse Harem Series)

Guardian

Guardian's Blood

Guardian Ascending

Collector's Division Omnibus

Neighpalm Industries Collective

(Enemies to Lovers Reverse Harem)

Abandoned Girl

Broken Girl

Tormented Girl

Wanted Girl

Cherished Girl

Loved Girl

Superficial Girl - Jacinta's Story Part 1

Superficial Girl - Jacinta's Story Part 2

Neighpalm Industries Collective 1-3

Neighpalm Industries Collective 4-6

Seductive Sins Collection

(Reverse Harem Series)

Glorious Gluttony

Gangs, Guns, and Glory

Galaxy Circus

(Sci-Fi Reverse Harem Series)

Apprentice

Stagehand

Whisperer

Mama - Galaxy Circus Novella

Performer

A Night Most Wicked - Galaxy Circus Novella

Broken Promises

(Dark Poly Romance Series)

Secrets Kept

Lies Untold

Trust Broken

Love Found

M.I.T.H.O.S

(Contemporary RH)

Spies Like Me

First published by Neighpalm Publishing in 2023

Spies Like Me - MITHOS 1

Mobi format: 978-0-6453753-3-6
Print: 978-0-6453753-4-3

Cover design by Dazed Designs
Editing by Elemental Editing

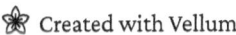 Created with Vellum

CHAPTER 1

"It's that time again, Kenzie."

My dad's back is to me as he stares out the big picture window overlooking the grounds of MITHOS's headquarters—Military Insurgent Tactical Homeland Operatives Secret. Really, it's a whole heap of words used to make up a fairly cool sounding acronym, but it also aptly describes what we are all about.

With his shoulders back and his hands clasped behind him, my dad's body is tight with tension. My eyes swing to where he's looking, searching for the source of his rigidity, but I see nothing. The acres of dark trees where his trainees can play super soldier appear ominous in the heavily clouded afternoon. The forest looks like something out of a gothic novel, beckoning a damsel to run toward it in the hopes of escaping whoever chases her, except instead of being saved, she would be swallowed up by the violent animals who roam it.

Unfortunately, nothing that exciting ever happens, and the woods are only home to a brutal version of capture the flag, but they are effective at teaching my dad's superspies in training to be on their toes.

As far as the world is concerned, the building we sit in this very moment is a private college, but it's a façade for what's concealed beneath. Deep below the wooded grounds is what we call the Lighthouse—an enormous, underground top-secret facility that trains some of the world's best spies and special operatives in the art of espionage.

Rolling my eyes at his words, I throw my boots up on his desk with a dramatic thump and rock back on the chair I'm sitting in. "When are you going to accept that none of them have been able to catch me and that there isn't much of a chance that they ever will? Give up on trying to add me to a team, Dad. It's *not* going to happen, so stop wasting our time." Yeah, I know I sound arrogant, but I have good reason to. I'm a fucking good spy.

He turns to face me, and when he sees my combat boots on his desk, he frowns and pushes them off before taking a seat across from me. He shakes his head, exasperated with me, and leans forward, propping his forearms on the desk.

"Don't be arrogant, it will be your downfall, but you're right. Up until now, nobody has caught you during one of these tests, and I agreed that if they didn't, you could remain as a solo operative, but your mother and I would worry a lot less if you had a team to back you up on your missions." The wrinkle that sits between his eyebrows is not a common occurrence. Seeing my unflappable father showing concern makes me feel guilty, so I sit up properly in my chair. If he's taking this conversation seriously, then so should I.

"Dad, you know I would annoy the fuck out of any team that ended up with me. I work well alone, and I'm damn good, even if I have to toot my own horn. Nobody looks at me and sees a spy. I'm good at blending in because they see me how they want to see me." I pause for a moment to gather my thoughts before continuing. "The reason you trained me separately from the rest of your agents was so I could be off the books. What happened that has made you and Mom paranoid? I've been in the field since I was sixteen, and I haven't had one failed mission against my name in the last six years. Not one single failure. How many other teams or operatives can you say that about?" I can hear the exasperation in my voice, and I'm sure my dad can too.

It's frustrating. How many times do I have to prove myself before they stop with these unnecessary games? Everything I just said has been repeated over the years, and even though I'm an adult now, it's still not enough.

He sighs heavily. "Only one other team has ever been that successful, but baby, Mom and I want more for you in your life than being an assassin and a ghost. It was never my intention for you to become what you have. We never wanted you to be a spy in the first place. We would have been happy with you doing anything, but you were so determined once you developed a sense of right and wrong that you wanted to be the one putting the bad guys away. You wouldn't take no for an answer, and we caved to your wants." He straightens up, the wrinkle in his forehead deepening. "I wish I'd been firmer." Guilt is thick in his tone, but I wave him off because it's not his fault.

"I know, Dad, and you have told me time and time again that it's my choice, but how could I live with myself if we let scumbags like the ones I've taken out escape and continue to commit the crimes we know they are guilty of? The justice system is heavily flawed, and I haven't assassinated anyone that I lose sleep over. Each and every man or woman I've killed deserved it, and we had the documentation to back it up. Trust me, Dad, my conscience is clear. I have to give your tech team credit, though, because they always give me what I need."

Lord fucking knows I wouldn't be able to do what I do without their help.

He scrubs a hand over his face, the stubble on his cheeks and the bags under his eyes telling me he hasn't been getting enough sleep. "Fine, but I stand by my deal. If a team beats you, then you will join them and become a permanent member."

I wave my hand again, dismissing his claim for the hundredth time. "Yeah, yeah, but we know that's not about to happen. I've beaten every single one of them before, and it's not like they are going to suddenly get the drop on me." I arch my eyebrow to emphasize my point. "Also, you know having me on an all-girls team would be a disaster. I watch some of the ones coming through the classes and want to shoot myself in the foot. What is it about women that make them so catty when they get competitive?"

I can't help the physical shudder that runs through me. Their behavior is embarrassing, and I want no part of it.

A small, secretive smile crosses his lips, but he quickly hides it and gestures for me to stand up as he walks around to my side of his desk. I stand and stretch, feeling the tension in my muscles, before giving him a hug and heading back out to the reception desk in front of his large office.

That's right, today I'm undercover as his secretary. Nobody looks twice at me as they come in for meetings with him. I have my hair pulled back in a tight bun, and I'm wearing a prudish sweater set over a beige pair of slacks. My tortoise shell glasses are large and make me look bug-eyed, aiding in the mousy secretary look. None of the teams that come here for their yearly evaluations would guess that I'm the target they are supposed to take down in their trial.

When they go through their yearly evaluations, they are given fake intel and are always instructed to capture me, the perp, for questioning. I'm then given some task I need to pretend to do, like rob a bank, assassinate a high-profile figure, or blow up a building. The teams are told it's a test, but all they will know is if they pass or fail. If they fail, then they get extra training. Sometimes they are clever enough to stop whatever it is I've been assigned to do for that trial, but none of them have ever succeeded in apprehending me.

It's a fun fucking time.

I love using my skills to thwart them. Thwart is such a great word. Anyway, it makes my life a little more interesting. I don't get sent on a lot of assignments because of my ghost status—only the most important and sensitive jobs—so there's not a whole lot for me to do, which is why I enjoy playing war games for my dad in my downtime.

Grabbing the clear-lensed glasses off my desk, I put them on and take a seat. I don't always act as his secretary, considering he has one that does the actual job, but one of his teams is coming in today. They are being assigned their yearly assessment, and they are the team I will be going up against in the hopes of beating them. Unless they upskilled since I went against them last time, I doubt that's going to happen.

Using the mouse, I bring up their file, not recognizing the mythical code name. Dad has an unholy obsession with mythical monsters. I'm pretty sure it's because his parents named him Perseus—like, what the hell, Gram and Gramps? Our bookshelves are filled with every book he can find on them. My reading material might be similar, although it has more of a paranormal romance bent than classic literature, but we choose not to discuss it.

Frowning, I double-check the file again. My head tilts to one side in curiosity as I try to rack my brain. I've never heard of Team Basilisk before, and it's throwing me off.

What the hell? Is this a new team? And why are they being tested so early in their career?

They usually get a year to settle in before they are pitted against me for their yearly evaluations.

Scowling, I flip through the pages. It's a team of seven men. There isn't a single photo of any of them in the file, nothing but their names, and that is the total extent of the information I've been given. All the other information—age, skills, and specialties—has been completely redacted. Thick black lines obscure everything that's truly important to my success.

What game is Dad playing? I press the intercom to ask him about the file full of nothing when the outer door to the office opens and in walk five men who look like they could be on the cover of GQ.

I snort internally, trying to school my features as I give them a good once over. These guys are going to be a piece of cake. I doubt there's a single one of them who has better training than I do. They are a bunch of pretty boys, though they seem to be missing two members of their team. I wonder if the file is current. Maybe they lost two members, and in punishment, Dad has them going around the country recruiting at colleges or something, because that's what they look like—quintessential college recruiters who haven't seen a day of a real assignment.

Piece of fucking cake.

I clear the file off my screen before plastering on a polite but slightly vacant smile. *Don't show too much interest, and don't look any of them in the eye.* They won't remember me, and that's the way it has to be.

"Can I help you?" I ask the one in front. Holy hell, it's all I can do not to swallow my tongue as he gets closer. The man oozes sex appeal. He's of Asian descent, and his dark gray suit looks like it's tailored to fit his body, meaning it doesn't hide the fact that he is fit. His short hair is as lustrous as onyx, but it's still long enough to run my fingers through it, and when his brown eyes meet mine, I can see flecks of red and orange in them.

Holy shit! I don't think I've ever had such a visceral reaction to a guy before, and right now, this stranger has me panting inside. In order to prevent myself from visibly reacting, I bite the inside of my cheek.

I'd always been warned about making intimate connections, and it's company policy not to date outside. It brings up unanswerable questions that, more often than not, make relationships difficult.

Also, due to my status as a ghost operative, I haven't had much contact with any of the other agents either, so I am a rather awkward loner who takes satisfaction in her job. Don't get me wrong, I'm not an innocent virgin. Sometimes I need to use sex to get the job done, but it's easy enough to detach oneself from the situation, especially if you're going to kill them or have them arrested. Feelings just never come into play, so this reaction to the yummy guy in front of me is completely unexpected. A feeling of unease starts to worm its way in, causing a rock to sit heavily in my stomach.

Give. Me. Strength.

A small chuckle has me blinking, and a light flush heats my cheeks as I realize I've been staring far longer than what's considered appropriate for someone who is supposed to act detached. Tearing my eyes away from Asian Hottie, I scan the rest of the group, trying to distract myself. Each and every one of them looks like they don't miss the gym, like ever, yet every one of them has a very different appearance. This makes sense though. When MITHOS allows teams to form, they are more likely to be approved if they offer a variety of options, so to speak, and this group seems to be very well-rounded. They also radiate this feeling of danger. Maybe there is something to this team that I need to be careful about.

Huh, Team Basilisk, why have I never heard of this team before or come up against them in one of Dad's tests?

They look too comfortable with one another and the whole process to be a new team. New teams walk into their first assessment practically pissing their pants, and these guys have an air of relaxation around them, like nothing fazes them. The sense of unease grows, and it's all I can do not to squirm with anticipation.

Jesus, send help, because this isn't like me. At all. What in the actual fuck is happening?

"You're not Gwen." My gaze moves to the man who points out the obvious, and I have to refrain from rolling my eyes. This one's wearing a black waistcoat and a long-sleeved button-up with rolled back sleeves, exposing dark mahogany tattooed forearms that almost make me drool. He has short cropped, curly black hair and eyes that are such a deep brown they are almost black as he stares at me like I'm a science experiment he wants to dissect.

"No, I'm not," I reply to Mr. Hot Chocolate, but I don't elaborate. I need to get them into Dad's office pronto before I do anything stupid or they ask too many questions and I stumble over my responses. I look back at the guy who I assume is the team leader and raise an eyebrow.

Again, someone snorts in amusement.

"Aww, pretty thing, don't be like that." This one is wearing jeans and a black, long-sleeved Henley with the sleeves pushed back over his forearms. I swear forearms are going to be the death of me. What captures my attention even more, however, are his vivid blue eyes, which sparkle behind black-rimmed glasses. He has that sexy nerd look down pat, with his tousled black hair that's long on top and shaved on the sides. "How about you tell us your name? That way we can all be friends and make this a bit more pleasant rather than awkward." The genuine smile on his face has me second-guessing my behavior. Fucking hell.

Hmm, using the friendly, boy next door routine to lull me into a false sense of security in the hopes that I might give them more information. Nice try, Nerdy Sexy, but no dice. I'm smart enough not to fall for that, so I continue to raise one eyebrow at the team leader and ignore the flirty nerd.

Again, someone snorts with amusement, and when my eyes swing to him, Mr. Latino Lovely is smirking at me, his hazel eyes crinkled with his barely contained laughter. He's wearing jeans and a T-shirt and holds himself with an arrogance that is familiar to me. This guy thinks he's all that and a bowl of sprinkles. "Well, would you look at that, someone is immune to your charm, Lathan." There's a slight hint of malice in his tone, and Lathan, Nerdy Sexy, scowls at him but doesn't respond. I feel my expression blank in response to his observation, but I don't engage.

"Hmph."

It's all I can do to stop my eyebrows from rising as the last one finally speaks up, or was that a grunt from a caveman? He has that stereotypical bad boy look with tattoos covering his arms and piercings in his eyebrow and lip, and he has shoulder-length brown hair that doesn't look like it's seen a brush recently. Apparently his face hasn't seen a razor either, considering the stubble covering his sharp jawline. Unlike the others who have put a bit of effort into what they are wearing, he has on a pair of ripped jeans and a band shirt with flip-flops. It's so totally not professional at all.

He sneers at me when my eyes meet his green ones like he wouldn't spit on me if I were on fire. Charming, but also fascinating, because the agency frowns on distinguishable features such as tattoos and piercings. They don't like it if you're easily identifiable, but from the looks of this team, that apparently means nothing to them, because Bad Boy is not the only one with tats.

"Team Basilisk, reporting to see Director Watson," Asian Hottie states, interrupting my stare down with Bad Boy, his face devoid of any emotion. It's like he's not impressed that he has to introduce the team and their reason for being here.

"Ah, of course, go right through the door, he's expecting you." I press the intercom on my desk. "Director Watson, your eleven o'clock is here," I tell him, but the team has already blown past me without another word, and I breathe a sigh of relief as they disappear into Dad's office, closing the door behind them. I can hear them through the intercom, which Dad deliberately left on, and while there's a jovial exchange of greetings, I quickly mute my end. I can feel my forehead crinkle and my lips purse. *What is Dad up to?* He's not greeting them in his usual, formal boss-like manner. It sounds like he's greeting old family friends, and that has me a little worried.

"Hey, Percy, who's the new girl out front? I haven't seen her before." That's Lathan asking the question. Dammit, I must have made an impression, and that is not what I was aiming for. Also, Percy? What the hell? Only his family calls him that.

"Gwen's out sick, so I had to call a temp agency. We have one we use occasionally, and their staff has been vetted and cleared to work for upper government agencies. She's no one important, just a pretty face with good clearance." *Ouch, Dad.* His brush-off seems to be good enough, because there are no more questions.

He invites them to take a seat and gets started straightaway. "Okay, guys, how is the new assignment coming along? Have you all settled in and established your cover?"

His question is met with grunts and groans. I can't help but roll my eyes at their reaction. Dramatic much?

"Yes, we're all firmly entrenched in the town in different capacities, but I'm going to be honest, we are really looking forward to a break after this one." That's Asian Hottie's voice, and it sends a shiver up my spine that's almost enough to distract me from gathering information, but not quite. Shaking off my reaction, I focus on the conversation.

"I know, I know. You've been undercover for a while now, and I have news on that front, but first, I have another quick assignment for you." He pauses to build up the suspense, and I roll my eyes. Again.

Dad has always had a flair for theatrics. From the outside looking in, you would only see a stern, authoritative director of a secret spy organization—or you would if it wasn't a secret, so maybe he seems like a banker or a lawyer—but the reality is, there's so much more to him. My dad has the best sense of humor. He's fun, and he's my best friend. Huh, maybe that explains why I'm so bad with people my own age.

"Intel says there's been a hit put out on me, and I need you to apprehend the assassin before they can kill me."

Did he just say what I think he did? I know he likes to surprise me with each assignment, and he's asked me to do some crazy things before, but this tops the cake. Fuck my life. I can't believe I have to assassinate my father—or at least pretend to. Surely that breaks the sacred father-daughter bond.

The team makes noises of surprise, but Dad goes on. "I'm making an appearance at a fundraising gala with my wife, and all intel indicates that they are going to make the attempt at that location. It's not like I go out in public very often, and I can't miss this one because Sadie is on the board." I hear concern and stress in his tone as he plays his role in setting up the assignment's background.

"Shoot to kill?" This voice is one I haven't heard yet, but goosebumps prickle my skin. It's silky smooth and sounds deadly. It has to be Bad Boy using more than grunts.

"No!" Dad sounds panicked, but he coughs and clears his throat before continuing. "Capture and detain only, Miller."

Miller! I quickly pull the electronic tab back up on my screen. Scanning the names in the file, I find the one I'm looking for—Miller King. At least I have one other name to put to a face, even if I don't have anything else. I tune back into the conversation.

"I want to see if we can find out who hired them. If

you can't apprehend them without lethal force, then let them go. Lathan, here's a thumb drive with everything we have on the assassin known as Phantom, which really isn't much except for a list of their escapades over the last few years. Maybe that will give you something, but they don't seem to have a solid method of operation."

"I'll check it out," Nerdy Sexy says confidently.

I know that list of information contains all my agency sanctioned hits, but apart from the name of the victims and how they were killed, there isn't any other information, nor will it tell them they were agency hits because they were all off-book and only run through Dad who acts as my handler. I don't even use the same method of assassination each time. If they dig too deeply into who the actual victims were, though, they might discover that they were all very bad people who deserved what they got, but I'm hoping they don't look that far into it. If they do, it might make them suspicious, but it won't change the parameters of the assignment. If they only stick to clues regarding my identity, then there will be nothing to discover. I'm very good at my job.

"I'll leave it to you guys to work out the details, but let me know what you come up with. Heaven forbid Sadie gets caught in the crossfire." Dad doesn't hide his concern for my mom. He's really putting on an act.

"We'll make sure they never get close enough to hurt you or your wife," Asian Hottie responds.

He has to be the team leader. I need to make notes

after they leave. It's not much to go on, but it's all I have. I'm even more worried now, because Dad usually tells them that this is their yearly assessment, but he's making it sound like a real threat against his life. What game is he playing?

"Now, have you had any luck gathering intel about the operation in Summerville? I am assuming you left the other two behind to maintain your cover," Dad remarks, moving on to a new subject, which also answers where the other two members of this team are. I guess they really aren't college recruiters, and I better not let my guard down just yet because their looks—as yummy as they might be—are deceiving.

"Yes, we are all established and getting to know the community. It's easy for them with who their dad is. He's smoothed everything over, and they are living in their family home. Anders and I have both secured jobs. I'm working at the local tattoo shop, and Anders is bartending at a popular bar in town. Lathan, Miller, and Bishop have all been attending the local high school and working that angle."

High school? How can they get away with looking like highschoolers? Is that what guys look like in high school? If so, then damn, I wish I insisted on going now. If they can pass as highschoolers, they must be pretty good at the job. I'm starting to feel a little suspicious about this whole thing, but I focus on the important details.

That's two more names. I run my finger down the list again. Anders Brooks and Bishop Ramirez. If I go by names, I would assume the latter is Latino Lovely, but I could be wrong. This information is helpful, though, and I'm glad my dad is asking these questions.

"And your backstory? Why are so many of you living together?"

"Rich parents who travel for work wanted to make sure their kids were all looking after one another. The town is stupid enough to believe it." I think it's Latino Lovely who answers. There's a hint of an accent, but not much.

"Good, good. Make the most of your downtime, because after the gala, you'll be headed back to Summerville. Hopefully, you can get the assignment wrapped up quickly, but there don't seem to be any solid leads yet, so you may be there for a while. I'm sorry, I know you were looking forward to a long break, especially because you've only just moved in. How are things at the new place? Do you like it? Sadie designed it with your specific tastes in mind."

All of our teams live on-site. Each time a new team is established, they are allowed to pick a location, and then a new residence is added. The teams always get to help with the planning. It's weird that an established team wouldn't already have a place here.

"It's amazing. You thought of everything we might need," Bad Boy asshole says.

I switch off the intercom. I don't need to hear anything else at this stage. I'm going to have to do some reconnaissance on the specifics of the gala. Mom will be the one to ask, since she is hosting it, and then

I'll scope out a place to take the fake shot from—one which is easily escapable. A closed session at the range is needed too. I haven't had to snipe anyone with a sniper rifle for a while, so it won't hurt to brush up on my skills. Not that I'll be using real bullets, just blanks, and I'll hit a place above Dad's head or something. At least I have something to go on now, but an uneasy feeling runs up my spine at the thought of the new test. Something just isn't sitting right. I don't know if it's because it involves *assassinating* my dad, or if it's the fact that I don't have much to go on regarding Team Basilisk, but I do know I need to be careful and make sure I dot all my i's and cross all my t's to make sure it goes off without a hitch.

I have to keep my perfect record of not getting caught, and I refuse to let Team Basilisk win.

CHAPTER 2

My nose wrinkles as I crouch down in a puddle of an unknown liquid and set up my sniper rifle. There were a couple of options for taking the shot, but with the knowledge that I have a team looking for me, I chose the least obvious, hoping they'll scope out the more apparent positions. I did consider a drive-by attempt, but there would be too much collateral damage, and it's hard to drive and shoot with any accuracy. I also considered taking a shot from inside the gala, but escape routes are limited within the building, so a rooftop shot it is, albeit from an extremely difficult angle.

I have my escape route already planned, and my motorcycle is parked close to the building. I expect to be home in time to order some takeout and watch a couple episodes of *The Witcher* before Dad calls me to debrief, and I can gloat about how I foiled his team once more. Henry Cavill is boyfriend goals and about as close as I'll ever get to one with my line of work.

I think back to the aftermath of me listening into that meeting between Team Basilisk and dad. My concern had risen to such high levels by the time they left, I actually confronted him as soon as I knew it was clear.

"What is this shit?" I demanded, waving the paper copy of the redacted file at him. "There's nothing about any of them except names. There aren't even any damn pictures so I can put those names to faces! And what's with the buddy-buddy act? Those men seemed to be a lot more than employees to you, so what fucking gives? And an assassination? You've got to be kidding me." I was angry because my parents didn't hide things from me, and this friendship my dad had with that team blindsided me.

When I met my dad's eyes, I knew I'd gone too far. He was wearing his Director Watson mien, looking cold and blank as he leaned forward in his chair. "This is as much of an assessment for you as it is for them, Kenzie. Your ghost status is dependent on your performance, and I can hardly give you an unfair advantage by telling you all they are capable of. You never know, this team may be better than you—in fact, they might be too good—but we will see what the outcome is on the day of the gala. I hope, for your sake, you're not cashing checks you can't afford." I wanted to stomp my feet in frustration, but I knew it'd get me nowhere when he was like this.

"I can afford plenty," I grumble out loud, thinking back to how I replied to him. The muted sound of traffic below pulls me from my musings. Up here, I can still hear a dull rumble and an occasional blast of impatient drivers' horns. A beep on my smartwatch alerts me to the fact that it's getting close to Mom and Dad's arrival time, and it's time for me to focus.

Stop replaying everything over in your head, Kenz, or you're going to fuck up.

I take a few calming breaths to center myself before I peer over the ledge and look down to see if I can spot their limo. I hope Dad told Mom what's about to happen. She will kick his ass if he didn't and lets her think he's been shot. He informed me he would be wearing a vest so I *should* hit him to make it look more real than aiming above his head. He also provided me with the bullet, said it was a blank, and that it wouldn't penetrate his vest. I, of course, checked when I put it in my rifle. It's better to be safe than sorry.

Fuck my life. The thought of shooting my dad is one I can't comprehend, but I know that in order to be successful with this evaluation, I have to follow through no matter how uncomfortable I feel.

Peering through my scope, I watch as various limos and town cars pull up, depositing their cargo of the rich and influential people in front of the hotel where the gala is being held. Women draped in jewels and luxurious fabrics and men in designer suits and tuxedos linger about, talking and posing, while paparazzi stand on either side of the red carpet, taking photos for their various gossip rags and news outlets.

I scan the waiting crowd, looking for at least one of

the five faces I memorized when I watched the security footage of them from Dad's office. I now have names to put to faces. That was the least Dad could help me with, though he refused to tell me anything else about the team or explain their redacted file. I still know nothing about their specialties or skills, which puts me at a disadvantage compared to normal assignments. When I tried to call Dad out on it, he just shrugged his shoulders and told me he was testing my skills too. I honestly thought we were already past testing my skills, but I guess not, so here I am, with minimal information and hoping for the best.

Asian Hottie is Dayton Wexley and team leader for Team Basilisk. Nerdy Sexy is Lathan Campbell and their team tech guru, but Dad told me not to underestimate him, because he's also a field operative. Latino Lovely and Hot Chocolate are Bishop Ramirez and Anders Brooks respectively, and the tattooed, pierced bad boy hottie with an attitude problem is Miller King. The other two team members who were not present had their names redacted. When I questioned Dad, he wouldn't explain why. He said I didn't need to know them unless I failed and had to join their team. I quickly shut up after that.

While I watch and wait, I pull out my laptop and try to hack into any radio feed that may be around. Teams usually work with ear comms, and I want to see if I can find their feed to give myself a little bit of an advantage. I shift slightly, trying to make myself more comfortable. I'm wearing my full-body armor today, which is bulletproof and all that other high-tech stuff. When Dad didn't tell them it was their yearly test, I decided not to risk anyone getting trigger happy despite him telling them it's capture and detain only. I know if I saw my leader and friend get shot, I'd be out for blood.

Finally, I find the right frequency and listen in to the chatter.

"Keep your eyes peeled. The director's limo is approaching the entrance. I repeat, the director's limo is approaching the entrance."

I don't really know their voices well enough to distinguish who is who.

"Anyone have eyes on the target?"

"How can we have eyes on the target? We don't know what the target looks like," one retorts grumpily. I can't help but smile at the sound of their annoyance.

"The target will look like an assassin. Probably in all black and maybe with a mask," comes the sassy reply. I've heard all of this chitchat before, and they haven't said anything yet to impress me or make me think they are close, so this should be an easy win.

A muttered, "Asshole," has me smiling as I pull down my ski mask and get into position. I track the arrival of Mom and Dad's sleek black limo and watch as Dad hops out before offering his hand to Mom. She steps out, and flashes light up the area. I blink, holding steady, as they step forward and she greets the press. Mom's dress is gorgeous, as usual, and befitting of her status, and my dad scrubs up pretty nicely in his suit. I smile at how good they look together.

This is the opportunity I've been waiting for. Blocking out the chatter in my earpiece, I hold my breath as Dad steps back, allowing Mom to talk to the waiting press, before breathing out slowly, sighting up his right shoulder, and pulling the trigger. The shot is loud, echoing off the surrounding buildings, and I watch as the bullet speeds along its trajectory. I'm about to start packing my weapon away when my stomach lurches in horror as it hits my father and red blooms across his chest, soaking his white shirt under his tux, and he falls to the ground.

I'm frozen as the screams from the street reach me. That wasn't supposed to happen. There should be no blood. That was a blank, I swear it was. Fuck. Did I just kill my dad? A crowd rushes to him and blocks him from my view as I lean to the side, pull up my ski mask, and vomit everything I ate earlier this evening onto the concrete.

Oh my god, I think I just killed my dad.

Wiping the back of my hand over my mouth, I pull the mask back down as the chatter in my ear has me unfreezing.

"The shot came from the building over there. Why in the fucking hell didn't we have eyes on that building?" I hear one of them scream, and I quickly pack my gear, throw it all into the bag, and race for the fire escape. Compartmentalizing my emotions is a priority right now until I can get to safety, and then I can address them.

"We ruled out that the angle would be too difficult," one of them shouts. I can hear the guys breathing hard as they run. I can't take pleasure in knowing I outwitted them by choosing a location they didn't think could work, but clearly it fucking did.

"We underestimated Phantom. Fuck! Percy warned us about this..." When I get to the fire escape, I look down and see there's already someone climbing up, so I run back to the stairs leading down the inside of the building, and when I yank the steel door open, I can hear more than one coming up that way too. *Fuck.* I look around to see if there is another way out. The next roof is close by. I guess I could leap to that one and use that fire escape. My hesitation at seeing my dad go down is going to be my downfall.

My decision is taken away from me as the door to the inner stairwell bangs open and two men come out. It doesn't take long for them to find me in the shadows, and they are too close for comfort. Dropping my bag, I run for the next roof. It was just going to weigh me down, and the laptop is a burner with nothing to give away who I am. I'll be sad about abandoning my favorite rifle later, but again, there's nothing that gives away whom it belongs to.

"Freeze, motherfucker!" one of them screams, but I ignore them, pumping my arms as I sprint to get away. The sound of a gun firing reaches my ears, and I brace for impact. It hits the back of my shoulder, but because of the body armor, it doesn't do more than hurt like a bitch and cause me to stumble slightly. I know I'll bruise from the impact, but I can't stop to look back, it will just slow me down even more, so I keep running. Why did I have to pick such a wide building? I'm close to the edge when I look up. On the other side, on the rooftop that I want to leap to, stands a man who's pointing a gun right at me. Double fuck! I'm going to have to fight my way out. My adrenaline increases. Even though I know this isn't real, they don't, so this is going to be rough.

Skidding to a stop, I whirl around and prepare to fight, but I'm slammed to the ground as someone tackles me. It's all I can do to stay quiet as the air whooshes out of my lungs. Rolling, I try to get on top of the person who has me pinned, but it's not easy. I buck my hips up to try and dislodge him from the full mount position he has me in, but he's all muscle and difficult to move. Shit, this is not going as planned, so it's time to improvise and let my instincts kick in. Reaching down, I pull my knife out of my sheath and slash back in the hopes that it might loosen his hold. I don't want to hurt him because he's just following orders, but I really need to get out of here so I can check on my dad.

My ploy works, and he leans back far enough for me to get him off. I pull my leg out from under him and use his body to push myself away with my foot. I quickly roll to my feet and take up a fighting stance. I'm now surrounded, with a gun trained on me from the other roof and the three men on this one with me. They are all wearing masks, too, so I don't know who is who. In the dark, they all look the same. I've had worse odds before and made it out alive, but I have a feeling these guys are much better trained than the ones I evaded previously.

"Dude, you're surrounded, there's no way out of here," one of them drawls with their gun pointed at my chest. "Come quietly, and we may be able to make a deal," he lies.

I scoff, knowing he's full of shit, but I don't respond. Right now, silence is still key in protecting my identity.

"Like fuck we're going to make a deal. This scumbag just *killed* Percy. I'm going to make it my job to see he gets the chair." The one who tackled me gets to his feet and pulls his sleeve back, showing me that I did actually connect with him. He has a shallow cut through a tattoo on his forearm that's oozing blood.

One of them actually shot me, so a little slice shouldn't make him cry. It's the least they deserve after the killer bruise I'm going to have on my shoulder. Clearing my head, I focus back on their conversation as I try to plot out my next move.

"Yeah, but we need the intel on who hired him first. We have to get him back to headquarters. Protocol dictates that if Percy is down, then Theseus is to be notified, and he'll fly in from the London office."

Fuck, that's just great, Uncle Theseus is going to piss himself laughing when he sees I got caught, though that will probably change once he finds out what I did. Dread runs through my veins at the realization that there's no coming back from my massive fuck up.

As much as I try to concentrate, my emotions are all over the fucking place, causing my brain to fog as more negative thoughts keep flitting around, picking at my invisible walls.

Seeing an opportunity, I lunge for the small gap between the two aiming their guns at me, feigning escape, and when they step together, tackle dude goes for me again. Clearly, he didn't learn his lesson from the first time. Spinning, I aim a punch straight at his head, but it grazes his cheekbone as I bring my knee up to kick him in the dick. I'm not afraid to use dirty tactics to get away, and this situation is calling for dirty tactics. I don't think he was expecting my knee to make such blunt contact, and he goes down hard, grunting in pain. I didn't hold back with that kick. I hope I didn't ruin his chances of having children.

One asshole down, two to go. I move again and lunge at the one who has his gun trained on me. I know they will be reluctant to shoot again, because they are good little soldiers who follow instructions, and I'm wearing body armor, so they have to know it's useless unless they take a headshot. I hope they are not that stupid. I grab the gun in one hand, releasing the magazine and pushing the slide back in one motion. It drops to the ground, and the bullet ejects out of the chamber. His shout of surprise would bring a smile to my lips if I wasn't in such a shitty position. While he's distracted, I do a spinning kick and hit the other guy in the head. He drops his gun, and his eyes roll back in his head—steel-toed boots for the win. He tumbles to the ground in a heap of muscle, and there's no denying he's out like a light. I can hear the guy on the other rooftop shouting in frustration, but I ignore his words as I square off against the last man whose gun I've rendered useless.

"What the fuck? Are you a ninja?" he growls, but I don't respond, I just run at him. I feint to the left, and as he tries to tackle me, I leap over him and run for the stairwell door. It's another long run back to the exit, but I still have wind left in my sails. I'm fit enough that even with all the adrenaline coursing through my body I can keep going. It's what I've been trained for.

I can hear him on my heels, but I wrench open the door and take the steps two at a time. The noise is loud, and I can hear his heaving breath in my ears. Just as I'm about to round the next landing, something hits the back of my heels. It's all I can do to protect my head as I stumble and fall down the next flight of stairs. Pain explodes throughout my body, and it feels like I tumble down one stair after the other in slow motion before landing at the bottom. I close my eyes against the pain, refusing to scream or acknowledge how injured I am.

"Holy shit, dude, what did you do?" a new voice from below asks.

"I did what I had to do," a voice growls back. "He was getting away."

"He wouldn't have gotten far. I'm here, and Anders left the roof on the other building as soon as Phantom did. He would have been at the bottom when the assassin got there." Fuck my life. The pain is too great, and as much as I fight internally, I can feel myself fading from consciousness. "Is he alive?"

"Who cares?" the man who tripped me responds as I pass out completely.

CHAPTER 3

A low groan leaves my mouth, which makes my head pound harder as I try to force my eyes open. I blink against the brightness of the light, unsurprised to find myself tied to a chair. I failed my assignment, was apprehended by the opposing team, and, to top it all off, I think I killed my own father. Blood wouldn't have spread across his chest with a blank. I'm not sure how it did. I checked it, it was definitely a blank, and nobody could have tampered with it before I took the shot.

I'm so confused. I don't understand what's happening, my head is foggy, and my body aches like never before, the pain making it hard to think clearly. I feel tears well in my eyes, but they soak into the ski mask I'm still wearing, so hopefully nobody notices my moment of weakness.

They are all too busy arguing to notice I'm awake yet, so that's something. My gaze skims my surroundings, and I recognize one of the interrogation rooms in the bowels of the Lighthouse.

"Any news of Theseus's arrival? Or should we start questioning this asshole without him?" Lathan asks Dayton, who shakes his head.

"Nobody could give me any answers. They advised us just to hold tight and make sure Phantom doesn't escape." I couldn't tell if there was genuine concern that I would try to escape or not, but the idea of being babysat because of the possibility clears my mind a little more.

"I say we beat the information out of him." Miller pushes his fingers together, cracking them aggressively. Fuck. That's just what I need, to withstand torture on top of everything else. I'm not sure if I'm strong enough for that. "And if that doesn't work, I have some tricks up my sleeve that will."

They all look so angry, and I don't blame them. I'm not looking forward to being on the receiving end of an interrogation for a change. I've been trained for this, but nobody likes pain, or at least most people don't.

"He's awake and has been listening to you assholes chatter for about five minutes." Bishop, Latino Lovely, has finally realized that I've regained consciousness, and they all turn to look at me.

"Why didn't you say anything, asshole?" Miller shoves him.

Bishop clenches his fists but doesn't retaliate. "You seemed to have it all under control." Wow, the barely contained malice between these two is super obvious. I wonder what has their panties in a bunch.

"Who hired you?" Anders demands, but I stay quiet. Dad told me never to give up any information without him or Uncle Theseus in the room despite us being on the same side—or at least that's what they lead you to believe.

Miller strides over to me, his hands already fisted, and I brace myself. He hauls back and slams one into my face, and a grunt leaves my mouth as my head snaps back as his fist connects with my cheek. "Answer the fucking question, or that is just the beginning."

My ears ring from the punch, but I stay quiet. Another fist comes at me, and this one hits me in the nose. I feel blood explode from it before it leaks down into my mouth, along with the tears I can't stop. It all rolls down my face, both fluids soaking into the mask.

Breathing through my mouth, I try to compartmentalize the pain, knowing I deserve every blow for killing my own father. I was overconfident and sloppy, and I must have missed something. I never expected my dad to put himself in a position where he could actually die during a training assignment, but here I am, at the mercy of Team Basilisk, and I'm receiving the consequences for my actions.

No, I deserve everything they dish out to me. I'm hoping they will just get it over with and kill me. I can't live with the knowledge that I killed my dad. A sob threatens to break through, but instead, it comes out as a whimper. My poor mom is never going to be able to forgive me, and I will never be able to look her in the face again. No, it would be better if I disappeared and she never found out what I did.

Shame weighs heavily in the pit of my stomach, and it deepens the heartbreak ricocheting through my veins.

"Fuck this, I want to look into the face of the person who murdered Percy." Miller reaches over and pulls the mask off my face at the same time the door opens.

The five men in front of me gape in surprise when they see me—a person who is definitely a female and *not* a male like they foolishly assumed.

"Fuck, it's a girl," Bishop announces rather unnecessarily as my dark blonde ponytail falls over my shoulder. I want to roll my eyes at the obviousness of his statement, but I manage to keep my expression blank.

"That's Percy's temp secretary from the other day," Lathan points out, and Miller hauls back to hit me again. He's even angrier than before, if that's even possible, but maybe it's from knowing they didn't recognize any warning signs indicating I could have been a danger to MITHOS that pisses him off.

"You fucking cunt." Spit flies from his mouth, but he halts, mid-swing, as a voice abruptly shouts out, "Stop!"

My heart skips a beat as I try to look around the men to see if my eyes can confirm what my ears are telling me, unsure if it's who I think it is or not.

"Don't fucking look at him," Miller growls and tries to block my view as he stands there with his arms crossed, but the man belonging to the voice pushes his way through the men.

"Daddy?" I can't help the word that leaves my mouth and the sob that follows as I completely break down. I give myself permission to be weak and vulnerable for the moment, but under any other circumstances, I would have done my damnedest to maintain control.

"Fucking hell, what have you assholes done to my daughter? I told you to *capture* and *detain*, not beat the shit out of them." Dad hurries toward me, the bright red blood blotch across the front of his white shirt as noticeable as ever, providing a shocking reminder of what I thought had happened. He undoes the shackles holding my arms and legs down before pulling me into his arms.

"I thought I'd killed you," I murmur around a mouthful of tears, blood, and snot, adding to the mess on his white shirt. "There was blood, a lot of fucking blood, and then I couldn't see you. I... I thought you were *dead*."

"Oh, baby, I'm sorry. I didn't play fair, did I? I set you up. I rigged up a blood pack under my shirt like they use in the movies. I thought if you saw the blood that you would be sloppy and get caught, I just didn't think it would go quite this far." Dad pushes strands of hair that escaped my ponytail back from my face as he scans it. His eyebrows are pinched together, and a frown completes the look of a devastated father who's seeing his broken and bruised daughter.

"Did he say daughter?" I hear one of them ask, but I don't hear the response because Dad tries to help me up, and I scream in pain because every bone in my body hurts. Fuck maintaining control and trying to be brave right now.

"Theseus, get me a medic, she needs to see a doctor." My uncle must be somewhere behind the others, because I hear him shout for medical assistance. Dad leans in, gently picks me up into his arms, and carries me out of the interrogation room. I pant heavily, closing my eyes and clenching my jaw as I breathe through the burning ache throbbing heavily throughout my body.

"Are you going to explain what's going on?" Dayton asks my dad tersely.

"Not another fucking word from any of you until I have made sure my daughter doesn't have internal bleeding, or worse," my dad snaps in response.

When he gets to the corridor, there's a gurney and medical staff waiting to fuss over me. I'm whisked away to one of the hospital rooms deep below the surface inside the Lighthouse, where I'm poked and prodded and sent off for various scans to make sure that nothing is broken or hemorrhaging from my fall down the stairs. They confirm my nose is broken and my cheek is fractured from Miller's hits. The doctor shifts my nose back into place and tapes it, shoving some cotton packing up my nostrils to keep it aligned.

"Well, this is just delightful," I grumble, sounding like I'm congested as I'm brought back into the room in a wheelchair and helped up onto the hospital bed.

Dad sniggers but winces with sympathy as he takes in the state of my face. The doctors hook me up to a drip with some painkiller in it, and I lean back on the pillow and close my eyes. I know I look like shit. Both of my eyes are black and swollen from having my nose broken, not to mention the first hit I took from Miller. I can't believe that asshole hit me even though he knew I hadn't killed my dad... or maybe they were just as surprised to see him as I was, and I just wasn't paying attention.

"Sweetie, I'm so sorry. I told them to catch and detain, but I guess they thought my death was real and took it out on you, disobeying my direct orders."

I try to lift my hand to wave him off, but I can't lift it high enough without it aching, so I drop it back down. "Don't worry about it, Dad. I totally would have done the same thing if the roles were reversed." My words start to slur, and I try to widen my eyes. "What did they give me?" I try to tug the drip out of my arm. I thought it was just a painkiller, but it must have a sedative in it as well.

Dad reaches out to stop me then runs his hand over my head, pushing my hair back in a soothing gesture. "Don't fight it, Kenzie, just rest, and we'll talk about your new team when you get up." His words register, and I try to fight the sedative.

"You cheated," I slur, but my eyes close as his chuckles reach my ears.

"Yes, yes I did. You shouldn't have underestimated what I would do to get what I wanted. I'm the boss for a reason."

His words echo in my ears as my mind slowly fades to black.

The first thing that registers as I wake up is how badly my body hurts. What the fuck did I do to it? Groaning, I try to roll over, but something stops me. Opening my eyes, I groan again. That's right, I fell down some stairs and then got punched in the face—twice. I squint at the bag attached to the tube in my arm and find the damn thing empty. I guess the drugs have worn off. Thank fuck. Trying to sit up in bed, I look around the room to locate a buzzer to call someone to help me, but I lock eyes with the black-haired, blue-eyed, bespectacled sexy nerd, Lathan Campbell.

"Great, just what I need, a witness to my humiliation," I grumble as I still struggle to sit up. He doesn't react to my movements or comment, just reaches for his phone and calls someone like a good little soldier.

"She's awake," he says to whoever is on the other end and then hangs up. No expression shows on his face, but he does run a hand over his stubbled jaw. I'm not sure what he sees, but he sighs and puts his laptop down before standing up and walking over to me.

He reaches out to help me, and I study his hand like it's going to bite me, not trusting him one bit. He sighs again, a bit more dramatically.

"Just let me help you, Kensington."

I look up, and his face is still expressionless, but there's something in his eyes, probably guilt, that's practically begging me to accept his assistance, so I take hold of his hand, and he slowly helps me into a sitting position before putting a pillow behind me to help keep me propped up. He leans over me, and I catch a whiff of something delicious as he presses the buzzer for the nurse before he straightens up.

He doesn't say another word as he goes back to his chair, and I wait for the medical staff to come check on me.

"Where's my dad?" I ask him, not liking the loaded silence sitting between us.

"He had a meeting he couldn't get out of, but he should be on his way." My dad must have been the one he called. Thank fuck it wasn't anyone else from Team Basilisk.

"What about my mom? Where is she?" A sudden spike of panic rolls over me. It's unlike my mom not to be here if I'm hurt. I've been injured a couple of times on assignments, and every time, I woke up to her hovering over me like a mother hen, berating me for my choice of careers.

Lathan's lips turn up in a slight smile at the worry in my tone. "Sadie was here, but I told her I would watch you so she could go home and get a shower and a nap. I promised I would call her if there were any complications."

He calls my mom Sadie? Only our family calls her that. Most people call her Princess Sadeen. How well do these guys know my parents? I need to get to the bottom of this, because not knowing this information doesn't sit well with me.

He chuckles at my frown, and it shakes me out of my funk. He's cute when he smiles. "You look as confused about that as we are about you. We have so much to talk about. Your dad and my team will be here soon."

At his mention of his team, I freeze. Fuck. His team, and if Dad gets his way, my new team. I think I just lost my ghost status. My stomach sinks in disappointment. I can't believe they caught me.

"Don't look so sad, Kensington, I'm sure everything will work out fine," he says, trying to reassure me and losing a little of the standoffishness that he's been portraying since I woke up. I think he is showing me a glimpse of his real self, and the robot from five minutes ago was an act that he just couldn't keep up. I could use a dose of honesty right about now.

"Kenzie," I mutter. "Only my grandfather calls me Kensington."

"Right, your grandfather. Would that be the

Jordanian king or the uber wealthy Lord Jonathon Watson? You certainly have an interesting family tree."

I scrunch my nose up at his words. "The latter. The first one calls me by my middle name, which is Jordanian."

"Ah yes, *Princess* Kensington Raina Watson. According to everything I could find on you, you are the quintessential bored royal socialite. You flit from continent to continent spending your family's money and rubbing elbows with the rich and famous, with a list of ex-boyfriends a mile long." He pauses for a moment, waiting to see how I'd react to the little tidbits of information he's dropping.

I arch an eyebrow, curious to see how much more he discovered.

"The only people seen with you on a semi-regular basis are your cousins, Katherine Watson, known as Katie to her friends, and Keely Simpson, also known as Kiki, and to round out your quartet is Flynn Johnson III. Speculation is rife as to which of you girls is sleeping with him. Now, what's funny is that Miller recognized Katie from a class he took at the academy a few years ago, but not one of us remembers *you* from any of our classes here, nor do we remember you attending any functions with your parents."

He spouts off the profile I have carefully crafted over the years, but I'm surprised that Miller recognized Katie. We were both very careful not to make friends when we attended school, and we also look very different than we did when we attended them for a reason.

I'm known as Phantom, Katie is Reaper, and Kiki is Specter. We call Flynn JB. He hates it, but we couldn't resist, what with the English accent and everything. He's a James Bond cliché, but he's known as Wraith. We are all ghosts for our respective branches of MITHOS—Katie's being the European branch, and mine the US. Kiki and JB go wherever they are needed, but quite often, they are based somewhere in Asia.

Miller would recognize her because we swapped and trained in the opposite academy so we would have anonymity. We lived on campus and didn't make friends with anyone in our year, and we also trained separately from them, with an occasional theory class on our schedule. That must be where Miller remembers her from. He must have a photographic memory or something, because we did our best to blend in. We also used pseudonyms, no one knew us as Lady Katherine Watson or Princess Kensington Watson. No, we saved them for real life, and they make such great covers, even though there is a level of truth to them. Nobody would ever glance at us in regard to the deaths of international criminals or crooked politicians, and it makes it easy for us to get into places we need to be.

"Well, what can I say? I'm good at my job." I shrug my shoulders, wincing at the pain as the door opens and a nurse bustles in.

"Hi, Kensington, I'm Nurse Florence. How are you

feeling today?" She has a soft smile on her face, and I instantly warm up to her.

"Like I was tripped down a flight of stairs and punched in the face," I tell her dryly. "Oh, wait, I was."

She tuts at my sarcasm and unhooks the empty bag, replacing it with a new one. I see Lathan cringe out of the corner of my eye, along with the expression of guilt on his face. Good.

"Let me just swap this over for a fresh bag. How is the pain on a scale of one to ten?" she asks, and I shrug casually like how I'm feeling is no big deal.

"Maybe a five," I answer. It's bad, but I've felt worse. She frowns like she doesn't believe me.

"Are you sure? You are quite beaten up. There are no broken bones with the exception of your nose or internal bleeding, but you're bruised from head to toe."

"What can I say? I have a high pain tolerance," I reply and try to smile reassuringly, but it hurts my face, especially my throbbing nose.

"Hmm, I think I'm still going to put some painkillers in the next bag of fluids. The last one might still be working." She rushes from the room, and I sigh.

All I really want to do is tear the port out of my arm and go home. Without waiting for her to return, I swing my legs to the side of the bed and pull at the tape holding the needle in my arm. Lathan notices and rushes over to stop me.

"What are you doing?" he demands, trapping my hand in his.

"Look, I just want to go home and rest in my own bed. I'll be fine in a couple of days," I tell him while pulling my hand back, but he shakes his head.

"Ah, no, you're not leaving. Your dad will be here any moment, and he'll be upset if he sees you out of bed."

I roll my eyes at his attempt to guilt me into staying. "My dad will understand my need to go home. Do you know if anyone retrieved my bag and gun from the roof? It's my favorite, and I want it back."

He just shakes his head again and refuses to release my hand. Another heavy sigh leaves my lips. I'm too sore to fight him, but I will if he won't get out of my way. Just as I'm about to open a can of whoop-ass on him, my door opens again. I'm expecting the nurse, but my dad strides in, stops, and frowns when he sees the position I'm in and Lathan's hand on me.

"Is she giving you a hard time, Lathan?" he asks, crossing his arms and raising an eyebrow in my direction.

Damn it. Dad knows me too well, so I won't be going anywhere anytime soon.

"No, sir. She just asked me to fix a new piece of tape across her port to hold it in place."

I gape at him, surprised that he didn't rat me out. Interesting.

"Hmm. I don't believe you, but it's cute that you're already sticking up for her. At least one of you won't hate having her on your team."

Now it's Lathan's turn to look at my dad in shock. "Excuse me, sir?"

Before Dad can respond, the rest of Team Basilisk enters my room. I'm *so* thrilled to see my captors again.

"Ah, everyone's here, so we can get started." Dad looks pleased with himself and gestures for all of them to find a seat. My room is big and private with plenty of seating, which is lucky, because it looks like we're debriefing here and now.

CHAPTER 4

The new arrivals take seats around the room, the tension escalating as Dad gives them a moment to get comfortable before he starts. He doesn't bother sitting. He always told me he thinks better on his feet.

"I owe everyone an apology. I lied to all of you, but I am not ashamed of what I did. I let you all believe, if for only a short while, that I had been killed. I have my reasons, which I will explain shortly." He turns to the guys, facing them directly. "I also didn't tell you that this would be your yearly evaluation, which you passed with flying colors, mind you, and that the assassination was set up by me to test your skills as a team, even though you were down two members."

Without waiting for them to respond, he comes over to sit next to me, picking up my hands. "And I hope you will forgive me for letting you believe you really killed me. I knew it would shake you, and I was hoping it would give the team the upper hand in catching you. I hadn't anticipated how hard you would fight to evade capture." He winces at the memory of my unsuccessful escape. "Or how hard they would fight to catch you."

"I don't care." I lean in and hug him slightly. "I've been hurt worse before, and I'm just so happy that it was all fake, but it *is* cheating, Dad. I'm pretty sure they wouldn't have caught me if I hadn't hesitated." I don't meet his eyes, because I don't want him to see how unsure I am about that statement. They were a well-organized machine. They were able to adjust their plan without hesitation. I might have gotten a little farther than I did, but I don't think I would have gotten away. I also knew this was a test, so shooting my way out was not an option.

"I can't believe you told us we were going after Phantom. We wouldn't have gone so hard on her if we had known differently," Dayton grumbles, not verbalizing the fact that I'm Percy's daughter, and the rest of the guys, bar Miller, chime in with their agreement.

Dad and I exchange a glance. I smirk as Dad sighs and turns to them. "I didn't lie to you about that. You did apprehend Phantom, it's just that he is a she, and she works for me. All of her kills were agency sanctioned hits."

The silence in the room is deafening as the five of them process what he revealed. Dad tried to hide the proud tone in his voice, but I heard it.

"Fuck off!" Miller growls, shaking his head in

disbelief. Anders and Bishop mirror his sentiment, while Dayton studies me as everyone else makes noise around him.

"Phantom is a girl, and she works for you? Not to mention she's your daughter, Princess Kensington?" Lathan looks at me with admiration in his eyes.

"There's no way she's Phantom and has that many kills under her belt. To do that, she would have had to have been killing for years. She can't be older than eighteen." Miller is furious in his disbelief. The clenching of his jaw and tightening of his fists almost make me laugh, because he really is taking this personally.

"Actually, I'm twenty-two, and I've been killing since I was sixteen. What, you can't believe I could have been so successful just because I have tits and a vagina? Believe me, it's because of said tits and vagina that I have been." I wink at Miller who scowls at me, and I notice Dad wincing out of the corner of my eye. Oops, maybe I shouldn't be talking about my tits and vagina and how I use them around my dad. My bad.

"I always knew you had a daughter, since she's not exactly discreet in the tabloids, but I had no idea she worked for you," Dayton says, trying to defuse the tension in the room.

Dad nods. "Yes, she has a very solid cover story, and the reason none of you ever saw her here is because she was trained in London with Theseus, while I trained Theseus's daughter Katherine. Both girls trained in secret to become the ghosts that they are, but now Kenzie will be joining your team."

There's another uproar, and a nurse sticks her head in the room.

"If you can't keep it down in here, I *will* make you all leave. Including you, Director Watson," she scolds, and they all pipe down. Even Dad looks properly chastised. I never thought I'd see the day when Percy Watson cringed under the glare of someone who wasn't my mom.

"Why are you making us take another member? Have we done something wrong to upset you?" Bishop asks as soon as the nurse closes the door. What a fucking cry baby. I don't want to join their team either. In fact, I had to be tricked to do it, but they should be thankful that I am, since I'm an asset.

Dad pats my leg and stands up, moving over to the guys again. "Not at all, but you know I like my teams to be mixed. You guys are the best I have." I clear my throat slightly at the insult, and Dad sighs. "The best *team* that I have, but you are a bit of a sausage fest. You will be a more effective team with a female on it, and who better than Phantom?"

I snort at Dad's words, and I see one or two lips tick up in small smiles, but they don't last. The guys aren't happy. At all. In fact, they look as disappointed at the idea as I am. I perk up a little, maybe this won't happen after all. I'll let the guys cry about the situation and see how my dad responds.

"So what? It's never been a problem in the past," Anders says lightly, and Lathan shakes his head.

"Well, actually, to be honest, it would have been better to have a female on a couple of jobs we've been on. There are just some places they can go where we can't. Women also trust women more." Fuck logic. He is not helping the situation.

"Shut up, Lath," Miller and Bishop both growl at the same time before scowling at one another.

"And that's exactly why you will have Kenzie. She will be joining you on your current assignment. Hopefully, she can find leads that are not available to you. She'll be going undercover as an aging out foster kid and potential victim." Now this has piqued my interest.

"What, you want to risk your daughter being taken for sex trafficking?" Bishop sounds incredulous and slightly disrespectful considering he's talking to his boss. I sit up straighter. Oh, this sounds even better than I thought. A new job, and one I can go undercover for.

"Trust me, Kenzie can take care of herself," Dad assures them, and I decide to add my input because I don't want them to fuck up my opportunity to do something outside of my normal assignments.

"Yup, remember? Phantom, ghost assassin." I point to myself, and Dayton frowns, not hiding his annoyance before standing up and pacing back and forth. I hide the smirk that wants to cross my lips. As much as I don't want to join a team, it seems as if they feel the same way, and I like this little bit of payback. Let them squirm after beating the crap out of me.

"Before you say anything else, let me just get Kenzie up to speed on the case and then I'll turn the floor over to you. For the time being, she is on your team. If you really feel so strongly against it after the job is done, then we can reassess, but for now, she stays. Who knows, you might be surprised by her." Dad has his *this is final* voice on, and I guess the guys have heard it before, because they don't argue. I'm actually a little excited to hear what the assignment is. My last few were boring.

He turns to me but sits down amongst the guys. "Right, Kenzie, there's a sex trafficking operation that is targeting girls and boys who are aging out of the foster system. A lot of them get kicked out of their homes when the money dries up from the state, and there are only so many options out there. They also target teenagers in group homes whose time and options are running out as well. Many disappear across the US daily, but in Georgia, it seems to happen almost double the national average. We suspect their base of operations is located there, but we haven't been able to narrow it down to an exact location. The governor has asked us to get involved as a personal favor. He and I go way back, and he happens to be on one or two of the committees that know about MITHOS. He's secured you a place at the local halfway house in Summerville, which happens to be his hometown."

"But... look at her." Dayton has been fairly quiet, happily pacing back and forth while listening to Dad, but now he stops and points at me. "She can barely get off the bed, let alone defend herself."

I'm insulted at the insinuation. Sure, I must look like shit, since Miller packs a mean punch, but at least I didn't lose too much blood this time. I'll be stiff for a few days from the bangs and bruises, but I'm sure the doctor will give me something that will help with that, and then I'll be right as rain soon enough. It's irritating that they won't give me the credit I deserve, instead viewing me as weak.

"She'll be fine. Actually, the damage to her face will help sell the story that she had to be removed from her last home." Dad smiles at me, appearing slightly apologetic, which I'm assuming is due to his enthusiasm over my injuries working well for my cover story... and his part in me getting hurt in the first place. I nod carefully, cognizant of said injuries despite the wicked pain meds in the IV.

"Sounds good to me. Just give me a couple of days for the stiffness to fade, and I'll be fine. I'm sure Nurse Florence will give me some kickass painkillers."

Anders snorts at my declaration. "I think it's going to take a bit more than a few painkillers to get you back up and running."

"I'm not even sure how you're going to be able to get out of bed, let alone function in any capacity," Bishop adds, sounding incredibly skeptical.

"Don't underestimate me, boys." I brush off their

concerns, though there's this warm feeling inside of me that suggests I might actually like their worry. Stupid emotions! I'll examine them later when I'm alone. "After a couple of days of rest, I'll be good to go. I've done it before."

"See, she said she'll be fine," my dad says to Dayton, who throws his hands up in exasperation, but Dad continues, ignoring his outburst. "We think a teacher at the high school may be scouting for them, or someone who is involved with one of the after-school programs. Dayton and Anders have jobs within the community, while Miller, Bishop, and Lathan will be attending high school with you. They have two other team members already established in the community. Between the eight of you, I'm sure you'll be able to figure it out well before Kenzie is targeted and taken."

"Oh, but if I allow myself to get abducted, we may be able to find out where all the other victims have been taken. This could also result in the assignment being a rescue mission as well," I suggest, and Team Basilisk looks like they are ready to blow a gasket. Rolling my eyes, I decide to add my feelings to the situation.

"Look, this doesn't thrill me any more than it does you. I'm used to working alone, used to having to rely on just me, and I prefer it. I won't fuck up, I won't miss a shot, I won't give away my cover. I now have to trust that none of you guys will do the same thing because of some false sense of concern that I can't handle myself," I deadpan. "I don't know how you work. You've all been together for years and know each other's strengths and weaknesses. I know nothing, so how about you cut me some slack and we do this job, and once it's done, you never have to see me again. I'll regain my ghost status, and you can continue on with your sausage fest or Dad can find you another female you might approve of."

Although I don't want to be a part of this team, I'm still hurt that they are arguing so hard against working with me. Is it me, or is it just a new person in general? Either way, it fucking sucks.

Dad stands up again and stretches, his hands coming up to his back as he does. He looks down at the guys, his face hard. "Look, you have no choice in this, so I suggest you accept it quickly and learn to live with it. This is happening, and you will work with one another. I'm not asking you to be best friends, but I need you to do this job. Innocent lives are at risk. We need to stop the sex trafficking. If we plug up this supply, then the assholes have one less. Kenzie will do her part and pass on any information she may get, and I expect you guys to do the same for her." Dad shakes his head. Now it's his turn to be exasperated with Team Basilisk's behavior. "I don't know why I thought this would work. You are all so set in your ways." He turns to me. "Kenzie, I'll be back to pick you up and take you home once Nurse Florence gives me the okay. Mom has your favorite mac and cheese waiting for you."

"Sadie made mac and cheese?" I see Lathan's face light up like a kid in a candy store, and I can't stop the growl that escapes my mouth. He raises his eyebrows in surprise, and I grimace sheepishly.

"It's my favorite, and I don't like to share," I tell him sternly, and he grins cheekily as if he just found a way to irritate me for the fun of it.

"That's okay, Kenzie, I do." He winks, indicating he means more than just food, and I feel slightly intrigued. I wonder who he likes to share with.

"Lathan, Sadie made you guys a tray, too, if you want to pick it up on your way home."

Mom is officially a traitor.

He fist bumps the air. "Yes!"

Anders and Bishop high-five one another. Miller is surly and staring at me with loathing, and Dayton seems troubled but manages a small smile at the guys' antics. It appears they've had Mom's food before, so my curiosity deepens.

"I'll leave you all to get to know each other a little better. Why don't you ask Kenzie some questions so it will make you feel better about her being on your team?" Dad suggests, hopeful that his recommendation will break the tension.

"Temporarily," Miller growls, and Dad rolls his eyes and throws up his hands.

"That's it, I'm out of here. I can't stand listening to you any longer. Get your shit together. I'll be back in a little while. I need to go find Theseus, and then I'll be back to get you, Kenzie. Can't trust my own blasted brother not to snoop through my files when I'm busy." He waves goodbye to the guys and gives me a kiss on the forehead before he leaves. The door closes behind him, and the room falls into uneasy silence. Wonder-fucking-ful. I'm starting to hurt a little more, so I lean back on my pillow and close my eyes to block out some of the light.

"Ask away. I know you have burning questions, but just know that I'm also owed some answers. I have never gone into a test with so little information about a team. I want to know skills and stats for all of you. None of this redacted shit like the file I was given." I put an arm over my face to block out even more of the light, but it doesn't seem to work.

I hear a shuffling sound as someone moves across the room. I should probably be worried that I'm going to get smothered by a pillow, but I also have a scalpel under my body if they try anything. I managed to steal one off the tray when they were distracted by Dad.

Nobody touches me, however, and instead I can see the light in my room dim from behind my closed eyelids. I relax slightly from the gesture.

"Would you like something to drink, Kensington?"

My eyes open in shock as I turn my head and find Dayton next to the bed, holding a jug of water and a glass.

"Ah, yeah, that would be great," I tell him, clearing my throat, and he pours me a glass before handing it to me. I take a sip, and the cool water soothes my dry throat. "Thank you," I murmur, and he nods before replacing the jug on a table on the side of the room.

"We never apologized for what happened. In our defense, we were under the impression you had killed our director." Dayton sounds slightly apologetic and defensive. It's like he can't make up his mind. I can relate.

I wave my hand away. "Don't worry about it. I've been hurt worse. At least you didn't stab or shoot me somewhere I would bleed. All of my blood is accounted for, and nobody had to open a vein to top me up. I call that a win-win situation."

He raises a single eyebrow in reaction, and I can see the others exchange looks.

"Okay, shoot. What do you want to know?"

CHAPTER 5

"Fuck this shit, I'm out of here." Miller pushes up out of his chair violently and, without a backward glance, storms out of the room. Well, that didn't last long.

"Miller." Dayton's tone sharpens as he calls after his belligerent teammate, but we just see a flash of his middle finger before he disappears from sight. Dayton sighs and scrubs a hand through his hair before turning back to me. "Sorry."

I shrug, and my aching body protests. I can't wait for Nurse Florence to return with my painkillers.

"It is what it is. Please don't think his temper tantrum is going to upset me, it's basically nonexistent on my radar. I'm not particularly happy with the situation either, but I'll suck it up because I'm a good little soldier and I do as I'm told. We'll do this case, plug up the supply chain for the sex traffickers, and go our separate ways. I'm not going to burst into tears because you guys don't want to work with me," I assure him. His eyes widen, and the four of them exchange a glance, and I snort. "For fuck's sake, what kind of female agents are you used to working with? You all look like you expected me to be upset about it."

Anders loses his surprised expression, putting his hands behind his head and placing his feet up on my bed before rocking back on his chair. "In the past, it has been our experience that women, or the women who have done trials with our group, have been overly emotional."

"Not to mention clingy and jealous," Bishop adds wryly, resting his chin on his hand, his hazel eyes studying me like I'm a science experiment. His description of other female agents doesn't surprise me one bit.

"Were you sleeping with them?" I guess, and Bishop shifts uncomfortably when I pin him with a look, which tells me everything I need to know.

"You need to establish boundaries. Your mistake was sleeping with the girls who thought they were becoming part of your team. That's just stupid. Yes, MITHOS encourages relationships within teams, but you have to be able to work with one another, and there's no place for jealousy or clinginess in our jobs. It complicates the assignment, which could cause failure."

Again, the four of them gape at me like they can't believe the words that are coming out of my mouth.

"What? It's true. Once you know you can work

with them, you could have fucked as much as you wanted. I judge no one. I've fucked some of the people I've killed, and I've used my body to get what I wanted, there's no shame in that. However, there is shame in expecting more than someone is willing to give."

Team Basilisk will learn soon enough that I say what I think.

Lathan starts to cough violently, and Dayton quickly pours him his own glass of water. Poor Nerdy Sexy. I'm guessing today is full of surprises for him. I bet he hasn't had to fuck a mark, though I don't doubt all of them have used their good looks to get what they want either.

"I can guarantee I'm not going to cause any problems. I have no desire to be part of your team, and you don't want me either."

"I'm not sure how your father thinks this is going to work. You're not exactly suitable for going undercover, Princess Kensington." Dayton's tone gives away how skeptical he is, and I snort.

"People see what they want to see. There's no way they are going to put two and two together and come up with four. All they are going to see is a foster girl who's been beaten by her foster parents who bears a slight resemblance to the socialite Princess Kensington. Why do you think I always look flawless and glamorous when I go out in public as her? Ghosts craft their personas very carefully. No one looks at us twice while we're undercover, and if we have to use a pair of colored contacts and a box of hair dye, we do that.

Neither of us have piercings or tattoos for that very reason. Nothing identifiable marks our skin."

As much as I understand their skepticism, it's fucking annoying. My record speaks for itself, and I shouldn't have to explain my abilities multiple times to ease their unreasonable doubt.

"Do you have the acting skills to pull off the beaten teenage foster kid act?" Lathan bites his lip, unable to hide the worry in his eyes.

"Please, beaten foster kid is one of the easier things I've done. If I can fake an orgasm, I can fake anything. Though I have to admit, I'm excited to experience high school. I never got to do it the first time around." A small smile graces my lips at the thought.

Once again, I stun the men into disbelief. They are all looking at me like I'm a little touched in the head.

"So what else do you want to know about me? You've read about my hits, but is there anything else?" Knowing that I have no choice but to work with these guys, I decide to make it more pleasant for all of us by being an open book.

"Why don't you just tell us what your special skills are, then we'll know what we're working with." Dayton sounds a little fucking condescending as he says that, and I get the feeling he's implying that my only special skill is on my back. What a stereotypical dick.

"Okay, well, let's see..." I tip my head to the side, but a ping sounds throughout the room, and Lathan pulls his phone out of his pocket.

"Oh, hey, your dad sent us your bio."

The other three scramble to get their own phones out, and Anders's chair almost tumbles over in his haste to read it.

They are quiet while they pull up my file on their phones, and then the room falls into an even heavier silence as they read through my skill set. It's almost comical how their eyes dart from what they are reading to me.

"There is no fucking way this is your resume." Bishop's accent thickens as he stabs a finger at what he sees on his screen. "You can't have all this training. You're a *princess* and the director's *daughter*. There is no way your parents would have allowed this."

He's partially right. Mom wasn't fond of it, but Dad knew I wouldn't settle for half-assed training.

"Okay, well, tell me what's there, and I can confirm or deny," I offer, knowing that everything will be confirmed. Katie and I were trained by the best to be the best. There are a couple of other ghost operatives, but we're an exclusive club. I smother a yawn, but eagle-eyed Dayton doesn't miss it. He frowns, but before he can say anything, Anders starts reeling off my resume.

"Sharpshooter, both close contact and sniper. Self-defense with weapons, hand-to-hand combat, and advanced driving."

"That's all standard MITHOS stuff, so I don't doubt you all have that as well," I point out, and there are small nods of acknowledgement from them.

Bishop takes over. "Interrogation and manipulations." Aka torture and lying, skills every proficient spy needs. "Diplomacy, first aid, and bomb making and defusing."

"Oh yeah, bomb making was a blast, if you'll excuse the pun. It's fun making shit go boom." Lathan smothers a smile, but the others don't find it funny. Well, at least one of them will be fun to work with. I think back to one of my favorite hits. I blew up the car of a particularly nasty pedophile while he was in it. I was sad to see such a beautiful car like that go up in flames, but it was worth it.

"Languages, psychology, and tech skills." Nerdy Sexy raises an eyebrow. "How many languages?"

I take a moment to think about it. It's one of the first skills my parents started me on because of my dual nationality. "Ten fluently, but I have a smattering of a few more."

"Fucking hell," he whispers, his eyes widening with surprise. "What kind of tech skills?"

I grimace. "Ah, I'm afraid that's the one thing I'm not great at. Some days I can't even get my phone to work. I can hack a communication signal or wipe cameras, but only because I have a program to do it. I rely on Dad's nerd herd for the rest. I have one who deals with me directly for anything I need, and he doesn't even know who I am."

He grins. "Phew, I was thinking we were working with Wonder Woman for a moment. It's nice to know you're human."

"Breaking and entering, sleight of hand, and seduction." Bishop sounds like he's judging me again.

"Look, you judgmental asshole. You can't tell me that not one of you has used your good looks to seduce someone into giving you information. We all do it. No man is immune to having their dick sucked by a pretty woman, and my body is pretty fucking distracting, if I do say so myself."

Lathan's grinning, but the other three just look at my poor, banged up body lying in the hospital bed and appear doubtful.

I flip them off. "Well, it's not like you're seeing me at my best. I have to ask, which one of you assholes tripped me on the stairs?"

As one, they look at Dayton, who has the grace to appear slightly ashamed.

"Who did I nail in the balls, and which one of you did I knock unconscious?" I'm dying to know which ones I got the better of. I know it wasn't Anders, since I heard them say he was the one pointing the gun at me from the other roof before I passed out, so that leaves Bishop, Lathan, and Miller.

"Bishop was the one you kicked in the head," Dayton tells me, and Bishop moves so I can see his other temple. Sure enough, there's a pretty purple bruise blooming on it. The look he gives me promises payback. Hmm, this is really not going well.

"And you rearranged Miller's balls." Anders snorts with amusement, and I feel all warm and tingly at the thought that I got the asshole good.

"Is that why he's being such a dick? I mean, he did break my nose and cheekbone, so I think we're kind of even now."

"Oh no. I mean, it didn't help, but he's normally like that." Lathan waves off the asshole's behavior.

"Wow, he must be a real asset to the team with that charming personality," I mumble, and he shrugs.

"Women like the silent, broody bad boy type. You'd be surprised at what he can do."

"Is that his superpower? He must be so proud." No one misses the sarcasm in my voice, but before they can answer or I can ask the relevant questions regarding all of their skills, my dad comes back with Uncle Theseus in tow, and he parks a wheelchair next to my bed.

Uncle T winces when he enters the room and sees my face. "Oh well, I guess it's not as bad as that time in Colombia," he says, leaning in and giving me a kiss on the top of my head. I couldn't agree with him more.

"What happened in Colombia?" Anders asks, but my dad frowns.

"It's classified."

"But we have level nine clearance," he argues, and it's my turn to be surprised. That's the highest clearance I've ever heard of a team having.

"Not high enough," my dad grumbles, and the team looks at me again. All I can do is shrug, but then I can't help but pull a few tails.

"Oh, so I guess that makes me the team leader

because I have the highest clearance, kills, and amount of skills out of everyone."

The four of them burst into protests, but my dad just looks at me knowingly, and Uncle T chuckles. It's going to be so much fun fucking with them. They take things way too seriously.

"Relax, boys, she's yanking your chain. She also has the least experience working with a team. She has only ever worried about herself before, so making her team leader would be a disaster." *Ouch.* Fair assessment, but still... ouch.

It seems to mollify them a little, however, and they settle down.

"Alright, trouble, let's get you out of here. I have your pain medication" —he taps the pocket of his suit — "and the car's waiting to take you home." Damn, I haven't had a chance to grill them about their own attributes. Dad better rectify that by giving me their unredacted bios.

"When are we going to get a chance to talk about the mission?" Dayton asks my dad.

"You're not. You're going to let Kenzie establish her cover while you four do what you need to do. Once there, you can use your best judgment for how you are going to exchange information. I will have the files sent to all of you to get her up to speed. You guys know how you work best, and I am not going to interfere with that, and neither will she. I just want you guys to collaborate, exchange information, and use one another if you need a certain skill. I know that by putting my best on this case, it will be closed in no time." Oh yeah, Dad is slathering that shit on thick, but I watch with amusement as the guys puff up and quickly agree. The man is a master manipulator, and they didn't even notice it was happening.

"Come on, sweet niece, your mother is at home waiting to smother you with love and mac and cheese. Shall we go?" Uncle T comes over and helps me swing my legs off the bed, but I can't stifle the moan of pain quickly enough, and once my legs are no longer covered by the sheets, everyone's eyes are drawn to the bruises on them.

"Holy shit." The words slip out of Lathan's mouth quietly as he grimaces like he's the one in pain.

"Yeah, at the moment, my body is just one giant bruise," I tell him, sliding off the bed and into the wheelchair. I don't even care that I'm naked underneath my hospital gown. There's no point in trying to put any clothes on. I'm just not capable without any assistance, and the only assistance I want right now is my mother's. I whimper as Dad helps me lift my feet up on the footrests, and then Uncle T spreads a blanket over my lap.

"Alright, Kenzie love, ready to go?" I look at my dad when Uncle T grabs the handles and starts wheeling me out.

"Aren't you coming?" I ask my dad, and he shakes his head.

"No, I'll be along shortly," he tells me, and I nod.

"Oh, okay." I look toward the team of men who I

will be working with in the near future. All wear various expressions—a sympathetic smile from Lathan, a contemplative look from Dayton, and frowns from the other two. Oh well, one out of four isn't bad. It could be worse, and they could all hate me.

"I'd like to say it was nice to meet you, but, well, it wasn't. I'm hoping the next time I see you, maybe you'll be able to figure out how we can work together without one of you beating the crap out of me, shooting me, or throwing me down a concrete stair-case. Hmm, maybe it would just be better if you all stayed away from me and we only communicated via email. Dad, give Lathan my secure email, and he can be my point of contact, because quite frankly, the other guys have done nothing but insult me since they walked into the room."

The six men explode into a cacophony of noise, but I just hold up my hand. "The four of you took one look at me and judged me on looks alone. Let me remind you that I very nearly evaded you, and I was rattled by the thought that I had just killed my father by acci-dent. Normally I am someone you wouldn't wish on your worst enemy. How about you wipe out every-thing you know about Princess Kensington Watson and focus on getting this job done, then we can wash our hands of each other and prove to my father that this was a bad fit."

"Kenzie," Dad growls, but I shake my head before he can chastise me for my lack of filter.

"No, Dad. I agreed to give it a try, but they already

have their doubts, so you're right. I will do my thing, they will do theirs, and we can exchange information. If any of us need something, then we can ask each other, but we need to work all angles of this, and I can't if I'm being judged for every move I make." I turn to Lathan. "Message me in a week. I should have something to share with you by then. I need a few days to recover, and I'll be good to go."

"A few days? Try a few weeks," Bishop mutters, and Uncle T gives him a hard look.

"If Kenz says she will be ready to go, then she will be. You guys worry about yourselves, because if a tiny, hundred and thirty pound girl can almost get the drop on you, then maybe your team needs to look at its own skills."

With that mic drop, Uncle T rolls me out, leaving the others behind with my dad.

CHAPTER 6

Uncle T pushes me through the underground facility which, thankfully, is not teeming with people. The elevator that runs through the middle of the facility takes us above ground, and from there, he helps me into a golf cart. We use the paths on the ground to take me to my parents' place, and I keep my head down on the way.

MITHOS is designed to look like a very exclusive college, and a lot of classes are held in those buildings, but the spy shit is held in the underground facility. Dotted around the large property are the houses belonging to various teams as well as my parents' large home, which is where Uncle T drives me.

You know what I love about my uncle? He doesn't feel the need to fill silence with useless, uncomfortable conversation. He's also not a stupid man, so he knows that I'm in an extreme amount of pain even though I'm hiding it well. Dad handed him my pain pills before we left, so I'm going to swallow a handful of those before easing myself gently into bed. Uncle T also knows that I'm berating myself for letting Team Basilisk get the drop on me. My perfect record was ruined in a matter of minutes, all because I let emotions overpower logic.

"You know this doesn't count," I tell him suddenly, needing to validate my feelings out loud. "Dad cheated. I didn't fail."

He just chuckles quietly. Speaking the words was more for my benefit than his. "But a deal's a deal. You agreed to the terms, and now you have to follow through. Despite the lack of a warm greeting, they are your team for the foreseeable future. You never know, kiddo, you might enjoy having someone to watch your back."

I purse my lips at his last comment. I've never needed anyone to watch over me before, so why would I want it now? Exhaling a deep breath to calm my frayed nerves, I shift my focus to something other than my internal shit show.

It's been a long time since I've used the trail we're on—I don't often go to the underground facility because I'm not supposed to make myself well-known —so when we pass a new home I've never seen previously, I say, "That one's new, I've never seen it before. Who does it belong to?"

Even though Uncle T doesn't live here, house approvals have to go through both him and Dad on both continents. I don't mingle with the other teams, but I know where each and every one of them lives and their identities. I guess that's why Team Basilisk threw me off, because I'd never heard of them before.

"Your new team has finally agreed to set down roots. They have been living out of a suitcase for so long, going where we needed them to, but Percy was worried about them and decided it was time they needed a foundation—somewhere for downtime, somewhere they can go and have space that belongs to them and actually be themselves. They were all starting to get a little lost from working undercover for so long. After this assignment, I don't think they will be sent out on one for a while."

What Uncle T isn't saying is that they will probably have to have some mental health counseling. Undercover assignments wear on a person after a time, and trying to keep who you really are straight becomes a struggle sometimes. I see someone after every assignment. It was one of the agreements I made with Dad when I first started six years ago, and I can't deny how much it has helped.

I scoff as he pulls up to our large two-story house, and I groan at the sight. Fuck, I had forgotten I have all those stairs to climb. Yes, I still live at home. I mean, where else am I going to live? I have no friends, it would be hard to explain to roommates where I disappear to all the time, and living on my own would just get lonely. This was the best solution, and to be honest, I like my mom and dad's company.

Uncle T helps me through the front door, and when the door closes behind us, a whirlwind of a woman comes running with a torrent of Arabic spilling from her mouth as she chastises me, my absent dad, and Uncle T for causing her to worry. My mother gathers me up in her arms, her signature scent, which is something exotic and reminds me of the souks in Amman, wrapping around me in comfort, but I grunt as a wave of pain washes over me.

She quickly steps away, gently holds me at arm's length, and looks me up and down as she catalogs every one of my bruises. "Why did you come home wearing that?" She turns to my uncle, raising a perfectly shaped eyebrow. "You couldn't be bothered to find her any clothes?"

I should have known she would pick up on my lack of clothing, so I jump in before he can defend himself. "Mama, I can't get dressed on my own, and I wanted your help."

Her scowl softens with my confession, and suddenly, she's all business—mama bear business. "Of course, *shazadi*. Why don't you go into the living room? Theseus can pull out the sofa bed for you there, and then you won't have to climb the stairs. I will get you something comfortable to wear and some of your favorite macaroni and cheese." She hurries off, muttering in Arabic about wayward children who enjoy making their mamas worry.

I shuffle slowly into the living room, and when I get there, Uncle T has already pulled out the sofa bed and is throwing pillows and blankets onto it from the little storage section. He helps me onto it, and I can't stop the low moan of pain that leaves my mouth, but he's a good uncle and doesn't say anything. Smart man.

Our family is incredibly close, and Theseus and his wife Felicity were basically my surrogate parents from the age of fourteen to sixteen while I trained at his branch of MITHOS. Same as my parents were to his daughter Katherine while she was here.

"How did you get here so quickly?" I ask him as he places cushions behind my back to keep me propped up. I slowly lean back before finishing off my thought. "I wasn't unconscious long enough for you to have flown from London."

"I was already here for a meeting. Your father never told me what the plan was, so when they hauled you in, I didn't even check that it was you. I thought it was real too. It wasn't until he barreled out of the elevator and into the interrogation room that any of us knew it was fake. I'm sorry, Kenzie. I would have stopped them from beating you if I had known."

He won't look me in the eye as he apologizes, and my mother bustles in to hear what he had to say. Her eyes flash, and her worry is replaced with a hot, burning fury. She slams the pile of clothes down on the bed before jamming her hands onto her hips. Uncle T steps back in the face of my mother's wrath. I smother a snort, but not quickly enough, because she turns that terrifying gaze my way.

"He didn't tell me either," she spits out, and I wouldn't want to be my dad when he gets home.

"Security separated us, and the last thing I saw was him being taken away in an ambulance. They hurried me to a car and drove me here, and it was only when the ambulance pulled up behind us and he climbed out that I knew the truth. He's going to wish it was real when I finally get my hands on him." I don't think I've ever seen my mother so angry.

"You haven't seen him?" I ask, and my uncle shakes his head, wearing a small grin on his lips, and answers before my mom can. He's brave for showing his amusement, because she's just as likely to take her anger out on him if he's not careful.

"Nope, why do you think he's dragging his heels about coming home? He knows how mad Sadie is, and he's not looking forward to her yelling at him."

"I also need to call my father and assure him everything is okay, otherwise he might send his royal guard on the next plane to the US." Mom sighs her frustration. "Perseus thinks he's so clever with his little war games and the deals he makes with you. I guess you have to join a team now."

Uncle T turns his back to me as Mom picks up the shirt she brought from the bed. I groan at the thought of moving again, and she just waves a hand. "Stay there. I will help you."

She peels the hospital gown down my arms, leaving me completely naked, and then she just holds out a shirt, and I slide my arms into each of the holes before she gently eases it over my head. Next, she pulls the blankets back and shimmies my legs into the pair of underwear she's holding out. I grit my teeth so I won't worry my mom, but as I lift my butt for her to slide them over, she doesn't miss the grimace, nor can she miss all the bruises on my body. I see her jaw clench as she takes a breath. She starts to say something, and I know it's going to be about how being a spy is not a proper career for a princess, so I distract her.

"Mom, whose clothes are these? Are these Dad's?" I ask, noticing that the T-shirt and underwear belong to a man.

"Okay, Theseus, you can turn around now," my mother tells him as she pulls my blankets up and over me. "No, we had some house guests for a few days while you were on your last mission. They left them behind, so I washed them and put them in a spare drawer. I was going to return them next time I saw them, but they are perfect for what you need—big, baggy, and comfortable."

She's not wrong. The boxers feel amazing, since they aren't riding up my butt cheeks or anything, and the shirt is old and worn, but super soft against my bruised and battered skin. It also helps that it's a cool band T-shirt. It's got a picture of Jim Morrison on it from The Doors.

"Hey, Sadie, the timer went off on the oven, so I pulled it out and grabbed myself a bowl. I hope you don't mind."

My mouth drops open in shock when a familiar voice has the three of us turning toward the door.

Standing there is Bad Boy Sexy, and he looks a lot less miserable than when he was at the hospital. He's also holding a steaming bowl of what I'm assuming is my mac and cheese.

I growl, and he looks at me with derision. "Still live at home, do you? Must be nice having your mommy and daddy picking up after you."

I gasp, speechless for probably one of the first times in my life, before all of my anger comes rushing back to me. "Seems like my mommy might be looking after you too. That's my fucking mac and cheese," I growl, and my mother gasps.

"Kensington!"

He smirks. "Well, it's in my bowl. It tastes amazing," he taunts as he takes a mouthful, and I feel my stomach grumble in protest.

"I'm surprised you're not still tasting your own balls considering how hard I launched them into your throat." Now it's my turn to smirk as he scowls at me, and I hear Theseus groan and my mother gasp again.

"Seriously, that is not princess-like behavior." Surprisingly, both Miller and I roll our eyes at the same time at her scolding.

Before I can say anything else, she puts her body between the two of us, cutting off my view of the asshole who's eating my home-cooked meal. She helps me shuffle back so I'm leaning on the pillows and then tucks the blankets around my legs. Finally, when she seems happy with her mothering and her successful attempt at heading off our argument—if her smug smile has anything to say—she steps back, and I can see Miller watching us very carefully, but then his eyes widen in surprise as I hear the front door open.

"Hey, that's my fucking T-shirt." He points his empty spoon at me as Dad and the rest of his team come into the lounge.

"Really?" I scowl at my mom before plastering on a smirk. "Well, it's on my body. It feels amazing," I taunt as I run my hands down the front of it.

Mom manages to hustle everyone out of the lounge before World War III can break out between Miller and me, but not before Uncle T slips me a gun to put under my pillow. I feel the tension drain out of me at the weight of the metal, and I give him a grateful smile. He just winks and follows everyone out. He and Dad both understand what Katie, Kiki, Flynn, and I have been through, and how even in my own house, I don't feel safe unless I have access to a weapon. You don't take out as many people as we have without constantly worrying about retaliation, no matter if it's done secretly or not.

Mom comes back with my own bowl of mac and cheese, and I desperately want to ask her why I'm wearing Miller's shirt, and why he was staying with her and Dad, but I'm so freaking tired. The painkillers Theseus gave me have kicked in, and although I still feel the dull remnants of it, they are working their magic for now. I let her fuss over me while I manage to eat half a bowl, and when Dad pokes his head in, I almost face-plant into it, so she takes it away.

"Come on, sweetie. Lie down now and get some rest. After a week or two of me looking after you, you'll be as good as gold again." My mother beams at me, and I see my father wince out of the corner of my eye. I haven't heard any screaming yet, so I guess she's waiting until our guests leave to unleash on him.

I scoot down, and she tucks me in. "Nope, I only have three days, and then I need to be in Summerville, Georgia, for my next assignment. I'm going to high school," I tell her, hearing my words slur, and then I see her glare at my father.

He comes over and grabs her by the hand, helping her up. "Come on, Sadeen. Let's let her rest, and I'll fill you in."

She huffs. "You have some explaining to do, Perseus Watson. She can barely walk, let alone go on assignment," she berates my father as he pulls something out of his pocket then puts it on the bed next to me.

"Oh, my phone that was in my bag." I struggle to keep my eyes open. "Did you get my rifle?" My mother huffs her disgust and storms out, and my dad leans in and kisses me on the head.

As my eyes drift closed, I hear him whisper, "Of

course. I made someone go and get it. Rest now, my fierce warrior princess. Tomorrow will be better."

My ringtone drags me out of my deep sleep. Normally I would ignore it, but it's "Don't Fear the Reaper" by Blue Oyster Cult, which I set for Katie—my best friend and fellow ghost—so I reach out and drag it to my ear.

"Yeah," I mumble into it when I swipe across the screen. A soft chuckle has me cracking an eye open. Fuck, I'm on FaceTime.

"Well, well, well, my dear Phantom, I must say you're looking a little worse for wear." Katie's posh English accent grates on my already sensitive nerves, so I flip off the screen. "Daddy says you got your ass handed to you. I never thought I'd see the day." She's practically gleeful. "Now you have to do what you agreed to and join the team that took you down. That has to hurt."

"They don't want me any more than I want them," I mutter, not bothering to move because my painkillers have worn off. "We agreed to get through this assignment, and then I'll be back to ghost status."

"I wouldn't be so sure of that." The glee is gone from her voice, and she sounds completely serious— serious enough for me to crack open an eyelid again. "I overheard Dad and Uncle Percy talking. I think both you and your team can kick up a fuss, but as far as they are concerned, it's a done deal."

Groaning, I sit up and pick up the phone. "Well, I know that if we don't get along, they won't force it, and trust me, we don't get along. I fed one of them his balls and head stomped another. The team leader looks at me like I'm just a honeytrap and worthless. They were skeptical about my resume too."

"What does Uncle Percy have you doing with them?"

"Apart from not killing them? We're trying to break up the supply chain of a sex trafficking ring. I'm going in as a potential victim. Oh, and guess what? I get to go to an actual high school." I wake up a little bit more at the thought of my next assignment. As much as I love hits, I really love undercover stuff.

"Seriously? Well, I guess that could be fun. Beats that last undercover job you did as the side piece for that arms dealer."

"Ah, Roman Bannister. That asshole liked to watch his guards fuck me before he would. I'm almost a hundred percent sure he was gay, and the only way he could get it up was by thinking about all the spunk that was already in my pussy before he shoved his dick in." I shudder at the memory. That was the longest three weeks of my life. "At least some of the guards actually knew what they were doing and I got an orgasm or two out of a couple of them."

"What's your new team like?" Katie sounds

curious and has a sly look on her face when she asks, "Are any of them hot?"

"Come on, you know the company doesn't hire ugly agents." I avoid answering the question, and I know I've made a mistake when a knowing grin crosses my cousin's lips. "Fuck."

"Maybe I should come out and visit with Uncle Percy and Aunt Sadie. I can keep you company while you recuperate and check out your new team."

"Nope, no can do. I'm due in Georgia in three days. The bruises are a good cover story since I'm going to be a foster kid who was beat up by their last foster parents. I'll be living in the halfway house in town. We think that's where they are getting most of the missing teenagers from."

"Well, you know where I am, so if you need help, just say the word. Oh, and we have that gallery opening in New York that we need to make an appearance at in a couple of weeks. Are you going to be able to get away for that one?"

Shit, I'd forgotten about that. Katie and I have to keep up appearances so that we have solid covers for other jobs, so Princess Kensington and Lady Katherine need to be seen rubbing elbows with the rich, famous, and influential.

"Yes, okay, I'll ask Dad if I can borrow the jet. I can spare forty-eight hours to do that. The team will have to manage without me for that long."

"Okay, I'll see you then, and Kenz, be careful."

The screen goes blank, and I realize my bladder is

telling me that I've been asleep a long time, so I ease the blankets back and, with my body screaming at me, I manage to get up. I shuffle to the bathroom that's on the ground floor before going in search of more painkillers and a big glass of water.

No one seems to be around, but I find my pills on the kitchen counter and grab a bottle of water out of the fridge, throwing two back. I chase them with a long drink before wiping my mouth with the back of my hand. Grabbing the rest of the pills, I shuffle back to my cozy nest on the sofa in the lounge. I'm going to make the most of the next couple of days, because I need to hit the ground running once I get to Summerville.

CHAPTER 7

My body is still a mottled mess of bruises when the bus I'm on pulls into the station, but with a few days of rest and some wicked good painkillers, I am just about functional again. I'm not back to full capacity, but I'm okay.

When I step off the bus, the driver has already removed my small, battered suitcase from below and is climbing back on without a backward glance. The backpack I'm carrying is the only other item I have. Looking around the quiet station, I search for the person from the halfway house who is supposed to collect me. Mrs. Standish is one half of a couple who runs the government funded home for teenagers who don't have anywhere else to go. According to my file, Serenity House can cater to fifteen teenagers all on the brink of aging out of the system or who already have and are trying to get on their feet. Most of them are high school students, and the Standishes help them gain skills to become fully functional members of society once they age out.

According to reports they filed with police, a few of their charges have disappeared, but it was never pursued because they were seen hopping onto buses much like the one I just got off, so it was assumed they were just finding somewhere else to put down roots, but they were never seen again. Somewhere between the time they got on the bus and it arriving at its destination, they disappeared.

The local police may have blown it off, but that's the kind of thing that raises flags at MITHOS, and a deeper investigation by the nerd herd discovered something more sinister than just itchy feet—a sex trafficking operation that all seems to start in this town. Over the last five years, more than thirty teenagers from this town alone have disappeared, but because they were all fosters or troubled teens, nobody paid too much attention. When we spread that search to all of America, the statistics were alarming.

That was when it was decided to send a team in undercover. I have a week to settle into my new role before I have to touch base with Team Bastards.

Just then, an out of breath woman runs into the station and waves her hand at me. "Oh my goodness, I am so sorry. Are you Mackenzie Walsh? I'm Martha Standish." The woman's cheeks are flushed, and she's breathing heavily as she waits for me to answer. She's probably in her early fifties and is dressed casually in a nice pair of shorts, a classy pale pink shirt, and sandals. Her blonde hair is cut in a short bob, and her makeup is light, her brown eyes framed with dark mascara-clad eyelashes.

"Yeah, I'm Mackenzie, I prefer Mac." I give her the name I decided to use as she scans the bruises on my face. Fucking Miller really worked me over, but the flash of sympathy in her eyes makes it worth it.

"Oh, you poor thing. Come on, let's get you home. I'm so sorry I was late. There was road work on the way that I hadn't anticipated, but we'll go home a different way and get you settled with a hot meal in no time." She picks up the suitcase at my feet and nearly stumbles when she feels how light it is. She frowns down at it, and I do my best to blush as I avoid her gaze.

"I was hoping maybe the town had a thrift shop. One of the nurses at the hospital was nice enough to give me that suitcase, but when the cops went back to the foster home, they had destroyed most of my things. I have some tip money from my waitressing job. It was in my pocket when this happened." I point to my face. "It's actually why this happened. They wanted it, and I wouldn't give it to them. How else was I supposed to eat and buy tampons?" I tell her quietly, and when I peer up at her from under my eyelashes, I see she's frowning, but it's a look full of sympathy.

Really, it's because none of my clothes at home say poor homeless foster child. No, my mother is big on designer labels and insists on still buying me clothes— not that I don't do my own shopping, but sometimes it's just easier to say yes to Princess Sadeen when she goes into royal mode. Both Dad and I have learned to pick our battles.

"We sure do. I can stop there on the way home if you want. In fact, one of my girls, Cassie, works there after school. She should be able to help you." She beams proudly, and I give her a small smile.

"That would be great."

When we get to her car, I'm a little surprised to see it's brand new and a luxury brand. She notices me staring at it, and her grin becomes smug. "My husband just got a promotion at work, and he bought it for me."

She opens the trunk and puts my case in before going around to the driver's side. She gestures for me to climb in, and within seconds, we're pulling out onto the road.

"Okay, let's go over the rules. No drugs, no alcohol, no boys. You can get an afterschool job, but your curfew is nine during the week and eleven on weekends, and there are no exceptions. You will also be assigned chores around the house and expected to maintain a 3.0 GPA." She takes her eyes off the road to look at me. "I know it probably sounds a bit strict, but we are trying to help you succeed in life once you leave our place. Now that you have arrived, we have five girls and three boys living with us. Three of you are seniors, but the rest are younger. Everyone has the same rules. If you need help writing a resume, James can help you with that. I know there are a few openings in some of the restaurants, and I also think the movie theater may be hiring as well. Meals are provided. You serve yourself breakfast and lunch, and dinner is served at six—no exceptions except if you have work or after-school activities. We have a white board in the kitchen where you can add those kinds of things to it so I can keep track of where you all are."

She pulls the car into a parking lot out in front of a large thrift store and shuts it off before turning to me. "We'll give you the week to settle in, and then you will be expected to pull your weight. Do you understand?"

I nod, not meeting her eyes as I roll mine internally. Playing meek and mild has always been difficult for me, but I suck it up.

"Good, I think you'll find if you follow the rules, living in my home will be easy, but there are consequences for not following the rules. I'd rather not have to punish you if I don't have to." There's a hint of coldness in her tone, but when I look up, she's all gentle smiles and soft eyes. Huh, maybe I imagined it.

"Why don't you run along and get yourself some clothes? I'll wait here for you. There's nothing worse than feeling rushed while trying to make decisions, and I'm sure my taste is very different from yours." She looks down at my ripped jeans and fitted T-shirt, unable to hide her distaste. "Maybe grab a few nice dresses and skirts while you're in there, and a pair of jeans that aren't so... ratty."

I smother my grin and thank God she can't actually see the designer label on the back of them. I'll have to tear that off before I wash them in case anyone else sees it. Usually I'm better organized and would have gone to a thrift store close to home, but with my injuries, I didn't get a chance to, and my mother wouldn't be caught dead stepping into one.

"Okay, I won't take long," I promise and climb out of the car, placing a hand across my still aching ribs. They are taking the longest to heal, but the bruise cream I've been rubbing in seems to be helping. I've been walking around for days smelling like arnica, but I can't deny the fact that the cream reduces the pain and bruising quicker than if I left it alone. I always have some on me just in case.

I put my backpack over my shoulder. Not only does it have my money in it, but it also has my gun, ammo, phone, and expensive laptop, which a foster kid definitely should not have. I can't risk Martha snooping while I'm gone.

Closing the door of the luxury sedan quietly, I head into the thrift store. There's quiet music playing and the scent of washed fabric. It's different than the smell of a store where you buy new stuff. That still has a chemical fragrance to it, while in here, the smell is cozy, comforting, and inviting.

There's no one else in here except me and the girl behind the counter. She hasn't even bothered to look up from the book she's reading since I walked in, and I'm okay with that. I'm not the greatest with people who live normal lives since I have trouble relating to them. Princess Kensington is great with the people she hangs out with because they are all superficial and self-involved and happy to talk about themselves, but that's okay because I want to appear standoffish. I'm not here to make friends, and making them could make my job more difficult.

I reach a rack of jeans and flick through them, pulling out a couple of pairs in my size. Hanging them over my arm, I move onto a rack of skirts. I decided before I came that I was going to style myself slightly gothic, so when I find a bunch of short tartan skirts with pins, I grab all three of them, as well as a couple of pairs of cutoff denim shorts. The shirt rack is a gold-mine of band shirts and fitted tops, and I choose a selection that I like the look of. After picking a few long-sleeved shirts to wear under them, I think I'm good to go.

As I approach the counter, I notice a table with new packs of underwear, socks, and stockings, so I grab a couple packs of panties and a few knee-highs and fishnets to add to my pile. Finally, I dump my haul on the counter and smile at the girl who's finally looked up from her book. Her eyes widen when they catch sight of my black eye and bruised cheek.

"Fuck, someone really worked you over." She puts her book down and starts ringing up my purchases. She looks over my shoulder, and I turn to see what she's looking at. My heartbeat rises minutely at the thought that someone may be behind me, but when I see where she's looking, it slows again. Martha has hopped out of the car and is leaning against the front, chatting on the phone. She waves at the two of us when she notices us looking.

"You must be the new girl. Martha said we were getting a new one today. Are you going to be attending school?"

"Ah, yeah. Senior," I reply, and she smirks.

"Well, you're going to stir things up with your style, that's for sure. The school isn't very tolerant of things that are... different, and from the looks of this, you're definitely different."

There's no nastiness or judgment, just her imparting knowledge to me. "Are you a senior?" I ask, and she shakes her head.

"No, I'm a junior. Only one of the other girls in the home is a senior, and you're going to want to avoid her. She has issues."

"I don't suppose you want to give me all the ins and outs on living at Serenity House, do you? It seems kind of..." I trail off, and she fills in the gap.

"Strict? Yeah, the Standishes are no joke. James works a lot, so it's mostly Martha, and she likes to run a tight ship." She says it mockingly, like she's heard it a hundred times. "But I guess you kind of have to with all of us. We're not exactly model citizens. Most of us have issues, either from our original homes or the foster ones we've been placed in. Cutters, depression, anger management, we've got them all."

My eyes drift to her arms, which are covered with long sleeves, wondering if she's the cutter, before returning to my purchases.

She finishes ringing up my clothes and starts shoving them into a couple of bags. "I don't have any homework tonight, so I'll offer to help you settle in after dinner. It will score me some brownie points with Martha, and I'll give you the rundown, but if Jessica sees us, I'm going to pretend like I hate you. I am not getting on her radar. The rest of us girls have learned to stay out of her way. Unfortunately for you, you're going to have to share a room with her."

Damn it, I was hoping I would have a room to myself. I'm going to have to find a hiding spot for my gun and things, because I don't doubt Jessica will want to snoop. "I'm sure she'll be okay. I tend to stick to myself."

The girl shakes her head. "Nope, you're new meat, and you're gorgeous, even I can see that through the bruises. You're instant competition for her. You see, Jessica is in the popular group at school. It's a surprise she was able to infiltrate it, but Queen Bitch took her under her wing on her first day, and it was all downhill from there. There are three of them that you're going to want to avoid, but I can tell you the rest later. It looks like Martha is getting impatient."

I turn back, and sure enough, she's off the phone and looking at her watch. I can see her huff.

"That will be fifty-two seventy," Cassie says, pushing the bags toward me.

I scramble around in the front pocket of my backpack where I shoved the cash Dad had given me. It's all crumpled and wrinkled like you'd expect from tip money, and it blends in with my cover story. Nothing says imposter quicker than pulling out a black credit card.

I count out the cents, and she takes it all, not even blinking at all the small change. "Well, I guess I'll see you at Serenity House then." She snorts. "Six on the dot. I'm starving, and there's no way I'm missing dinner and having to go to bed without."

I wave goodbye and walk out thinking about what she said. Is being late and not being allowed dinner one of those consequences Martha mentioned? I need to study the board in the kitchen with everyone's schedules. I have to snoop, and that's not going to be easy. If I'm only allowed out for after-school activities or a job, then I think I'm going to have to hit up Team Basilisk already. I heard them mention one of them has a job managing something in town. He's going to have to be my cover, because I'm not going to find out much if I'm confined to school and the house.

Martha beams at me and my bags, though I'm pretty sure she's going to change her attitude when she sees my purchases. "All done?" she asks like she wasn't just looking at her watch.

"Yeah, but I was wondering if there is a drugstore we can stop at on the way as well."

Her smile drops. "What do you need from a drugstore? I won't stand for sexually active people in my house, so I don't condone birth control." Whoa, talk about leaping to a conclusion. I have an IUD, but she doesn't need to know that. I won't risk a random pregnancy, not when I use sex like I do. The risk of STDs is my biggest problem, and thankfully I'm all clean after that last fucked up job. I hate it when the marks refuse to use condoms, but a good course of broad-spectrum antibiotics covers most STIs

"I just need some tampons and things," I assure her, shrinking away from the angry woman. The anger clears and is replaced with that serene smile once more. Hmm, this woman's mood swings are off the charts.

"Of course, dear. There's one just down the street a little bit." We climb in, and the silence is awkward between us. "Make it quick. I need to get dinner started so it's on the table by six."

Once again, she parks in front of the building, and I hurry in. I don't dawdle, I just grab the things I need. I wasn't lying about tampons, but I also wanted to grab some makeup. I couldn't very well turn up with a case of it. Luckily, they have the brand I normally use, so I just grab my favorite items and quickly pay for those as well before rushing out to the car.

"That was quick. It's great that you can follow instructions," Martha praises as she starts back down the street. Maybe she thinks foster kids need all the praise they can get.

The car silently glides through town, leaving the shopping precinct and heading into suburbia. Pretty little houses with neat, tidy gardens line either side of the road. We drive a little farther, and that gives way to a more affluent area. Large mansions on even larger blocks are spread in a way that assures privacy for the wealthy people. We pass one particularly spectacular place, and she points it out.

"That's Governor Turner's house. He's a local man and maintains a place here. His sons have recently moved back to town. The youngest one was going to an exclusive boarding school out of state, and the oldest just finished college and is home while he decides what he wants to do." She imparts that gossipy bit of knowledge reverently, and I can hear the hint of envy in her tone.

We soon pass it, and once more, the scenery changes. The mansions give way to open space, and then we enter an area that is most definitely the poorer section of town. We pass old, run-down, decrepit buildings with tireless cars dumped in front and houses with leaning porches and broken shutters until we finally turn down a dirt road. Fuck, Serenity House is located in the middle of nowhere. Without a car, I'm going to be stuck walking everywhere.

"How does Cassie get to work?" I ask Martha, wondering if maybe there is at least public transportation.

"There's a bus that will drop you at the end of the lane," she tells me, and I breathe a sigh of relief. "It runs until nine in the evenings, and then it stops." Of course it does. Sneaking out at night just became a little harder with both a roommate and no transportation, but I've dealt with worse.

Finally, the little lane opens up to a large, two-story, clapboard house that looks like it's seen better days. The whitewash is a grimy gray, but the garden beds are well-tended, and none of the shutters are broken. I know from the file that this is not actually their house and is private property that the government rents for the purpose of housing unwanted teenagers. The Standishes are just the caretakers and live-in chaperones.

She pulls the car into a carport attached to the house and turns it off. "Well, don't just sit there, let's move."

CHAPTER 8

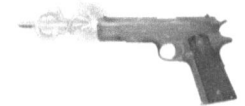

Martha helps me carry my meager belongings into the house. We put my purchases and the suitcase down at the bottom of a staircase, and she gives me a tour of the downstairs. Martha shows me the master bedroom, which is hers and her husbands and off limits, office, again off limits, large living area, and combined dining room and kitchen. All are old and in need of updating, but the house is clean and tidy.

She points out the white board where there is a whole heap of initials in columns with different days of the week. I run my eye down the Tuesday column, and the initials CH sit next to the word "work." That must be the girl at the thrift store. Under it are the letters JL, and they have "cheerleading practice" next to them. I wonder if that's the Jessica that Cassie warned me about. Next to the schedule is a chore chart with the same initials beside various chores like washing, garbage, dusting, and bathrooms. As I run my eye over the chart, I get the feeling that Martha doesn't actually have to lift a finger, since she has all the live-in help to do it. Even dinner prep has initials next to it a couple of days a week.

Next, she takes me upstairs. I grab my bags as we go past them. She points to a door where I can hear the low sounds of music playing inside. "This is the boys' room. Under no circumstances are you allowed in there." The next door we come to has a lilac-colored star on it. "This is Cassie, Sally, and Stephanie's room. You met Cassie, she's a junior, and the other two are sophomores. There are two bathrooms on this level. One is for the boys, and one is for the girls." She points at two doors at opposite ends of the long hallway. Holy shit, one bathroom for five teenage girls. That must be a shit show in the morning.

She stops in front of another door. "This leads to the loft. The oldest boy has his room and a bathroom up there. Again, you are not allowed up there. Don't let me catch you trying to weasel your way into using his bathroom or anything," she threatens, and I just about tell her to chill. There's no way I'm going to be inter-ested in high school kids, but I can't very well admit that, can I? I wonder what she would say if I told her I wasn't interested in boys. Would she still put me in with a girl? Man, I really want to fuck with her assuming ass, but I won't.

"You don't have to worry about me, ma'am. I just want to keep my head down, work hard at school, and get myself a college scholarship." I lay the good girl act on thick, but it must work, because she beams at me and pats my hand.

"Now that's what I like to hear. Someone who has their priorities right." She keeps moving to the last door. "This here is your room. You'll be sharing with Jessica. She's a senior just like you and popular to boot. I'm sure she can help show you around school tomorrow." She pushes the door open, and a wave of sickly sweet perfume wafts out.

She gestures for me to enter, so I step over the threshold and look around the room. Twin beds sit on either side, with two sets of drawers separating them. There's also a desk and chair against a wall next to the door, but that's about it. Above what is obviously Jessica's bed is a shelf with knickknacks, perfume, and girlie things, and the chest of drawers on her side is covered in the same.

"This will be yours." Martha goes over to the other side and points at the bed and drawers. "I expect your room to be kept neat at all times. I don't tolerate messiness or laziness. The five of you rotate cleaning bathrooms, and you and Jessica will share dusting and vacuuming in here. Now, if you want to get settled in, I need to get started on dinner. You can meet everyone else then." Without waiting for a response, she turns and bustles out of the room, leaving the door open behind her.

Heaving out a huge sigh, I take a seat on the bed and look around the room. There's absolutely nowhere to hide my things. The room has no carpet, just floor-boards, so maybe there's a loose one I can pry up where I can hide something in the gap. Jumping off the bed, I crouch down to look under it. I shimmy beneath it and tap the floorboards in the hopes of finding something that is usable. Nothing moves an inch. Fuck! I climb back out and then look at the drawers.

After pulling out the bottom one, I breathe a sigh of relief. There's a gap between the bottom drawer and the base, which can't be seen unless you pull the drawer all the way out like I just did. What are the chances that Jessica will snoop that diligently? I look at her set. Unless she's got something hidden too. Standing up, I walk to the door and peer around the frame. There's no one in sight, and I took note of how the stairs creak and groan when we walked up them. If I'm quick and I keep an ear out, then I should be able to hear if someone comes.

Hurrying back to her drawers, I crouch down and pull hers out, checking that she has nothing hidden in the gap. Thankfully, there's nothing but dust bunnies, and I quickly close it and grab my backpack. I pull out my laptop and iPhone and push them into the gap, then I grab my gun and the two spare maga-zines I have. I wrap them in an old T-shirt from my suitcase and then shove them in as well. Leaning back on my heels, I survey what I've done. If she does end up finding everything, hopefully she will be distracted by the phone and laptop and won't think to check what's in the shirt. Both devices are password protected, and what are the chances she's a hacker?

Placing the drawer back in the sliders, I push it in. All that's left in my backpack now is a paperback book I grabbed at the bus station before I boarded the bus, as well as my wallet and cheap burner phone that's for my cover. I toss it back onto the bed and open my suitcase. In it is Miller's T-shirt, which I refused to give back. I also kept his boxer briefs. Who knew men's underwear was so comfy? I would have brought them and more with me, but I thought that might confuse Martha, so I reluctantly left them behind. There are also a couple of other things that I thought would work for this assignment and some bras and shoes. I pull everything out and shove it into the top drawer before placing the shoes at the end of the bed. I put most of my purchases from the thrift shop in the next one, and lastly, I shove the jeans in that bottom drawer. There is nothing exciting to see, and hopefully she stays out of it.

I push my now empty backpack and the bags the clothes came in under the bed before standing up and brushing myself off. Jessica obviously hasn't vacuumed under that bed for a while. Now, there's nothing left for me to do for the moment.

It's half past five in the evening. I'm assuming everyone will be arriving home soon or emerging from their rooms, so there's no point in getting my laptop out to see if the nerd herd has come up with any more information. So far, there isn't much to go on. I'm going to have to do some snooping and poking around. There's bound to be people who know things. It's just a matter of turning over the right rock and flushing them out, but that's a worry for tomorrow, because right now, I'm going to suss out this household. I need to ask questions about the teens that went missing, and I'm not sure how to do that with Martha without seeming suspicious. Why would a foster kid know about that kind of thing? I'll need to ascertain who's been here the longest and then tell them I heard rumors about missing kids or something, but to do that, I need to play happy family. Well, not too happy, since I'm a shy, beaten down foster kid.

I make my way downstairs, moving slowly so I can take note of all the creaks and groans the floors make. I'd like to know if they can be heard downstairs just in case I need to sneak out. I didn't think to look out the window and see what my chance would be for climbing out there. Hopefully there's a tree or a gently sloping roof as an alternative option. I'll check them out when I get back.

The music is still playing in the first boys' room as I pass it, and I'm tempted to knock and introduce myself, but that won't fit my character. Instead, I slink downstairs, avoiding all the creaky parts of the steps that I noted on the way up and finding a couple more. Jesus, I hope Martha and James are heavy sleepers, otherwise it's not going to be as easy as I hoped.

Noise coming from the kitchen/dining room tells me more than just Martha is in there, so I wrap my cover persona around myself and slink in, darting my eyes around the room to take in everything. Two teenage girls are setting the table and chatting animatedly to Martha as they do. They are telling her about what happened at volleyball practice, and how one of their teammates spiked the ball into another teammate's face. Both girls are tall and slim with red hair and freckles, and I'm guessing they are twins but not identical. There are differences in the shades of their hair, and when they look up at me, I can see one has green eyes and the other brown.

"Holy heck, you look like you got spiked in the face with a volleyball too," the green-eyed girl exclaims as her eyes widen when she sees the state of my face.

"Nope, it was a fist," I tell her, not having to lie, and she winces and exchanges a glance with her sister.

"Ah, Mackenzie, there you are. Come in and sit down. Sally and Stephanie were just telling me about their day." She points to each of the girls. Sally is the green-eyed one, and Stephanie has brown. "Girls, this is Makenzie. She's going to be a senior, but I hope if you see her looking lost, you'll help her out. Sally and Stephanie are sophomores, but they are both on the junior varsity volleyball team. Both of them are super athletic, and we're hoping they'll be able to get scholarships for college," Martha says, sharing personal information with me, and I have to frown. I'm practically a stranger, so why is she telling me this? Stephanie's and Sally's backs are to her, so she doesn't see the annoyed eye roll either. I guess they feel the same way.

"In fact, all of my kids are on track for scholarships," she brags, bringing a large, steaming casserole dish over to the table the girls have finished setting, just as the back door opens and Cassie and a pretty black-haired girl walk in. Ah, this must be the famed Jessica.

"Oh good, girls, you're right on time." Martha beams as Cassie smiles at me, and Jessica eyes me with icy indifference. "When you put your things in your rooms, please tell the boys dinner is ready."

They both go and do as Martha instructed, leaving the kitchen just as the back door opens once more and an older man walks in. Martha beams as he leans in to give her a kiss, and I study them together. He's a hand-some man with broad shoulders and gray streaked dark hair. His facial hair has the same smattering of gray in it as well. When they pull apart, he turns to me, and his piercing blue eyes seem to see right through to my soul. I can't control the goosebumps that break out across my skin. Holy shit, that's one hell of a visceral reaction, and I always trust my gut, but in a blink, the look is gone, and he smiles warmly at me.

"You must be Mackenzie. I'm James." He walks toward me and holds out his hand. My reactions are a little slower than normal, but that fits with my persona, so I give him a small, limp handshake before snatching my hand back.

"Nice to meet you," I mumble, not looking at him.

"Why don't you go and wash up, dear? The girls are just getting the boys, and we should be ready to eat." Martha shoos her husband out of the kitchen and gestures to the table. "Take a seat, Mackenzie. Sally, show her which one is hers." Martha bustles back to the counter to grab another pot of steaming something.

"You sit here." The green-eyed twin points to one of the seats. "I'm sorry. It's between the boys, but if we don't separate them at dinner, they end up squabbling over who gets the most food."

Before I can respond, there's a clattering of feet on the stairs. Whoever it is isn't even trying to avoid making noise. Two boys tumble into the room, and they seem to be doing their best to keep each other away from the table. One of them is basically the spitting image of the two girls, so I'm guessing they are triplets, not twins. He's slightly taller and lean as well, with the same red hair. The other is a little more solid, with dark skin and tight, curly black hair that sticks out all over his head like he stuck his finger in a light socket. It bounces with every movement. They shove and jeer at one another, but Martha quickly puts a stop to it.

"Boys, that's enough. Sit yourselves down." They quickly do as she says, and that's when they catch sight of me. A grin spreads across the face of the redhead, and he winks at me, his eyes brown like his sister Stephanie's.

"Oh look, Ty, new meat," he jokes, but Ty is looking at me with a frown on his face.

"Yeah, Will, and she looks like she's already been tenderized for us." The boys quickly take a seat on either side of me and start peppering me with questions. I'm not sure what to answer first, but again, Martha jumps to the rescue.

"Oh, for goodness' sake, leave her be. You have plenty of time to get to know her." She places a steaming bowl of vegetables on the table and takes a seat at one end just as Cassie and Jessica return. Cassie takes a seat on the other side of Ty, and Jessica sits opposite us where Sally and Stephanie are, but there's still one empty seat on their side, as well as the chair opposite Martha. The table is loud and chatty as Martha asks everyone about their day. Nobody touches the food on the table, so I guess they are waiting for James and whoever sits in the other empty seat.

Five minutes later, Martha sighs and looks at the clock on the wall. "Where are the other two? They know how I like to keep to the schedule."

Just then, two things happen. James reappears and takes his seat, and the back door opens one last time. The person who saunters in gets a reaction from Martha, but they also manage to get one from me. My mouth drops open in surprise as Miller peels off a leather jacket and hangs it on the hook before taking the last seat at the table. When he turns around, he catches my eye, and his green eyes widen minutely as he catches sight of me. I guess he wasn't expecting for me to look like I do. I dyed my blonde hair black, and I have long wear lavender contacts in my eyes. I didn't bother with makeup because I wanted the sympathy my bruises would bring me.

Our eyes meet, and I think there's a small hint of appreciation in his gaze, but I must have been mistaken, because all I see now is cold indifference before he looks away.

CHAPTER 9

"**M**iller, that was cutting it close," Martha scolds, and he gives her a smile much like the one he had given my mom a few days ago. It's like butter wouldn't melt in his mouth.

"Sorry, Martha, my lift home had to run an errand on the way," he apologizes politely, ignoring me completely.

I catch Jessica eyeing me carefully, and I have to quickly snap my mouth shut and look down at my hands. I can't appear to be interested, or I'm going to blow this right here and now. Why the fuck didn't anyone tell me he was a plant in this house? I thought I was going to work the foster angle while they did something else.

"That's alright, dear," Martha coos at Miller inappropriately. "Now that everyone is here, this is

Mackenzie. She's going to be with us for a while, so I hope you make her feel like family."

"What happened to your face? Did your pimp beat you up?"

Cassie gasps in shock, but I hear Jessica snicker as Miller's silky tone floats across the table. I don't look up because I'm worried if I do, they'll see my desire to grab my knife and stab him in the thigh with it. Did my pimp beat me up? Is he implying I'm a whore? Scratch that—not the thigh, the balls. I've done that before, pinned a man to his chair by his balls. The sounds of his screams were magical to my ears because that cocksucker liked little boys and girls just a little too much.

"Miller, that's enough," James snaps and holds out his hands. "Let's say grace so we can eat the delicious food Martha and the girls made for us."

Everyone does as asked, and I find myself holding both Ty's and Will's hands as James thanks the good lord for our food, and to keep us all healthy and safe, and to watch over those of their children who have left to go on for new things, and to keep the ones who have gone missing safe.

A foot nudges me under the table at that, and I lift my eyes to see Miller looking at me. He nods at James, like he's trying to get me to listen to what he's saying. I roll my eyes at him and look back down. Of course I heard it, moron. Has he never been undercover before? That wasn't subtle at all.

James finishes with, "Amen," which is echoed around the table, and people start reaching for food.

"So what year are you in, Mackenzie?" Jessica's voice has a little girl quality to it, which is annoying as fuck, and she's only said a few words. I'm going to want to gag her if she talks to me too much. "Sally, Steph, and Will are sophomores, and Ty and Cassie are juniors, so I'm sure they can help show you around."

And the claws come out, but what does she think that implying I look young is going to do? Fuck me, I'm still recovering from having the shit beat out of me, so her pathetic attempt to make me feel bad is nothing.

Before I can answer, Martha does. "Oh no, dear, she's a senior like you. I thought maybe you or Miller could show her around school tomorrow."

Jessica's eyes widen dramatically, and she puts her hand on Miller's tattoo covered arm. "I couldn't possibly. I have my Divinity of Morality Club meeting before school tomorrow, and Miller is helping me with that. Maybe if you call the school, they can assign someone to help her out."

She's smiling, but I can hear her politely covered threat. Jessica just staked her claim on Miller and basically told me I was nothing and no one, and I better not get in her way. That's no skin off my nose, she's welcome to the asshole. I wonder what she'd say if she knew he was the one who did the damage to my face. She'd probably congratulate him.

"Of course I'll do that. Don't worry, I'll make sure they look after you," Martha assures me.

"Of course we will. We take really good care of our foster children. We want you to be the best you can be," James adds, smiling at me, but once again, it doesn't reach his eyes.

Dinner chaos goes on around us, and he breaks our stare off when Miller passes him a basket of rolls, but I can't suppress the shudder that runs down my back at his words. The dude gives me a creepy feeling, and he just became my number one suspect.

"We sure do, so you can go on and live happy, successful, and productive lives," Martha chimes in, sounding like a propaganda ad. They are laying it on a little thick, and I can see I'm not the only one who thinks so. The twins roll their eyes good-naturedly, and Jessica simpers at the adults.

Dinner is a noisy affair, and thankfully, everyone leaves me alone after that, giving me enough time to observe the dynamic. It seems much like the triplets—Ty, Jessica, and Cassie—have been with the Standishes for a while. Miller is quiet and only responds when asked a direct question. I can tell that Martha thinks he's wonderful, even though she does try to convince him to take his piercings out. James eats his meal and contributes now and then to the conversation, but otherwise he's happy to let the others carry it.

The reminiscence comes to a screaming halt when Ty chuckles about something Slater used to do. The loaded glances exchanged by the teenagers at the table has me champing at the bit to ask a question, but I don't have to.

"Who's Slater?" Miller asks casually before taking a sip of water from the cup in front of him.

Martha crosses herself before replying. "Slater was one of our foster kids. He got a job offer for an apprenticeship at a tattoo place down in Brunswick, but he never made it there. He went missing, and the police haven't been able to find him."

She exchanges a loaded glance with James, and he sighs, putting his knife and fork down. Leaning back in his chair, he crosses his arms. "I guess we should probably have a conversation with Mackenzie and Miller, because he's only been here a couple of weeks too. The rest of you kids have heard this, but it's not going to hurt for you to hear it again. Slater isn't the only one of our foster kids who have gone missing. In the last year, we had another four kids age out and get great jobs or scholarship offers. We were so proud of them, and we thought what we were trying to achieve here was working. Kids who had difficult childhoods were getting their lives straightened out and achieving things they had only dreamed of."

"Yes, Rory had received a scholarship to the University of Georgia. He wanted to study agriculture, buy a farm, and raise goats. Fletcher was obsessed with those Japanese comics and gaming. He was going to do graphic design and art at the Savannah College of Art and Design." Martha sounds proud, but it's tinged with sadness.

"Sybil had been scouted by a modeling agency,"

Martha continues, "and she was moving into a shared home in New York. They already had jobs lined up for her. Lastly, there's Lydia. We have a friend who has a club in Savannah, and she asked us if we could organize an interview for her. She wanted to earn some money while she was figuring out what she would like to do. She talked about how traveling and gaining some bar experience would be beneficial to her."

Martha sighs. "We were thrilled, of course, for all of our kids, and we put them on buses and happily waved goodbye. For a while, we weren't worried that we hadn't heard from them. They were moving on with their lives, and they were making new friends and creating new routines, but when I invited them back for Thanksgiving and didn't get a response from any of them, then we got worried."

James takes over again. "Turns out that none of them ever made it to their destination. At some point between us dropping them at the bus station and where they were going, they just disappeared."

Martha sniffles and dabs at her eyes with her napkin.

"Missing?" Miller sounds incredulous.

I glance around the table, and the kids look haunted. Even bitchy Jessica looks sad, so I don't doubt that this is not news to them.

"Yes, we alerted the police, but they have no leads. The reason I'm telling you this is because I want you all to be careful. It's why we're so strict on curfews and needing to know your whereabouts. We don't want anything to happen to any of you." James is somber but firm.

"No, I don't think I could live with myself if any more of my kids were to go missing." Martha sniffles as she stands up and takes her empty plate over to the sink.

A small pang of doubt worms its way into my conscience. Would they be so upset and determined to keep their other kids safe if they were involved? Or are they just that good at pretending?

Dinner wraps up after that, and everyone disperses. Jessica disappears back upstairs as I help Martha clear the table, but she quickly reappears with her coat and bag.

"Sophie is picking me up, and we're going to work on our history assignment together," she tells Martha, who beams at her.

"That's great. I'm so glad you are friends. She's such a good girl. You should introduce Mackenzie to her," she suggests, and I can see that Jessica doesn't think it's a good idea by the way she screws her nose up when Martha turns her back. "Sophie is my niece, and she's the head cheerleader and president of the yearbook committee. I bet she'll even get nominated for prom queen." She sounds like a real overachiever.

I smile noncommittally as I wipe up the dining table.

A horn honks outside, and Jessica dashes out of the house. Martha pulls back the curtain on the window and waves before dropping it again. "Thanks for your help, Mackenzie. You didn't have to do it on your first day, but I appreciate it. Why don't you watch some TV with James and the boys?" she suggests, but what I really need to do is check out my escape options from my room.

"I'm kind of tired. I might get ready for bed and read for a little while," I tell her quietly. "What time does the bus leave in the morning?"

"Of course, it's been a long day. You need to be at the stop at the end of the road at seven, so I wake everyone at six."

I thank her for the lovely meal and walk through the living area to get to the stairs. James and the younger boys are watching a football game, but there's no sign of Miller or the other three girls.

"Hey, Mackenzie, you want to watch the game with us?" Ty's friendly grin is welcoming, and he gestures to a spot between him and Will on the couch.

"No thank you, I think I'm going to get an early night. Maybe next time." I wave at them, and they all wish me good night. I practically feel eyes on me all the way up the stairs, but I don't want to turn around to see who it is. My money is on James. My spidey senses are tingling, and they are screaming that man is no good.

Once I'm back in my room, I check my bottom drawer and find everything is as I left it, so I guess Jessica hasn't snooped yet. Once I'm reassured, I head over to the window. It's going to be the only other place to get out, but it's inconvenient because it sits between the two beds. There's no screen on the window as I lift it up, but it screeches in the frame and gets stuck halfway. Fuck! I poke my head out of the little gap and gaze around. There's actually nowhere for me to go anyway. I thought there might be a bit of roof to climb out on, but it's a straight side of the building. As I look up, I see that the window of the loft has a tree right next to it, which would be easy enough to climb down. There's a light on in the attic, so I decide to go and check it out.

Pulling the window closed, I head back to the door I'm assuming is Miller's. That must be why she told me I couldn't go up there, but there's no one around, and I guess now is as good a time as any to touch base with him. I won't have to wait to get started if we can exchange some information, but I wonder if he's going to be a dick or not.

I look at the door of the other girls' room, but it's firmly closed, and I can hear them chatting behind it, so I quickly turn the handle and slip quietly into the doorway, pulling it closed behind me. The set of stairs that leads upward is dark, but I run my hand against the wall and feel my way up them. Surprisingly, they are quiet compared to the others in the house, and I find myself at the top of them in no time.

There is another doorway with an open door that leads into the attic, and when I peer around it to check if Miller is in here, I just about swallow my tongue. He's stretched out on his bed, naked except for a tight set of boxer briefs, ones that match the pair I now have, but they fit him much better than mine fit me. The fabric is tight against what looks like a generous package, but I can't see because his hand is shoved down there, and he's slowly stroking it.

CHAPTER 10

My eyes roam over his ripped physique as I try to catalog all of the tattoos that cover his body, but my eyes keep drifting back to where he has his hand. I really wish I could see what he is doing better. I wonder if his junk is pierced too. I've never had sex with someone with pierced junk. In fact, of the two times I've had sex that was by choice and not part of the job, it was completely underwhelming. Miller looks like he'd know what he was doing. Fuck, I bet he could hate fuck me into oblivion. He's so pretty, and if I could gag him, it would be perfect. My core tingles with the thought, and I pinch myself hard. What the fuck am I thinking?

"Like what you see?" His husky voice startles me from my dirty thoughts. Fuck! He's staring at me with a smirk on his face, but his eyes are molten heat as he continues to stroke his length. "You can come over here and give me a hand if you want. I hear that you're no stranger to using sex to get what you want. How about if you suck me off, I'll let you ask me five questions?"

I must take too long to think about it, because I see his eyes widen in surprise, and I chuckle. "Dude, did you expect me to get upset about you propositioning me? Like you said, I use sex all the time. You're right, I did want some questions answered, but I was wondering if I had enough time for an orgasm before someone noticed I'm missing and came looking for me. I wouldn't want to be caught breaking the rules on the first day."

His hand hasn't stopped moving while we've been talking, and as I step into the room, his gaze wanders over my body. "Gothic princess was not what I was expecting when I pictured you undercover. I have to say I'm surprised. I thought you'd be a Jessica clone, a perky cheerleader. This is a good look on you." His gaze comes back to my face. "It makes me hard as fuck to see my marks on your face. I liked marking you. Would you let me mark you again? Come closer and take your top off so I can paint your pretty tits with my cum."

Holy hell, this guy is filthy as fuck, and I would be so here for it if he wasn't such a dick. I spy a tissue box on a cabinet, so I step over and pull a couple free before tossing them at him. "Can you just hurry it up? I want a briefing, and then you can go back to loving on yourself."

He smirks and calls my bluff, or what he thinks is

my bluff, but I desperately want to see what he looks like when he comes. He pushes his briefs down with his other hand, and holy shit, his dick is big. My mouth waters, and I have to check that I'm not actually drooling as I watch his hand speed up. A glint of metal catches my eye, and I step closer for a better look. He has piercings in it, and not just one. He has a row of five bars lining the shaft. It's all I can do to maintain my nonchalance and not reach out to touch them. I pretend to check my watch for the time just so I can hide my fascination, but when my eyes flick back to him, I see his abs contract before thick, white cum paints them. My gaze flies back to his face. He has his eyes closed and his head thrown back in pleasure, his neck muscles straining, and I almost fucking spontaneously orgasm at the sight. Biting my lip, I contain the groan that wants to escape.

"Want to lick it clean?" he asks, jolting me out of my own fantasy, and I wrinkle my nose in pretend disgust.

"I have no interest in playing games with you, Miller, so just get on with it."

Sighing and pouting with mock disappointment, he uses the tissues I threw at him to clean up his ripped abs and then tosses them in a nearby trash can before righting his briefs and covering his still semi-hard cock. He grabs a shirt off the bed and pulls it on over his head.

"Happy now?"

"Perfect, thanks." I look around his room, spying

the window I think leads to the tree, and without asking permission, I head over to it. Again, it has no screen on it, but this time when I lift it, the window slides smoothly and quietly. I breathe out a sigh of relief as I feel Miller at my back. Poking my head out, I see it's an easy leap to the tree in either direction and decide this will be my way in and out. Now I'm stuck with the issue of how to get to town quickly.

I pull my head back into the room and slide the window closed before spinning and looking at the asshole who is now right up in my personal space.

"Do you mind?" I ask and push him back, and he moves, but he's lost his trademark smirk, and he's frowning.

"What are you doing?"

"Well, I need a way to get out of the house undetected, and I can't go out through my own bedroom window, so it will have to be yours. How do you get to town if you need to?" I ask him, leaning back against the window frame and crossing my arms.

"I message one of the guys, and they pick me up at the end of the road." He seems happy to share information now, so maybe we can be professional about this after all. He takes a seat at the desk chair nearby.

"Is the wooded area the driveway runs down on public land, or does it belong to this place?" I ask him.

"It belongs to this place. Why?"

"Well, I was thinking we could hide a motorcycle in there, and then we wouldn't be at the mercy of your team. Leave it with me, I'll come up with something.

Now, I can't say I wasn't a little surprised to see you here. Dad never told me that he had another agent in the house. How long have you been here?"

"A little over three weeks. And your dad lets us run our ops how we want. He's our handler and tells us only to contact him if we need help."

Huh. I didn't know Dad handled another team. I thought it was just me.

"We thought this would be a good place for one of us to be, since five of the more recent missing teens originated from here. I didn't know he was going to send you here as well."

"It probably won't hurt to have us both here. They don't seem to specifically target male or females, so either of us could be considered a target. Have you looked into the Standishes?"

He rolls his eyes at my question and sighs like he's annoyed, but he answers it. "Yes. They were the first people we looked into. They are upstanding citizens in the community who are praised for their charity work with unwanted children. They attend church regularly, and James works for a law firm." He spins around and opens up the laptop on the desk, tapping at a few keys until five photos fill the screen. "These are the five who went missing from here."

I push off the windowsill and peer over his shoulder. Each of the kids are attractive teens with smiling faces and nice bodies. I can see why they were targeted.

"All were good students and worked part-time

jobs, from what we can ascertain. The only thing they had in common is that they all came from families where there was no chance of reconciliation. The parents were either dead or incarcerated, and they had no extended family. There's nothing to suggest that any of them were doing anything illegal on the side like dealing drugs or flesh. They were genuinely good kids."

"So the only reason they were picked is because nobody would miss them, and the only reason anyone noticed they were gone was because Mrs. Standish invited them for Thanksgiving. What about school friends? None of them know anything or have heard from them?"

"No, we checked. They tended to stick together and didn't really have any outside friends."

"Which made them an even better target," I muse.

He opens another file. "These are the other kids from this state who have gone missing, which is what prompted the governor to bring us in." There are about twenty faces looking back at me. Again, he clicks on another file, and in it are hundreds of headshots of attractive teens. There isn't an ugly kid in the bunch. "Lathan did some digging, and when he put in the parameters of foster child, no relatives, and missing, this is what he came up with. Every one of these kids have disappeared in the same kind of circumstances as the ones here." A few of them have red marks on them.

"What does this mean?" I ask, pointing at the mark.

"Lathan also ran a broad-spectrum facial recognition software through the internet. All of the ones with red have either appeared in porn or have been sold through an auction site on the dark web."

A wave of nausea has me swallowing at the thought of all of these kids being abused and used against their consent. Unlike me, who uses sex as a weapon by choice, they are having it used against them and don't have the choice to say no.

"Do we have any leads?" I ask, ready to nail some assholes to the wall.

He runs a frustrated hand through his dark brown hair and shakes his head. "A few. We think that the school counselor is a groomer. You will be called into his office in the first couple of days, so I'd like your opinion. He asks questions that no school counselor should be asking."

"What do you mean?" I ask. I've never been to school, and my upbringing was far from normal, so getting him to explain what he's talking about will help me.

"He was a little overly friendly and not professional at all. He asked me how I was settling in, if I enjoyed living with Martha and James, and how I was getting along at school, which are all normal things, but then he started getting personal. Was I interested in any of the girls? Had I checked out the cheerleader practices and noticed how tight their warm-up outfits were? Or was I more into the chicks like me with tattoos and piercings? Then he had the audacity to ask me if they put out. It was like he was trying to be my friend instead of an adult partly responsible for my care. It was gross, and I told him that. He didn't like that one bit, and the meeting finished shortly after that."

"Hmm, okay, so when it's my turn, what if instead of getting upset about it, I go along with it? I can say that I don't like teenage boys, since they don't know how to give a girl an orgasm, and I much prefer older males."

He turns quickly in his chair, wearing a scowl on his face as he looks up at me, his head in line with my breasts. "Fuck, you're just asking to be taken, aren't you?" He sounds pissed, and I step back—not because I'm afraid, but because I really like how he's looking at me. His fury is fucking sexy.

"Yes, Miller, that's why I'm here. We want me to be taken. The quicker that happens, the quicker we have a chance to save these kids." I wave at the laptop behind him. "Most of them won't even be in the country anymore. We'll be lucky if we can even retrieve half of what is there, and most of them will be traumatized beyond belief. We're their only hope at this stage, and you can damn well bet I'm going to do what I can to find them. If that means I get taken, then I get taken. It's not like I haven't had to fuck my way out of bad situations before."

"You can't be serious!" He gapes at me, and I roll my eyes.

"I am not sure what female agents you've worked

with in the past, but I can absolutely fucking guarantee that I'm not afraid of doing anything to get my mark or resolve an operation, and I have the skills to fucking back that up."

He just continues to look at me in surprise, and I sigh and sit down on the bed.

"I know it's hard for you guys to understand my mindset, but I've only ever had me." I stop and think about how to explain this to him. "You know that MITHOS is a family organization run by my dad's family, yes?" He nods. "And you know about Dad and Uncle T, but you might not know about their sister Jillian. She was the OG ghost operative, and when it was decided that Katie, Jillian's daughter Keely, and I were going to be ghost operatives, she decided we needed to be... schooled, I guess you could say, in the fine art of using our bodies as weapons."

He blinks, still not comprehending what I am saying.

"Fucking, Miller, she got us lessons in fucking."

His mouth drops open, and he starts to sputter, and I laugh.

"Yup, that was Dad and Uncle T's reaction too. Man, that was not a pleasant conversation. Imagine a conference room with three sets of parents sitting around the table, and then Aunt Jillian announces to them that us three girls needed sex lessons. I thought our dads' heads would explode. Surprisingly, Mom and Aunt Flic were supportive and said it would be smart for us to know how to use all the weapons in our arsenal. The men eventually came around, and Aunt Jillian hired each of us an escort to teach us about sex."

"You lost your virginity to an escort?" Miller looks like his head is about to explode as well.

"Yeah, but it was no hardship. Sampson was fucking gorgeous. All three of them were, and none of us girls were under the illusion that your virginity needs to be saved for your husband or anything else. And hey, at least he knew what he was doing. How many virgins can say that? Over the next six months, I had my mind expanded on everything sex related so I would be comfortable if I needed to use it for a job. Look, Miller, I think you're under the impression that women can't have sex without there being emotions involved, and it's just not true. Sometimes a girl just wants to get off, and no cuddling or pretty words are needed." I pat him on the leg and stand up. "So you don't need to worry about me. If I get taken, then I'll do what I'll need to until you guys can find me."

"And how do you think that's going to happen?" he spits out, and I point behind my ear.

"I have a tracker, and by now, Lathan will have access to the program. To be honest, the fact that you are here as bait tells me that you might need one as well." Then I think about the previous conversation. "Are you prepared to do what you need to do to survive? Because if you get taken, there's no guarantee that you're going to be sold to a woman. Or should I apologize for assuming something about you?"

"You just worry about yourself, and I'll worry

about me," he snarls, avoiding the question. "Now get out of my room before anyone finds you up here."

"Alright. Is that information in the MITHOS database?" I ask, pointing at his laptop, and he nods abruptly. "Okay then, I guess I'll see you around."

I leave it at that because I can see I'm not getting through to him. I'm sure we will have a team meeting soon, and maybe dealing with one of the others will be easier. He's silent as I leave, and I don't look back.

Deep breath, Kenz. It's only one assignment, and then you will go back to being blissfully alone and not having to rely on anyone.

Back in my room, I pull out my real encrypted phone and send Dad a message about needing to have a tracker planted in Miller and asking if he could organize a motorcycle that I can hide in the bushes. If I conceal it far enough away, no one should even be able to hear it up at the house. Reluctantly, I ask for two helmets. I don't really want to share it with Miller, but it's not always going to be practical for him to wait for a pickup.

Once I'm done, I shove the phone back into my hiding spot and change into my pajamas. Although the shirt smells nothing like the spicy scent that encompassed Miller's room, I still stick my nose into it in the hopes that I can catch some of the residue, but alas, all I smell is laundry detergent. With images of him pleasuring himself washing through my mind, I fall asleep with a smile on my face.

CHAPTER 11

I take special care with my makeup and outfit the next morning, and Martha's expression is hysterical when I come downstairs in my fishnet tights, boots, and skirt. I smother the grin when she looks me up and down and crosses herself.

"Mackenzie, that's really not trying to fit in. Are you trying to get ostracized?"

I look down at myself and smooth out the tartan skirt. "You think so?"

"She looks hot," Will remarks from the table, where he's shoveling cereal into his mouth. His sisters both nod, but Jessica scowls.

"No, Martha is right, she looks like a tramp. She'll fit right in with the losers and deadbeats."

I didn't hear her come in last night, which is concerning because I should have. I guess everything is catching up with me and my body needed the rest after the long day yesterday. I heard her get up this morning but pretended to stay asleep because I didn't want a confrontation first thing this morning. She's wearing a skirt and top too, very much like mine. In fact, the skirt is even shorter, but because it's in pastel colors, I guess it's more acceptable than what I'm wearing. Miller is sitting next to her, wearing all black much like I am, but he doesn't get compared to a loser or a deadbeat.

"Oh well, I don't need to be part of the popular group. I just want to get good grades and graduate. I'll probably just stick to myself. I'm not really good with people anyway," I tell her as I grab a mug and fill it with coffee before joining the others at the table.

"I think you look great," Cassie whispers to me.

"That's what I like to hear," Martha says. "You're going to work hard and stay out of drama, which seems like a great idea to me. Hurry up, you lot, you still have to walk down the drive, so you better get moving if you don't want to be late. Cassie, can you show Mackenzie to the office? I've organized to have someone show Mackenzie around. Oh, and show her the supply cupboard so she can grab some things for school." Martha grabs a mug, pours some coffee into it, and places it at the head of the table where James sat last night. I guess he doesn't need to start as early as we do in the morning.

Everyone pushes away from the table and gets moving. I quickly drain my coffee and put my mug in the dishwasher as Cassie opens a cupboard near the back door. She pulls out a couple of notebooks and pens for me. I shove them into my backpack as everyone starts to leave out the back door with noisy goodbyes for Martha.

"Come on, we don't want to miss the bus." Cassie tugs me out the door, and we hurry to catch up to Sally and Stephanie. Ty and Will are in front, roughhousing as they walk down the drive, and just behind them are Miller and Jessica. Jessica has her arm tucked into the crook of his elbow, and their heads are close together. I hear Cassie snort next to me.

"Jessica has been trying so hard to get his attention, but he usually brushes it off. I wonder what made him accept it today." I can see her look at me out of the corner of my eye, but I don't engage.

"What happens if we miss the bus?" I ask her.

"You have to ask Martha to take you, and she doesn't stop berating you the whole entire time. It's not worth the hassle, trust me. Okay, so the quick rundown of who's who in senior year. You heard Martha mention her niece Sophie yesterday. She's the queen bee of the girls, and she's a viper. I'm not actually sure how she even accepted Jessica into her fold. I think it was probably more about keeping your enemies, or the pretty girls, close so she could manipulate them. Avoid them if you just want to keep your head down. They are nothing but drama, and you're going to send them into a frenzy. Lucy and Michelle round out their quad."

The air is a little chilly this morning, so I pull my long sleeves down over my hands, and I'm thankful I wore the fishnets. Even though they don't block a lot of the wind, I bet my legs are warmer than Jessica's.

"As for the boys, Ryland Turner, who is Governor Turner's son, has recently returned to town to go to school. Rumor has it he was kicked out of his exclusive boarding school, but he's the most popular boy in the school at the moment, which pisses off Billy, the quarterback for the football team and the former most popular boy. In fact, all of the football guys lost their top spot because we also brought three other new guys to school, and they are all hot and mysterious, so instant popularity." She waves a hand at Miller. "Perfect example. He's a foster kid but he oozes sexy bad boy, so instant popularity. You know all the good girls are hoping he will corrupt them. Somehow, he fits in with Ryland's group, which consists of two more boys who are new to the town as well."

Hmm, it doesn't seem like they are blending in all that well if they hang out together, and how the hell are they going to find out any information if people think they are just teenagers? Maybe we're all potential targets though. I really need to talk to Team Bastards and grill them over their plan.

"Okay, so avoid Jessica's and Miller's groups if I want to be left alone?" I ask.

"Yeah, that's about the gist of it, but I'm sure you're going to cause waves anyway. You're a threat to Sophie, and she'll be in attack mode. I'm not so sure of Ryland and the boys. I haven't seen them be nasty to anyone, even Billy who tries to start shit with them.

They just pat him on the back and wish him luck with his game. It infuriates him because he desperately wants to start a fight."

"How do you know all this?" I ask her, and she shrugs.

"I have the same lunch as them, and I'm a watcher. Societal interaction fascinates me," Cassie says as we reach where everyone else has gathered, so I'm guessing it's the bus stop. Cassie may very well be my ticket to finding out about the missing kids. She obviously sees more than others do.

Before I can ask any questions, a shiny red four-door Maserati pulls up and a back window lowers. Bishop sticks his head out. "Hey, Miller, you want a lift?" Bishop doesn't even acknowledge me. I'm not sure if it's because of our cover or because he doesn't recognize me. Miller untangles himself from Jessica.

"Yeah, that would be great," he says as he opens the back door and climbs in.

"Can I come too?" Jessica leans down, giving Bishop a clear view of her cleavage.

His lips turn up in a wolfish grin. "Yeah, sure, jump in."

Jessica follows behind Miller and pulls the door closed. There's someone sitting in the passenger seat, but from this angle, I can't see who. I'm assuming it's Lathan though. It doesn't take them long to pull away, leaving a cloud of dust in their wake. We're all waving it away as the bus lumbers to a stop.

The school bustles with activity when the bus pulls up and drops us off. I get a few side glances, but I'm mostly ignored, and I'm happy for that. Cassie leads me to the office and introduces me to the lady at the front desk.

"Mrs. Steed, this is Mackenzie. She's new at our home. Mrs. Standish said she organized to have someone show her around."

The gray-haired woman eyes me with sympathy. Sure, I could have covered the remaining discoloration on my face with makeup, but this is the exact reason why I didn't. "Of course. Welcome, Mackenzie. Here's your schedule, and your escort should be—" She breaks off as the door opens behind us. "Ah, here he is now." Cassie and I turn around, and she gasps quietly next to me. "Ryland, this is Mackenzie. She has the same classes as you all day. Could you be her guide for the day? Mackenzie, this is Ryland Turner, Governor Turner's son and one of our top students."

The blond-haired hottie smiles at the lady behind me. "Of course, Mrs. Steed, I'd be happy to. Hey, Cassie, how are you?"

Cassie grabs my arm briefly before quickly recovering. "Hey, Ry. I'm good, thanks."

He turns his attention to me, and I see him scan my body as I do the same thing to him. Ryland Turner is smoking hot. He's wearing a pair of loose-fitted jeans that hug his legs but aren't skinny jeans, and a T-shirt fitted tight enough that I can see his abs ripple underneath it. His shaggy blond hair is artfully styled, and his sapphire blue eyes twinkle as he peruses my form. Pouty full lips draw attention to his mouth, and I watch as he uses his tongue to wet the bottom one. Fuck! Inner me is drooling over a teenager. I should be arrested for the thoughts I'm having.

"Hi, Mackenzie, and welcome to Summerville. I'll be happy to be your escort for the day. Come on, we have French first." Ryland startles me out of my dirty thoughts, and I'm guessing from the smirk on his face that I may have been projecting one or two of them.

Fucking hell, Kenz, get your shit together. You have a perfect poker face.

He opens the door and gestures for Cassie and me to go first.

"I'll see you around, maybe at lunch," Cassie says as we enter the teen-filled corridor. She quickly disappears, and I find Ryland looking at me intently.

"It's Mac," I tell him quietly as he leads me down the locker lined hallway.

"Oh okay, cool. How do you know Cassie?" he asks, making polite conversation.

"Oh, I live at the foster home with her."

"Oh, I'm sorry about that," he replies, and I shrug.

"Don't be, it's better than the last place I was at." I point to my face, and he winces slightly, and then there's an awkward silence.

"So what do you do for fun around here?" I ask him, changing the subject as we walk toward our first class. Thankfully, French is one of the languages I'm fluent in, but I'm not sure whether to play it cool and pretend I'm not or to just own that shit. I'm supposed to be a good and studious teen, so I'm leaning toward fluent.

"Um, well, I guess there are sports if you're inclined, but mostly we hang out at the Mug Shot Diner with friends. There are places to party, too, if you're interested in that." He sounds almost as awkward as I am when he tells me about it, like he's not used to it, but I guess he has been in a boarding school for years. This must be a new experience for him too.

I need to figure out where the kids that are missing used to hang out and with whom, but they are all from last year's graduating class, and Ryland is new at the school, so he's not going to be any help in that respect. I need to ask someone else. I think I'm going to ply Cassie for information. She seems to be a fount of knowledge, plus she lived with the kids, so she'll know what they used to do or if any of them were particularly friendly with others.

Thankfully, we stop at a nearby door. I hadn't noticed while we were walking, but now that we're stopped, I can see we're getting all kinds of looks from the students around us. I guess we must make a weird sight with big, blond, beautiful Ryland walking next to little old goth me.

"Ryland," a husky female voice calls out, and when I turn in that direction, I see Miller, Jessica, Bishop, and Lathan, who's grinning at me, with three other girls. The one who's in the lead is tall and has hair so blonde it has to be from a bottle. She's wearing an outfit much like Jessica's, all pastels and pretty, and she has a smile on her face that doesn't quite meet her eyes.

"You must be the new street trash Jessica was telling me about." She eyes me up and down. "Goth sluts aren't welcome in this school. You alternative freaks are nothing but trouble, with your drugs and wild ways. It's all a sin in the eyes of the church." Oh my lord, what kind of backwater, alternative reality did I just fall into? Hello, *Footloose*, you're missing some cast members.

"Seriously?" I ask, raising an eyebrow.

Lathan is still grinning, while Bishop and Miller hide smirks.

"Sophie," Ryland chides gently. "Don't be like that. It's okay to be different, and I'm pretty sure that the church preaches acceptance, not prejudice."

"Not the church they go to," I hear Lathan mutter, but no one else does because they are all raptly waiting for the drama to unfold, but the last thing I need is attention, so I decide to diffuse the situation.

"Thanks for showing me to class, Ryland," I say politely before I push the door open and walk in without a backward glance. I am going to cut my losses there, since I'm not interested in the drama that comes along with being his friend, not to mention I'm not sure if I could stop lusting after him, and nobody wants pedophilia on their record.

After being so excited to go to high school, I have to say it's completely underwhelming and fucking cliché, like every book I've ever read. Sophie is obviously the mean girl, and I don't have time for that shit. No wonder Team Basilisk hasn't got anywhere in the investigation if they are drawing attention to themselves and hanging around with that crowd.

I know Anders and Dayton are established in the community, but I wonder where the last two members of their team are. I must remember to ask one of them when I get a chance. Probably Lathan because he still looks happy to see me.

I take a seat at the back of the classroom as the rest of the students flow in behind me now that the drama didn't escalate. Ryland, of course, is in my class, as are the other boys and girls who were in the circle. Not long after, another group walks in. The boys are all wearing letterman jackets and are large and beefy. I'm going to guess they belong to the football team. The other group couldn't be more opposite. Instead of strutting and being loud like the football guys, these kids practically slink into class and take seats in the front row. They are so involved in their conversation about what I'm assuming is a video game—because I'd hate to think that they know about kill shots in real life—that they are oblivious to everything around them.

Lathan takes a seat next to me and the other guys and girls, with his group spread out around us. Sophie sits next to Ryland and engages him in conversation about an upcoming party, and Jessica's doing her best to draw Miller's attention, but he's sketching on a book in front of him and only responds with single word answers. Bishop has a pretty chocolate-skinned girl on his lap, and my eyes widen minutely before I look away.

Holy fuck. These guys are too old to be messing around with these teens. I hope it's for show, but out of the corner of my eye, I see her lean in and kiss him. He doesn't push her away. In fact, I see him slide his hand up and under her shirt. It only stops when Lathan loudly drops some books down on the table next to me. Bishop removes his hand before pushing her from his lap and sits her on a chair next to him. She pouts, but he ignores it and keeps talking to her.

"Hi, I'm Lathan." His friendly voice has me turning to look at him.

His glasses are slightly crooked on his face, and I reach up to straighten them as I reply, "Hi, I'm Mackenzie, Mac if you want." He startles slightly until he realizes what I'm doing, and then he beams at me.

"Ew, Lathan, what are you doing talking to her and letting that skank touch you? You should probably wash your glasses now." The annoying voice comes from behind me, and I drop my hand.

"Thank you," Lathan tells me before scowling at

whoever is behind me. "Lucy, just leave her alone. It's never easy being the new kid."

The tiny Asian girl looks me up and down. "Oh, I bet it's really easy for her. All she has to do is spread her legs and she'll fit right in."

Lathan grunts and looks disgusted, but it's all I can do not to laugh out loud. Oh, for fuck's sake, are teenagers really this fucking ridiculous? Is it too late for me to pretend to go to college?

Before either of us can respond to the load of garbage that just came out of her mouth, the door to the room opens once more.

"*Bonjour! Asseyez-vous et sortez vos livres s'il vous plaît.*" A beautiful blonde woman glides into the room and instructs everyone to take a seat and get their books out as she puts her bag down on the desk.

What is it with the women in this town and all their pastel colors? This one is wearing a pastel pink pencil skirt that is so tight, she needs to take little steps in her four-inch heels, and her tight, black top is really indecent if she's going to lean down in front of teenage boys. She looks around the room, smiling until she gets to me.

"*Oh, je vois que nous avons une nouvelle étudiante. Eh bien, je n'ai pas le temps de te dorloter donc tu devras te rattraper à ton propre rythme.*" She condescendingly tells me she doesn't have time to baby me and that I'll have to catch up in my own time.

"Oh, I'm fairly certain I can keep up," I reply in

English, and I see her eyes widen before her brows furrow in a frown.

"We speak only French in this class, Miss..." She draws her pink polished finger down a sheet of paper on top of her desk. "Walsh, is it?"

"Oui je m'appelle Mackenzie, mais vous pouvez m'appeler Mac. Je m'en excuse. Je vais m'en tenir au français à partir de maintenant," I reply, apologizing and promising to use French from now on.

She purses her lips like she's annoyed, but there's nothing else she can say without seeming like she's a bitch. I also bet only a quarter of the class is fluent. While Ryland, Sophie, and one or two others seem to have kept up with the conversation, everyone else seems to only be catching bits and pieces. The groans when she tells everyone we're having a pop quiz basically confirms it for me.

The rest of French class is quiet after she hands out the quiz, and I breeze through it in no time and finish halfway through the allotted time. The teacher, who still hasn't introduced herself, sits at the front of the class and sends text messages for the whole hour, not even looking up once she's made herself comfortable.

When I get up to hand her the quiz, I get incredulous looks from everyone around me as well as the teacher before she dismisses me with a wave of her hand, so I gather up my things and wait outside. Just outside the door is a trophy case that contains shiny silver trophies and a whole heap of photos and things. I step up to examine it, my eyes sweeping over the various achievements from years past. A familiar face in an old photo catches my eye. When I look closer, I see that it's a group of people. Divinity of Morality, class of 1990. What the fuck is that? Some chastity group? Martha and James are both recognizable. They are standing with a number of other men and women, one of whom I recognize as Governor Turner.

Before I can take out my phone to google that club, the bell rings and people spill out of the classroom. I quickly take a picture of the photo as Ryland approaches with Miller. Their heads are close together, and they have small, secretive smiles on their faces. I feel my cheeks redden as I wonder if Miller is telling him about what happened last night. Surely he wouldn't involve a teenager, but they quickly break apart as they get to me. Miller's face blanks once more, but Ryland smiles brightly.

"Oh good, you waited. We have history next. It's this way. Come on."

I put my phone back in my pocket and follow them like a little lost puppy, making sure I memorize the way because I don't want to have to rely on him tomorrow.

CHAPTER 12

I'm quiet as we walk along the crowded hallway to our next class. I let the two of them walk in front of me, and I'm happy to follow behind, but they soon stop and wait for me to catch up.

Ryland breaks the awkward silence that had fallen over us. "Ms. Standish was not happy about you showing her up. She's a bitch like that."

"Standish? As in Martha and James?" I ask, looking from boy to boy. They have me pinned between them, so I have to swing my head from side to side.

"Yeah, she's their niece and Sophie's older sister." Well, shit. I guess the two sisters both took an instant dislike to me.

"Fuck," I grumble quietly to myself, and the two boys chuckle as we enter the next classroom.

Like the last one, it's filled with many of the same people, and there's only one seat left once Miller and Ryland hurry to two vacant ones at the back. It's in the front, and I quickly slide into it as a teacher enters the room. He closes the door behind him and steps behind his desk, and I just about swallow my tongue. What is it about this school? Is there a rule that you must be attractive to work here?

The man in front of me is young, maybe twenty-five or twenty-six, and he's wearing a pair of black slacks with a light blue button-up shirt with the sleeves rolled up, showcasing his sexy forearms. His face is a work of art, with blue eyes that really pop with his shirt and sinful lips that make me want to take a bite out of them. He has a chiseled jawline and blond hair that looks to have some curl to it, but it's cut short enough to disguise it. His narrowed eyes sweep around the room, eventually landing on me.

"You must be Mackenzie Walsh. I'm Mr. Turner, welcome."

I give him a little smile. The man is surprisingly intimidating with his intensity, and I quickly break eye contact.

Fuck, Kenz, get your head in the game. You've faced arms dealers, dictators, and mob bosses with ease, and one hot high school teacher gets you to crack.

Someone needs to slap me now. Maybe Miller's hit to the face and the tumble down the stairs did more damage than I thought.

"Okay, let's get back to what we were working on last week. Can someone explain to Ms. Walsh what we are studying at the moment?" He looks around the room and points a finger. "Yes, Sophie."

I tune out as Sophie talks about what they did in class. I don't really care, because I'm not actually here to learn. I really need to set up a meeting with Team Bastards so we can come up with a game plan. Working with other people sucks, but I don't want to investigate in places they already have. Not to mention if they are so distracted by teenage girls, I bet they haven't gotten anywhere at all. They really need to be exploring business connections in town and seeing if anyone is earning more money than they should be. Lathan may be my best bet to work with. His computer skills far exceed my own, so maybe we could work that angle together.

"Do you have anything to contribute to that, Ms. Walsh?" Mr. Turner's smooth timbre shakes me out of my thoughts, and I startle slightly, not having paid attention to what they were talking about at all.

He's frowning at me, and I know I'm about to be reprimanded when a knock at the door has the whole class looking to see who it is. An older man, who's maybe in his late forties or early fifties, opens the door with a smarmy grin on his face. I just saw a younger version of him in the picture in the trophy cabinet. The guy has not aged well. He had a full set of hair and was wearing a letterman jacket in the photo. Now, he's balding, but instead of embracing it, he's combing his hair over to hide it, and he's certainly not going to be making touchdowns anytime soon carrying that belly.

He catches sight of Mr. Turner who is now leaning

against the wall at the back of the classroom. "Ah, Max, there you are. I was just after your new student."

Mr. Turner waves a hand at me. "Mackenzie, this is Mr. Marshall. He's the guidance counselor, and it's school policy for any new students to see him. Take your things with you, since class will be over before you are finished."

This must be the guy Miller was telling me about, and when I get out of my seat and grab my things, I catch his eye, and he gives me a small, almost unperceivable nod. Right then, I guess it's go time. I pack up my things and head out of the classroom.

Mr. Marshall guides me to his office and gestures for me to take a seat. He takes the one behind his desk and steeples his fingers in front of him while taking me in. It's all I can do to not squirm as his frowning perusal takes a little longer than is appropriate.

"So what did you want to see me for?" I ask, not willing to wait any longer.

The frown clears, and a half-hearted smile spreads across his lips. "How has your first day been?"

What the hell? He pulled me out of my second class to ask that question? I gaze around the room, looking for some sort of evidence of his qualifications, because surely he's not as dumb as he seems.

"Okay, I guess. I mean, you did pull me out of my second class."

He seems to ignore what I'm saying. "And have you made any friends?" He eyes me up and down much like Martha had this morning. "Dressing like that really isn't going to win you any popularity contests. People don't like different."

"Yeah, that's kind of what I've been sensing." I don't hold back on my sarcasm, but it goes right over his head.

He lifts a file on his desk and reads through it, his eyes widening slightly at something he sees. I have no clue what that file says, since Dad was in charge of sending my "school records" here, but now I'm curious about what he had the tech team put in them.

"Well, from what I read here, Mackenzie, it seems that you've been on a rocky path for a while. You were arrested for soliciting twice, and then you were beaten up by your foster father and you reported him to the police, claiming he was forcing you to prostitute yourself to bring in money for the family."

What the actual fuck? I'm going to kill my dad when I see him. It's all I can do not to react in a way that would give myself away, so I cross my arms defensively. "Yeah, and? So what? I had to do what I had to do. That man was batshit crazy, and if I didn't, he threatened to make the younger kids in the house do the same thing. I was protecting the younger foster kids the state had placed with those two despicable individuals." I jut out my chin defiantly, and there's a gleam in his eye now.

"Was it something he made you do often? Or was it only the two times you were arrested?" he asks, sounding curious.

"No, I did it all the time. I had to bring in a

minimum of five hundred a week, or he would have started selling the others."

He leans forward. "Would you like to talk about the things they made you do? It might make you feel better if you got some of it off your chest." He wets his lips with his tongue, practically salivating.

Now, if this dude isn't part of the sex ring, he's definitely a grade A fucking pedophile, and I'm going to make sure he pays one way or another, so I look down at my lap and twist my hands in agitation.

"You really don't want to hear about the depraved sexual acts I had to perform," I whisper loudly enough for him to hear, feigning embarrassment.

He gets up and comes around to the chair next to mine, and then he grabs one of my hands, stopping them from twisting.

When I look up at him, there are tears dripping down my face. "Because the sicker the act, the better the money, so I didn't have to do it as many times."

His hand tightens on mine, and when I drop my eyes away from his again, I can see a bulge in his pants. Even if this man is not involved in any ring, there is no way he should be a counselor, and before I leave this town, I will make sure he fucking pays.

"Oh, I can assure you that talking about it will make it so much better," he tells me. "Getting all the sick and dirty things that happened to you off your chest will allow for your soul to be cleansed. In fact, I think you should attend the local church on Sunday and speak to Father Daniel about it. You can go to confession, or even book a one-on-one session with him."

"And you're not going to tell anyone about this? I'll never be able to start fresh if everyone knows I used to get paid for sex."

"Oh no, it will be our little secret. I promise," he assures me, and when I look up, there's a calculating gleam in his eye, which he tries to hide.

"Thank you," I whisper gratefully before pulling my hand out of his and reaching for a tissue from the box on his desk. If I hold his hand any longer, I might slip and break it. I blow my nose noisily and grab another to wipe my face. "I don't suppose you have a list of after-school work that might be available in town, do you? I still need to earn money to buy the things I need."

He beams at me. "See, you're already moving in the right direction to change your life." He pats me a little too high on the leg, considering I'm wearing a skirt, and stands up.

I can still see that he has a boner, and he does nothing to hide it now that it's basically directly in my face. Is he hoping that I'll drop to my knees and beg to suck it? When I look up at him, he winks, acknowledging it, but he doesn't go as far as propositioning me.

He walks back around to his desk and sprawls in his chair with his legs spread. "I could ask around and put in a good word for you. I have a few connections, but I guess I really need to know what your skills are."

He puts his hands behind his head, and I don't miss what he's implying as I hear the bell ring out in the hallway.

What a fucking cunt. I can't believe I'm going to have to give this douchebag a blowjob. I could just kill him now and make it look like an accident, but so far, he's my only lead, and he could just be a slimy asshole and not even involved in the trafficking ring. I really need to set up a meeting with Team Bastards and find out if they have any leads. Miller and I didn't exactly get very far last night.

"Come on, Mackenzie. I think you'll find that if you're a very good girl, then I can be very good to you."

Sighing, I stand up and smooth down my skirt. His eyes roam over my figure, but just as I'm about to move around to his side of the desk, someone knocks on the door.

"Fuck!" he exclaims, straightening himself out and pulling his chair up to his desk so he can hide his erection under it. "Come in," he calls, and the door opens.

Ryland pops his head in and looks around, smiling when he sees me. "Oh hey, Mr. Marshall. I thought I should show Mackenzie to her next class. If you're done, that is?" He tips his head to the side questioningly, and I quickly grab my bag and throw it over my shoulder, taking the out he's offering. I can find a job myself.

"Thank you for speaking to me, Mr. Marshall," I say demurely, and he smiles, although it doesn't reach his eyes.

"Anytime, Mackenzie, and remember if you want that list of jobs, my door is always open."

The audacity of the fucking creep. I feel bad for the poor females in this school. I need to ask Cassie if he's tried anything with her. Does he only try this with the foster kids, or is it any of the girls? Waving goodbye, I follow after Ryland, ready to just about lay a kiss on the poor teenager for his timely rescue.

I shudder as we walk away, and he drapes an arm around my shoulders. I look down at his hand and then back at him, and he smirks.

"Cold?" he asks, and I shake my head.

"No, creeped out."

He nods but doesn't remove his arm as we keep walking, and the weight of it is nice. It's weird getting affection from someone that's not a mark, but I don't hate it. It kind of makes butterflies swarm in my stomach.

No, Kenzie, bad girl. Even if he's eighteen, he's off limits. He's still in high school.

"Yeah, that's not the first time I've heard that about Mr. Marshall." We walk past a group of athletes, who are all whispering like teenage girls. Bishop is goofing off with them, but he stiffens up when he sees us coming. One of them steps in front of us, halting us in our path. He looks me up and down, eyeing Ryland's arm around my shoulders.

"Oh, so maybe you're not a fag after all, you just like the freaky bitches. This one is just as freaky as that new guy Miller. Hey, I don't blame you, the freaks are always grateful for anything you give them." The group around him chuckles and jeers at Ryland as his hand tightens on my shoulder, his whole body growing tense.

Before he can say anything, I jump in, looking the asshole up and down. "No, the freaky bitches aren't grateful for anything you would give them. Judging by the overabundance of muscles, I'm assuming all your junk has shrunk beyond recognition. Freaky bitches like to be able to feel the cock they are being fucked with."

"Oh damn!" one of the other athletes calls out, and the others snigger quietly as a look of fury washes over the asshole's face, and he clenches his fists at his sides.

Bishop places a hand on his arm. "Steady, Billy," he cautions, but Billy shakes him off.

"You watch yourself, bitch. My dad is the chief of police, and he can make your life very difficult."

"How about you watch yourself, bitch, because my dad's the governor, and he can make your dad's life very difficult, Billy." The chilling threat comes from the boy beside me, and I watch the color drain from Billy's face before he steps back. When I turn quickly to look at Ryland, he is all smiles. Ryland has barely moved, so I wonder what Billy saw on his face to cause such an extreme reaction. "Yeah, that's what I thought. Now why don't you get the fuck out of our way? I'm sure Mackenzie doesn't want a tardy on her first day at school."

Billy and his meathead friends shuffle to the side,

allowing us to pass, but he can't help taking a last dig. "Or maybe you are tag teaming her. You and the freak Miller. Dude, I'm fucking impressed. Maybe there's hope for you yet."

Ryland ignores him and drags me away, but I can't help wondering if Billy is onto something. Is Miller working on Governor Turner's son? Are they just friends, or is there more? Has Miller been getting close to Ryland for the same reason I had considered? Maybe he saw the picture of Governor Turner with that group of people. I mean, it's a long shot, but at least it's something. I know I can always ask my dad to get in touch with the governor, but working his son first is not going to hurt. I just hope Miller isn't seducing a teenager.

They might just be friends and Billy is a homophobe, but what if he's right? I really don't want another run-in with Miller, so maybe I'll speak to Dayton about it once we all touch base. There's also Bishop's actions to consider too. This whole team doesn't seem above seducing teenagers to get what they want. I have nothing against their technique, but I do question the ages of the girls. Does this make us any better than the people we are trying to bring down?

CHAPTER 13

We finally make it to lunch, and I'm freaking exhausted. The girls have continued to throw sly, nasty remarks in my face, and they are in most of my classes. It's taken all I have not to put my fist in their faces, but that's not going to help my cause at all.

I tell Ryland, Lathan, and Miller I'll meet them in the lunchroom, needing to use the bathroom before I sit down to eat.

When I finish my business, I wash my hands and step out into a now empty corridor. My steps are silent as I walk toward the cafeteria, but a voice in an alcove has me stopping to listen.

"Hey, Brock, how did your meeting go with the new girl?" I hear Mr. Turner ask.

"Oh my goodness, that girl is troubled," I hear Mr. Marshall reply, and I roll my eyes.

"Oh?" Mr. Turner prompts.

"Yes, prostitution, can you believe it?" Wow, so much for confidentiality. I feel my cheeks blush red at the thought of the hot teacher thinking I'm a whore. I mean, it's not far from the truth, but come on.

"Wow, okay. Did she tell you about it?" Mr. Turner asks, and he plummets in my esteem. What a fucking creep, but hot people can be criminals too.

"No, she was just about to give me a demonstration, if you know what I mean, when your idiot brother walked in."

"Sorry about that. Ryland's sense of timing has always been off. What a shame. She would look pretty on her knees."

Jesus Christ, there's another one I need to put on my kill list. Does this town breed sleazy men? Maybe Dad misjudged Governor Turner all these years. How could he be friends with a man who produces a predator for a son? I guess Miller is on the right track with working the Ryland angle.

"Well, yes, I suggested that she head along to church on Sunday with the Standishes and have a meeting with Daniel to admit to her sins. I'm sure he will have a list of her skills for us in no time."

"I would be very interested in that list," Mr. Turner tells Mr. Maxwell.

"I'm sure Daniel would make it available to you. After all, we need to know how to guide a troubled youth in our school. I suggested that the other new foster kid go and see the priest too, but he seemed reluctant."

"Yes, well, we can't force them to comply. They need to go in under their own volition. Maybe I'll pull Miller aside and suggest that it would be a good idea. He's quite close with my brother, so maybe he will take it better from me."

The conversation is deliberately vague, but it's enough to put the two of them and the priest at the top of my suspect list. Surely it can't be that easy. I've been here all of two days, and I've already found the culprits, though I guess that explains why the others haven't. None of them are troubled foster kids except for Miller, and he looks to be on their radar as well. I wonder if Ryland is in on this also and becoming friends with Miller is his contribution.

The voices start to move, and I hurry back to the bathroom and pretend to be leaving it just as the two of them come around the corner.

"Ah, Ms. Walsh, we were just discussing you." Mr. Marshall smiles brightly at me while Mr. Turner's face stays particularly blank. "You need to make sure you catch up with Max and get any homework you may have missed while you were meeting with me. How about after school?" He looks at Mr. Turner, who nods slightly.

"That would be fine. I would like to talk to you about what you were doing at your last school to make sure you can keep up with the curriculum here."

I just bet he does, but this works to my advantage. Maybe I can seduce the history teacher. That would be preferable to getting down on my knees for Mr.

Marshall. Men do tend to over share when they are getting their dicks wet.

"That would be great, thanks. I'm so worried that I'm behind, and I really want to get good grades so I can get a scholarship to college." I smile, making sure I put enough bright and bubbly bimbo into the tone. "I would do anything to ensure I get a scholarship." No one misses the innuendo, and despite his blank face, I see Mr. Turner's jaw tighten, but Mr. Marshall just beams at me.

"That's great, Mackenzie. We do love it when a student takes control of their own education." He slaps Mr. Turner on the back. "Don't we, Max?"

"Yes indeed," Mr. Turner says. "I'll see you in my office after school then," he tells me before I brush past them, my boob pressing against Mr. Turner's arm more than what's considered appropriate.

I don't look back, but I can feel their eyes on me, so I put a little more sway into my steps. My tartan skirt barely covers my ass, and I know my legs look amazing in the fishnet tights. I work hard to keep my body looking good so I can trap my marks.

When I push open the door to the cafeteria, the noise drops minutely as everyone turns to look, but it quickly picks up again as I head to the lunch line. There are a few people in front of me, but there's still plenty of food left when I get to the front of the line. Eyeing the selection, I decide on a slice of pizza and an iced tea.

Taking my tray, I look around for somewhere to sit.

I see Ryland wave at me, but when I notice who he's sitting with, I smile and shake my head before walking to an empty table, but another waving hand catches my eye. Cassie is sitting at a table with the triplets and Ty, so I change direction and head over to sit with them.

"I thought you were going to pretend to hate me so you didn't get on Jessica's bad side," I say to Cassie as everyone greets me.

"Fuck Jessica." William grins, and the others agree. "Us outcasts need to stick together."

They continue gossiping, and I let the happy chatter wash over me as I eat my lunch. It's greasy and delicious and oh so bad for me, but I figure I can go for a run.

I hear my phone beep inside my bag, so I reach in and pull it out.

Transport has been approved and will be situated this evening.

Ah, good, my motorcycle. That means I have a way to get into town. I just need to be able to sneak out. I'm not sure how I'm going to manage that yet without waking Jessica. I may need to drug her, but I'm not sure how I can do that without getting caught. Maybe I need some tranquilizer so I can dose her once she's already asleep, ensuring she doesn't wake up before morning. Anders is the medical guru for Team Bastards, so I'll have to ask him if he has anything I can use. Otherwise, I'll need to make another request to Dad.

I quickly delete the message, shove the phone into my backpack, and tune back into the conversation. The two guys are laughing about something, and when I hear them mention the Divinity of Morality, I butt in.

"I saw a photo in the trophy cabinet mentioning that club. What is it?" I ask, and the five of them roll their eyes.

"It's basically an excuse for the popular kids to get together and talk shit, but it's supposed to be a chastity club. Everyone wears rings indicating what level of chastity they are," Stephanie explains.

"If you are saving yourself for marriage and a virgin, you have a ring with a diamond in it. If that boat has sailed but you are repentant, then you wear a ring with a ruby in it," her sister adds.

"Are you fucking serious? I thought that kind of thing was a joke." My mouth drops open in disbelief.

"Oh no, here in the South, they take your virginity very seriously." Cassie almost manages to keep a straight face, but William snorts, and the five of them start to giggle like kids.

"We all know most of them regularly mess around with each other. Lucy has been known to blow the entire forward line of the football team for good luck before a game," Sally explains.

"Oh yes, and don't forget that if you let them fuck your ass, you still count as a virgin," Tyrone says a little too loudly, and the table next to us looks around.

He ducks, and I think if I could see him blush, he would be doing that right now.

I chuckle. "So it's been around for years? Because the photo I saw had Martha and James in it, as well as Governor Turner."

"Oh yes, that photo is the who's who of prominent people in Summerville."

I grab my phone and open it up to the photo I took. "Show me," I demand, and William and Tyrone move closer and start to point people out.

"That's Father Sweeny and his wife Melissa." Tyrone points to a fairly serious looking couple. They look like teenagers who don't know the meaning of fun. "You know James and Martha, but that is Ted and June Standish. That's Sophie's mom and dad and James's brother."

I look between the two men and can see the family resemblance.

"Ted runs an import-export business out of the docks here and is quite wealthy," William tells me, and I'm almost giddy with excitement. These foster kids are giving me all the good information, and I don't even have to work hard for it.

"I recognize Mr. Marshall there." I point out the guidance counselor. "And of course Governor Turner."

"Yup, and the man next to him is his brother Kevin," Cassie chimes in. "He's the black sheep of the family and owns the tattoo parlor in town." Governor Jeffery Turner has his arm slung around a man next to him, and I wouldn't have thought they would be related. Kevin is dark-haired and stocky, whereas Governor Turner is blonde, tall, and slender. "Kevin is the president of the local chapter of the Raging Scorpion MC. Not long after this photo was taken, he was kicked out of the group because of his unsavory acquaintances. I think Governor Turner left at the same time."

I look at Cassie with wide eyes. "Wow, you are a real fount of information."

She just rolls her eyes and grins. "You would not believe the things women gossip about when they come to the thrift shop. And everything Governor Turner was fair game recently with his sons returning to town."

"Okay, what about the others?" The boys are about to continue when Sally reaches over and steals the phone out of my hand. I raise my eyebrows, and she grins.

"What? I want to be involved too." She and her sister put their heads together to study the photo. "Okay, these two, Rebecca and Timothy, are married and own the Mug Shot Diner. I think they are friends of Kevin's. I've seen them having lunch together there sometimes, and Ryland is always given preferential service whenever he's hanging out there." Sally rolls her eyes.

"I can't believe they have all been happily coupled up since high school. That's got to be what, over thirty years?"

"Who says they are happy?" Cassie counters,

pointing a carrot stick at me. "Remember, no one notices the foster kid at the checkout at the thrift store. I can tell you that most of those men are not faithful to their wives. Timothy and Rebecca are solid, and Governor Turner is a widow, but there are whispers about all of the others."

"What about the last two men?" I point out two guys who aren't with women, and the five of them exchange a glance.

"That's Matthew Stewart. He owns that club in town, and the other is Isaac Palmer. He's the captain of the coast guard outfit here in town," Stephanie says before leaning in. Everyone gets closer, and she whispers, "It's rumored that they are lovers, and that the club actually has a secret society underneath it. Apparently this specific Divinity of Morality chapter still exists because they run a sex club under the main club. Secret membership only." She hands me back my phone, gesturing to the photo. "And it's not just a basic sex club, but something more depraved."

Holy shit, how does everyone not know about this if my fellow teenage foster kids do? Or is it one of those not so secret secrets that everyone is in on? They must see the question on my face, because William puts his arm around me and pulls me in for a side hug. "See? Being invisible does pay off. Stick with us, kid, because we have all the good gossip."

My table laughs, but a louder, shrill peal of laughter draws our attention. We all turn to find

Sophie glaring at us while the three girls with her try to outdo our laughter.

"Oh shit, how did you manage to get on Sophie Standish's shit list after only half a day?" Tyrone asks as we turn back.

I shrug. "I think just breathing was enough. So tell me more about this chapter. I'm assuming Sophie runs it. Are all of the people at her table in it?" When I looked, I noticed that Lathan, Miller, and Bishop are there again, as well as Jessica, Lucy, and the last girl whose name I now know is Michelle.

"Sophie, Michelle, Lucy, and Jessica are, as well as Billy, a couple of his teammates, and Ashley, who is Father Sweeny's son. I think they are trying to recruit the new boys too. Traditionally, people who have paired up in the Divinity of Morality group go on to get married. It's almost like a cult. Michelle and Lucy are actually both exchange students who live with Sophie's family. Before Ryland arrived, they were all paired up. Sophie was with Billy, and Michelle was with Ashley. Jessica and Lucy weren't with anyone in particular, and they seem to float week to week, but now that Ryland has arrived, Sophie dropped Billy like he was a grenade and has been working Ryland like a two-dime hooker." Cassie sounds scornful.

"I think the other guys are just pretty eye candy. None of them have connections with the town, and Miller is a tattooed and pierced foster kid. That doesn't really fit in with their code. I'm sure Sophie will try to drive a wedge between Miller and Ryland's friendship as soon as she can, and Miller will find himself sitting over here with the rejects. If Jessica was smart, she would be working Billy instead of trying to get her hooks into Miller. Billy is from a prominent family and her ticket to easy street if she wants it." Cassie sounds wise beyond her years, and I can tell she's been through shit. All five of them have.

To be honest all five of them show the kind of smarts my dad is always looking for. If the Standishes end up being a part of this, then I will make sure my dad offers all five of them a place at MITHOS. I think they would make a great team. I also see the way William looks at Cassie, even though she seems to be oblivious.

The bell rings before I can ask any more questions, but I count lunch as a win. There were no snide remarks, and I got a shit ton of information. We may be able to wrap up this investigation quicker than I thought, and then I can go back to being a solo player.

CHAPTER 14

My last class after lunch is PE, and it requires me changing into a uniform that the PE teacher throws at me when I make my way to the gym.

"Make it quick, Walsh. I don't have all day to wait for you to primp." Her voice is gruff and low, and from the muscles bulging under her own tight PE shirt, I'm going to guess that maybe she has been indulging with roids.

Ignoring the urge to say something back to her, I hurry to the locker rooms. It's empty of people, and I find myself a spare locker to shove all my crap into. I quickly change into the PE uniform and scowl down at my boots. Nobody told me that I needed to bring a change of footwear. This is going to suck. Hopefully we're only playing some lame team sport and won't be required to run far—not that I haven't had to run in combat boots before.

Of course my luck is against me, and when I get out to the gym, everyone is filing through a door that leads outside.

"Listen up. We're running the cross-country track today," Coach Barlet announces.

There are a large amount of groans but also some cheering. I scan the crowd, and it looks like the whole senior class has PE at the same time. There are more kids here than there have been in all my other classes.

"Footballers, you go first, I don't want anyone holding you up. You will be timed." A group of boys, some that I recognize from my first class, pushes to the front, and when the Coach blows the whistle, they start off toward the forest that is nestled behind an oval field. There looks to be a path leading into it, and sure enough, the footballers enter and disappear.

"Remember to stick to the trail and look for the red flags that are placed everywhere. I do not have time to come and look for you if you get lost, so don't fall behind." She directs that last bit specifically to me, glaring down at my boots.

Bitch, please, what do you think our armed forces wear and run in? I am going to be fine. If I can run in high heels, I can run in anything.

She blows her whistle, and the rest of the class starts across the expanse of mowed grass. I hold back a little. I don't need to prove anything, and I don't want to fall victim to being tripped by anyone. I'm already banged and bruised enough, so I don't need to add to them on my first day.

The popular group leads the rest of the senior class. All four girls have PE uniforms that are almost two sizes too small for them. The shorts, which are slightly baggy on me, hug their asses like booty shorts, the bottoms of their butt cheeks hanging out, and the tops are indecently tight. Team Bastard and Ryland fall in behind them, and then there is the rest of the class with me bringing up the rear. I could probably outrun everyone, but I don't want anyone to know I'm athletic. I want to be underestimated at every turn.

When we reach the forest, the bright sunlight disappears and becomes mottled shade. The track is well defined, and it's obvious many sneakers must have run this course because there is no way you could miss it. The trees and bushes are thick, and as I scan either side, I realize I can't see more than a couple of yards before the wall of foliage blocks out any chance of me seeing farther into the bushes.

Ahead of me, the senior class has eased to a walk. Frowning, I slow down as I catch up to them and listen in to the conversation around me. There is chatter about the weekend, the upcoming football game, and some church social thing, and none of them seem concerned about running the track.

I'm not sure what to do. Do I overtake them and keep on running, or do I try to fit into the crowd? I really don't want to draw attention to myself. As I'm still trying to decide what to do, Lathan drops back and starts to walk next to me, and I'm kind of relieved to see a familiar face.

"What is this?" I ask him, waving to the walking seniors.

"A few years ago, some enterprising students who hated running created a shortcut. None of the faculty knows about it, and it's passed down from senior class to senior class. We can walk from here until just before the end when you leave the forest and have to cross the parking lot to return to the gym," he tells me, and in silent agreement, we drop even farther back.

"How are you feeling?" he asks quietly, and I can hear the concern in his voice. It gives me warm and fuzzy feelings that I want to slap myself for.

No, Kenz, do not get attached to one of the team members. Despite him being sweet, sexy, and kind, the rest of them are douchebags.

"Are you still in a lot of pain?"

"Nah, I'm okay." I play it off lightly. He doesn't need to know that my ribs are still fairly sore. "Listen, I know I'm supposed to settle in for a week and then touch base with you, but I'd like to do it sooner rather than later. I need to know what you do, because I don't want to double up on investigating the same things."

He nods. "Yeah, that sounds smart. I'll talk to the others after school and let you know a time and place. How was your appointment with Mr. Marshall?" He grimaces slightly, and I chuckle.

"Did you have a run-in with him too?" I ask as we continue along the dappled path.

"I had an appointment with him, but it was completely above board. He asked about my future plans and stuff, but Miller said there was something off about him. He made some insinuations about how, as a foster kid, Miller needed to work extra hard to succeed in life."

I snort, muttering, "I wonder if he asked Miller to suck his dick too."

Lathan stumbles and looks at me incredulously. "He asked you to do that?"

"Yeah, but apparently my transcripts say I'd been arrested for prostitution in the past, so I guess he thought there wouldn't be anything I wouldn't do to get ahead. He promised to find me a good job." I shrug my shoulders, and he shakes his head.

"I can't believe he had the nerve to do that."

"Oh, for sure. Either he's involved or he's a predator, but either way, he's going down. I'm just glad Ryland walked in before I got down on my knees."

Again, Lathan's eyes widen in surprise, and I hide my smirk. He really puts off an innocent air, so maybe he spends more time behind a computer screen instead of in the field. It's a shame, because he would be the perfect honeytrap. Women are super attracted to the sexy, nerdy shy thing.

"I knew you were lying." A voice from behind us has me jumping and spinning. Somehow, Miller managed to get behind us without either of us noticing.

"Where the fuck did you come from?" I exclaim, looking around, and he points to a big tree off the side of the trail.

"Some spy you are. I was hiding behind there."

"What did you mean about me lying?" I stop and put my hands on my hips, not willing to take any shit from his guy.

"That you would do anything to get the job done. You just said you were grateful you were interrupted."

"Just because I was grateful doesn't mean I wouldn't have done it. Have you seen the dude? Sucking his cock would not be fun. I wonder if I could even find it under his pot belly?" Lathan and I shudder in unison before laughing at ourselves, while Miller scowls at both of us.

We start walking again, but before I can grill the two of them any further, I notice that some of the senior class has stopped. Jessica has noticed Miller's absence and is looking around for him.

She sneers when she sees both of the guys with me. "What are you doing back there with the trash? If you want to raise your standings in this town, then you need to be seen associating with the right kind of people."

"Is that what you're doing? Because as far as I can see, there's no difference between you, Miller, and me," I retort, already over all the petty teen bullcrap. If this is what high school was like, then I didn't miss out on a thing. Katie is going to tell me she told me so.

Before she can answer, Ryland joins the conversation. "Come on, if we don't keep going, we will be late even with the shortcut."

It's only then that I notice the small trail leading

off the main one. The rest of the people who stopped and waited start down it. It's not easy, and we have to watch where we go, stepping over fallen branches and ducking under the low hanging ones. We're silent, the single path not making conversation easy for any of us. I think we've been walking for fifteen minutes or so when the trail opens up into a clearing. It's weird! There's this one open spot in the forest, and there's a wooden house in the clearing. There are a few deck chairs on the front porch and some beer bottles scattered around what would be the front yard, but mostly it has a run-down, abandoned look to it.

Bishop must see me studying it, because he stops and waits for me to catch up to him. We don't need to stay single file in the clearing, and no one else seems to pay attention as they keep walking until the trail starts again.

"It's the old ranger's home. He died a few years back, and the city didn't bother hiring a new one. They cleaned out his personal possessions but left some of the furniture. The teens in town use it to throw parties. Someone managed to have the power and electricity turned back on, but I'm not sure how. There is a party coming up at the end of the week after the football game." He keeps his voice down, his slight accent melodic in the quiet clearing.

"And the adults don't know about it?" I sound skeptical even to my own ears, and he shrugs.

"If they do, they turn a blind eye to it." He doesn't seem particularly suspicious about it, unlike the weird vibe I feel just from looking at it. The location appears to be so very out of the way. Unless you knew it was here, you would never find it, and the forest surrounding it is so dense. "We've had a few here already. Lots of sex, alcohol, and drugs. It's a blast."

I can't stop my mouth from dropping open in surprise. "Are you here to work or to have fun? What the fuck, man?" I ask, unable to hide my annoyance.

His grin drops, and he sneers. "Why can't I do both?" He whirls around and follows the rest of the crowd as I shake my head in disappointment. His attitude is becoming a problem. I look back at the cabin, trying to picture it surrounded by drunk teenagers.

From what I know about this town already, that seems to be weird, but what the fuck do I know? Maybe that's what happens in small-town America. I just get the vibe that this place is rather straightlaced. Church and Divinity of Morality Club all point to it, or it's a carefully cultivated facade to hide the dark underbelly of what's really happening in the town.

"Come on, the trail isn't well marked, and I don't have it down completely yet." Lathan grabs my hand and pulls me across the now empty clearing, following after the rest of the senior class. His hand is warm in mine, and it feels nice. I leave it there and let him help me over a big log not far into the track. My ribs are starting to ache even more now, and having someone to boost me means I don't have to scramble over it, possibly hurting them more if I were on my own.

"Thank you." I smile at him on the other side, and

he smiles back, although there is still a wary light in his eyes, like he's not sure if he can trust me yet or not. I know how he feels. This whole assignment is going to be full of uncertainty until we decide we can. I just hope their problem with me doesn't interfere with finding justice.

"Hey, what is Bishop's malfunction?" I ask, and he sighs deeply.

"He has a big ass chip on his shoulder, and he was the last person to join the team, so I think he feels like he still has something to prove. Truthfully, he does. He hasn't impressed any of us so far."

Oh wow, okay. I didn't expect him to say that. We fall silent as we catch up to the larger group. I don't want them to overhear anything relevant.

The rest of the walk is quiet aside from an occasional murmur or two breaking the eerie silence of the thick forest. Sporadically, other trails break off from this main one, but we don't detour. Finally, it opens out onto the bigger track. I guess we cut across where it looped around. The football boys are just passing where our trail ends, but Billy sees us and stops, jogging on the spot.

"Just give it another ten minutes. If you arrive straight after us, the coach is going to be suspicious, and she'll make us do extra sprints," he huffs out, his chest heaving and sweat beading on his brow.

I guess not everyone cheated, and I have a small amount of begrudging respect for the athletes for taking it seriously, unlike the rest of the class who treated it as a blow off session. Maybe in the future I'll ask if I can jog with the athletes. I can't afford to let myself get lazy, though with my injuries, it was nice not to have to today.

The ten minutes pass quickly, and soon enough, everyone starts jogging. I'm not sure how the coach doesn't suspect anything, since no one is breathing hard and there isn't a drop of sweat to be seen, but she hardly pays attention to any of us as we enter the gym since she's too busy barking instructions at the football players.

"So you can probably guess that unless you play football, you don't register on Coach Bartlet's radar," Lathan tells me as we cool down after our run, stretching out on one side of the gym.

"That's a nice change from my first couple of classes. I got the feeling that Mr. Turner and Ms. Standish are going to be hard taskmasters."

Lathan grins at me. "Well, it seems like you're smart enough that it won't matter."

"Hey, Lathan, let's go," Miller calls across the gym, where he's waiting with Bishop and Ryland.

Bishop doesn't acknowledge me, but Ryland gives me a small wave. Of course Miller just scowls.

"That boy has some real issues. He acts like I pissed in his Wheaties when I was just acting on orders," I mutter, and Lathan's smile drops.

"Yeah, it's going to take him a while to get over it all. When he thought you killed Percy, he was murderous. You're actually lucky he didn't disobey orders and kill you then and there."

"Well, I think he got his pound of flesh." I point at my face, and Lathan wrinkles his nose in a cute way that makes me want to reach out and boop it, but I resist.

"Lath." Miller's voice is more insistent, and we look back at them. They've been joined by all the girls.

"I'll catch you later," I tell him, not wanting to draw more attention to myself. I have things I want to do this afternoon after I see Mr. Turner. I want to get the layout of the town, and I need to do it so that I'm home in time for dinner. I wouldn't want to get on Martha's bad side on the first day.

He looks reluctant to leave, but after studying me for a moment, he waves goodbye and hurries over to the others.

I need to change out of my PE uniform and then go see Mr. Turner. I'm not sure what I'm going to tell him I learned at my last school. Shit, I probably should have googled senior history curriculum.

I don't bother putting my fishnets on when I don my other clothes, I just bundle them up and put them into my bag. The hassle of taking off my boots and putting them back on is going to slow me down. I don't want to be late to meet one of my suspects. A little shiver of excitement rolls over my skin as I push the locker room door open and hurry back to my history class. I'm finally going to get somewhere on this case.

CHAPTER 15

There's a note on the history room door telling me to meet Mr. Turner in his office, with instructions on how to find it. That was strangely thoughtful of him. I follow the directions, and before long, I'm knocking on the closed door that has a plaque with his name. Breathing out a sigh, I smooth the fabric of my skirt while I wait for him to answer, replaying the conversation I overheard earlier in my head. It made it sound like Mr. Turner has a predilection for young girls. Saying that, though, he can't be that much older than me, maybe twenty-five or so, so even pretend Mac isn't that much younger. Maybe he's into some kinky shit. He did mention wanting to see me on my knees. Perhaps he wants a slave. Why else would a gorgeous man be interested in someone like my cover? He could easily find a girlfriend.

I'm mulling over all the information in my head

and not paying attention, so I jump when the door suddenly opens in front of me. Gasping, I grab at my chest in fright. Mr. Turner's eyes follow my hand. Looking down, I notice that my breasts are really prominent like that. Oh yeah, he's interested alright. I hide the smug smile that wants to cross my lips. It wouldn't pay for me to show that I know his game.

"Oh goodness, you scared me. I was daydreaming." My voice is low and breathy as I pretend to be frightened.

Mr. Turner steps back and gestures for me to enter the room. "I'm very sorry. Why don't you come in, take a seat, and get your breathing under control?" He peers out the door and looks either way down the corridor as I enter before pulling the door closed behind me. The sound of the lock engaging is deafening in the awkward silence.

He goes around to his seat on the other side of the desk and sits down, shuffling a few papers. He's quiet, and it gives me a chance to study him. He and his brother could almost be twins, but Ryland is not as broad as Mr. Turner, and his hair is longer and there's no hint of a curl, but they both have the same blue eyes and pouty lips. He keeps glancing to the corner of the room, which makes me suspicious, so this time when he looks back down at the notes in front of him, I turn my head slightly. Up in the corner of the room is a flashing red light—a camera. Well, it looks like I'm going to have to perform after all.

"So, Mackenzie—"

I interrupt him. "Please call me Mac."

He frowns. "Please don't interrupt me when I'm speaking," he scolds in a delicious growly voice, and I feel my nipples pebble with excitement.

Holy shit, Mr. Turner puts off some serious dom vibes. If he wasn't a suspect in a sex trafficking ring, I'd be all over him. I'd love to find out what it would be like to give up control to someone. I've spent all my life looking after myself and making sure I wasn't captured or killed on assignment, so I think it would be freeing to give myself over to someone.

I drop my head and lower my eyes. "I'm sorry, sir," I murmur.

"See that you don't do it again. Now, I'd like to know where you were in your last school. What were you studying?"

Fuck! How do I play this? I need to get my shit together. I'm not prepared for this, so I take a deep breath and uncross my legs before recrossing them, letting my skirt slide up to give him a good look at my panties before pulling it back down again.

"I'm sorry, Mr. Turner, but history is not my best subject. I think we were working on world history."

He leans back in his chair and steeples his fingers, frowning in disappointment. "Well, that's not going to work here, I'm afraid. We take our students' education very seriously, and as a foster child, you should be making every extra effort to try harder and make something of yourself. What are your plans for your future? Do you want to attend college, or are you just planning on paying your way on your back?"

Oh wow, so we're not even going to pretend that he hasn't heard about my "record."

I urge a blush to my cheeks and shake my head. "No, sir. I would really love to get into college."

"How far are you willing to go to get good grades, Mackenzie?"

Whoop, there it is. He's hooked, I just need to reel him in. I look up at him from under my lashes. "I'd do anything to get good grades, sir."

"Hmm, why don't I believe that?" He pushes his chair back from his desk and adopts a relaxed, spread-legged pose. I see it for what it is and see him look up at the camera once more. I guess he must have been tasked with getting proof of my promiscuity. I must be seen as a sure thing by the ring, one who probably won't put up too much of a fight.

"Please, sir, I promise to be good," I beg, shifting forward on my seat eagerly. I run my tongue over my lip before dragging it between my teeth, and I watch as he breathes deeply, his eyes locked on my lips, before he shakes himself and pats his lap.

"Why don't you come over here and show me how good you can be," he says through gritted teeth like he's trying to hold himself back.

Mr. Turner puts out this air of restrained violence, one I am very familiar with, and it makes me excited. I'm not sure if my adrenaline is running because I'm gearing up for a fight, or if it's because I want to fuck. I kind of feel a little gross that this perv gets me excited. It's never happened before, but maybe it's just the thought that after this, we'll have him hook, line, and sinker. I get to my feet and go around to his side of the desk, placing myself directly in front of him, my head bowed in submission.

"What do you want from me, sir?" I ask, and he pats his knee.

"Peel your panties down, sit on my lap, and tell me what a good girl you can be." His voice is all growly, and I can see his erection straining against his dress pants. Swallowing down my own groan at how big it looks, I go to toe off my boots, but he holds up a hand. "Leave them on," he orders, so I do, and I slide my panties down and over them, discarding them on the floor.

I quickly straddle his lap, my chest pressed to his. Still looking down, I feel his breath stir my hair.

"Good girl," he praises in his growly voice, and a shiver runs down my spine.

I take a deep breath, inhaling Max's scent, and just about swoon. He smells like sex and decadence, and I involuntarily grind myself into his erection. He stiffens slightly like he's surprised by my reaction.

"Lift that skirt a little bit so I can see that pretty pink pussy. Is it wet for me?" he demands, and I do as he asks, still not looking at him. "That's a good girl," he praises and quickly spins his chair so that the high back is to the camera, blocking us from its view. "Oh yes, look at how wet you are, how it glistens for me. I would love to run my tongue through that mess. Why don't you take my cock out and slide it through there for me?" he continues, seducing me with his words, and I am so here for this despite everything.

Fuck, maybe I've been doing this too long and it's time I got out, because this mark is causing me to become such a mess.

I do as he asks, the zipper loud in the quiet room apart from our ragged breathing. I'm concentrating so hard on what I'm doing that I startle when his hand stops mine, and he lifts my chin with his other hand. Gone is the seductive dom, and in his place is someone who looks rather uncomfortable.

"Can you make it look like we're fucking?" he whispers quietly so the sound doesn't carry to the camera. "Make it loud and active, and they will never know the difference."

"So you don't really want me to fuck you?" I ask, feeling incredibly disappointed and confused.

He smiles wryly. "Believe me, if we ever fuck, it won't be because a perverted fucking asshole wants to know if you will put out or not," he growls into my ear, and I do a double take. "But I need to prove my dedication to their cause."

"Team Basilisk?" I ask.

He nods before loudly saying, "That's it, bounce up and down on my cock and show me what a good girl you can be." Our eyes are locked, but I run my tongue along my lips, and his gaze shifts to follow the movement.

"Oh, sir, your cock is so big and thick, I'm not sure if I will be able to," I say loudly and wink at him.

He rolls his eyes but nods his encouragement. This is so weird. I've never actually had to pretend before, I always just did it, so I shuffle around like I'm trying to slide my pussy down his cock, faking my moans and groans.

"I'm not sure if I can take any more," I protest loudly.

"You can and you will, let me help." He shoves me back down onto his lap like he's shoving me onto his cock, and I howl like he hurt me. I'm sure the people behind the camera are getting off on the idea that it caused me pain.

I fake sob. "Oh my god, it's too much."

"Oh yeah, your pussy is so tight wrapped around my dick. Now start moving. I want you to ride me and milk my cock until I fill you with my cum."

Placing my hands on his shoulders, I grind against him, moaning and panting while he continues to encourage me. His filthy words combined with my own movements do some very nice things to my body.

"Pull that shirt up and show me those titties," he commands, and I stop, raising an eyebrow and silently asking if he really wants me to.

"They actually can't see your chest with the chair turned, they can just see general movements," he whispers, so I drop my hands from his shoulders and cup my boobs over my shirt before continuing my grinding movements, but it's not long before I'm not even faking the sounds.

Mr. Maxwell's cock is long and thick, and I don't have any panties on, so it rubs against my clit in just the right spot. Thank God his slacks are black so that no one can see the wet patch I'm leaving behind. I wonder if he can feel what he's doing to me.

The orgasm builds quickly inside of me, and I throw my head back and ride the wave of pleasure as it bursts over me. It's not until I'm coming down from the intense feelings that I realize what I've done. My cheeks heat slightly, and I can't even look at Mr. Turner.

I have never been so embarrassed before, not even the first time I had to sleep with someone to get the job done. I try to scramble off his lap, but he clamps his hands on my hips and doesn't let me move.

"Well, watching you get off was hot as fuck, but now it's my turn," he growls, the heat in his eyes real as he bounces me on his lap, pretending to thrust up into me.

I grab his shoulders and hold on. I can feel his thick thighs tense and relax beneath mine with each movement, his hard dick rubbing against my sensitive clit, and I feel another orgasm start to build. My nipples are tight and achy, and I grab them to get some relief.

He's muttering more dirty words and grunting and groaning like he is about to come too. Either he's a fantastic actor and has experience at this, or he's as turned on as I am and about to come in his pants. This just makes me feel even hornier. I'm dying to reach down into his slacks, pull his cock out, and slowly slide my pussy onto it. I want to feel it deep inside me to ease the ache that I'm going to have to take care of later.

I grit my teeth and make loud, enthusiastic noises, praising him for his skills as he mutters more dirty words to me. Suddenly, he lifts me up and shoves me down onto my knees. I grunt with the pain, my body still recovering from the beating his teammates gave me, as he grabs my hair and shoves my face into his crotch.

"Now drink down my cum like a good girl, and we can overlook your lack of knowledge in my class," he growls, and I pretend to gag like he shoved his cock too deep before bobbing up and down. "Can't risk knocking up a dirty slut like you. What would my father say?" He chuckles and then groans, pretending to come for our audience. "Oh yeah, that's it, drink it all down. Such a good little dirty whore."

Finally, he releases my hair and sneers down at me. "Get up and get out, and next time you're in my class, make sure you're paying attention if you want to pass my class." The venom in his voice has me flinching back, and I stumble to my feet, tugging my shirt down quickly so the camera doesn't see that I'm still wearing my bra. He bends down and picks up my panties, tossing them at me before turning his back on me and picking up what he was reading when I walked in.

Okay, I've been dismissed. I grab my backpack and

hurry out of the office as quickly as I can, not having to pretend that I'm shaken by the whole experience. What the actual fuck? Why didn't anyone let me know he was on the team? He seemed to know who I was. And does that mean Ryland is the other member, or is it just a coincidence and it's someone else altogether?

I hurry along the hallway, not wanting anyone to find me with my panties in my hand. I slip into a bathroom and wince when I see myself in the mirror. My makeup is smeared slightly, and my hair looks like it's had someone's hands running through it. My breath heaves out of my chest like I really did have sex with him. I'm so discombobulated right now. Before, when I only had myself to worry about, I only had to worry about what angle the bad guys were playing, but now I have a whole team that seems to be working different angles. I don't really have a choice now. I need to talk to Team Bastards. We need to collaborate, or we're going to end up stepping on each other's toes.

Tonight I'm going to have to sneak out and take Miller with me, and demand a meeting with the whole team. We all need to be on the same page if we're going to get to the bottom of this trafficking ring, and there are obviously things I need to know—things they know and haven't shared with Dad, because my file contained nothing that said one of their team members was working this angle. It's smart, very smart actually, especially with the Turners' previous connection with the town, but we all need to be on the same page. I can't be blindsided again.

With that decision made, I clean up my face as best as I can, wiping away the smudge marks from around my eyes, and step back into my panties. I need to check out the town. I want to visit the tattoo parlor, the cafe, whose name I can't remember at the moment, and the club that the foster kids told me has some kind of secret club below it. Hopefully one of them is hiring so I can at least have a cover for the Standishes, an excuse not to be at the halfway house.

Stepping back out into the hallway, which I assume also has cameras in it, I hold my head high and put my shoulders back. Anyone watching will see a resilient foster kid who can roll with the punches and isn't afraid of doing what she has to so she can get ahead. Hopefully I will be targeted by the ring soon. Working with Team Bastards is messing with my mind and my abilities, so the sooner we can wrap this up, the better.

CHAPTER 16

The school isn't very far from the town center. After a short fifteen-minute walk, I'm on a quaint bustling main street. There are tall magnolias throwing shade all over beautiful rest areas with seating. Groups of people are enjoying the afternoon sunshine, but they all look at me and frown before turning their backs and ignoring me. Hmm, I guess the bruises make people a little wary, or they are all judgy as fuck. It doesn't matter to me, I'm not here to make friends. I keep walking a little farther toward what seems to be the retail hub of this small town.

There is a mall off to one side, which seems to have some interesting boutiques and shop fronts, but I bypass it completely. It looks high end, and my cover as a foster child makes shopping there an impossibility. Down the street is a café called Mug Shot Diner, and I can see a whole heap of kids inside. I stop pretending to look at the phone in my hand while I suss out who is in there. I can see a group of boys in their letterman jackets, so it must be the football team. They are surrounded by a group of girls wearing cheer-leading uniforms, but not one of them is Sophie and her friends.

I keep surreptitiously scanning the crowd until I get to who I'm looking for. I find Ryland, Miller, Lathan, and Bishop in a booth in the back surrounded by the girls. I don't know what they are playing at, but Jessica is on Miller's lap, Ryland has Sophie, and Michelle is with Bishop. The last couple are making out hard core, but Ryland and Miller look like they are trying to fight their lap sitters off. I'd giggle if I didn't think it would draw attention. Lathan is the only one without a girl on his lap, but I can see Lucy pouting next to him. He has a laptop in front of him and seems to be fully involved in what he's doing. Well, I guess I can ask them about what their game plan is later, but I feel a wave of irrational jealousy as Jessica leans in and presses a kiss against Miller's pouting lips. I'm not sure what that's about, and I plan on ignoring it completely.

Turning my back to them, I hurry down the street, trying to get the layout of the rest of the main shop-ping precinct. There are few more cute cafes, a book-store, and a hardware store, and across the road is the town library, the town hall, and the police precinct. On the next corner over is the fire station and the coast guard headquarters. At lunch, Cassie said that the wharf is a dock for one of the many ships that patrol the waters off the coast.

I contemplate turning back, but as I scan the rest of the street, I see a small sign with an arrow pointing into an alley. The sign says, "The Inkubus," and has a stylized tattoo gun next to the fancy words. I wonder if that's the tattoo parlor one of the guys is working at. There's no time like the present to check it out. I head in that direction, keeping my eye out for anything that may be suspicious, but let's face it, a sex trafficking ring is not going to be operating on the main street of a small town. It will be hidden in the shadows and camouflaged by the glossy, superficial goodness the South is so famous for.

The alley is clean and neat, and it must be swept on a daily basis because there is no litter or weird, funky smells that you often find in alleyways. That shows the owner is smart. Nobody wants to visit a shady tattoo parlor unless they are desperate and cheap. The shop is about thirty feet in off the street, and there is a glass shop front that is covered in vinyl tattoo designs with the words "The Inkubus" with a sexy as fuck male demon blowing kisses next to the letters. It's fucking cute and not what I expected. Cassie said this place was owned by Kevin Turner. He is Governor Turner's brother, and I guess Mr. Turner and Ryland's uncle, and the supposed black sheep of the family and the president of the Raging Scorpion MC. It's such a complete contrast to Governor Turner, but apparently they are close.

The store is lit up inside, with white lighting illuminating a number of tattoo stations. I can see a woman getting a tattoo. A man with dark hair leans over her back, holding the tattoo gun in his hand as he applies whatever design she decided to put permanently on her body. I shudder at the thought. Putting something permanently on my body like that would be the end of my career, especially if it was in a spot everyone could see. No, if I got a tattoo, it would have to be cleverly hidden from public view, but I need a reason to go into the parlor. I can't very well admit I'm snooping. Another sign catches my eye in the window —piercings. Well, I always wanted to have something pierced, and I guess now is as good a time as any.

I push the door open, and a small bell chimes above my head. "I'll be right with you," a voice calls, and my eyes widen when I recognize it—Dayton Wexley, Asian Hottie, and team lead of Team Bastards, and I guess undercover tattoo artist. I never would have guessed. I was sure I was going to find Anders here. I had pegged Dayton as too uptight to be creative, but I guess I was wrong. I should know better than to judge a book by its cover.

I take a seat on the plush sofa in one corner and pull over the portfolio albums to browse through. The room smells like antiseptic and something else, something I think is possibly the smell of blood and ink combined, but since I've never had a tattoo, I can't know for sure. There are four different stations, even though Dayton is the only artist I can see at the moment. I start with his portfolio, and my eyes widen at what I see. I expected it to be practically empty, but Dayton has obviously been tattooing for years. The book is stuffed full of photos. When did he find the time to do all of these? Or is tattoo artist his usual cover wherever he goes? It's a good one if it is. No one questions tattoo artists looking for a job.

A noise has me looking up, and a blonde man enters the shop from a side door. He's older, probably around my parents' age, and his shoulder-length hair is neat and clean. He's wearing an Inkubus Tattoos T-shirt and jeans, and he has three takeaway coffee cups in his hands. I recognize the older version of Kevin Turner. He's aged well and is a hot older man.

"Here you go. Black for you, D, and a chai latte for you." He places one cup on the counter next to the tattoo bed before holding the other one out to the girl. The sound of the gun turns off, and I watch as Dayton wipes the girl's back with a paper towel.

"Okay, Charity, you can have a break," he tells her, and she sits up, gripping her top to her chest before reaching out for the coffee.

"Thanks, D, and thank you, baby."

Kevin leans in and gives the girl a kiss before winking and turning his attention to me.

"Hi, how can I help you this afternoon?" He smiles politely, but I see his eyes widen when he notices the state of my face. "Oh my god, are you okay? Do you need help?" He hurries over to me and squats down at my level, grabbing hold of my hands. His eyes are filled with concern as he scans the rest of my body. Without my fishnets on, you can see the mottled bruising on my legs, and my arms still have a few too. "Who did this to you? Tell me, and I will deal with it." His concern turns to fury, and I know that if he could get his hands on who caused the bruises, then they would be dead. Unfortunately, that doesn't work for the case, because I'd like to see this guy go up against my team, so I shrug and pull my hands out of his, hunching in on myself.

"It was a foster father, but he's been taken care of," I mutter, and he looks carefully into my eyes for signs of lies. I guess he's satisfied with what he sees, because his whole body relaxes before he gets up from his position.

"As long as you're sure." He doesn't seem to want to let it go.

"I swear, I've been placed at a halfway house here in Summerville. You might know the people who run it, the Standishes."

He frowns and nods. "Yes, I know them. I'm not sure they are any better." He mutters that last bit to himself, but I still hear it. "So what are you here for today? I'm afraid we can't tattoo any of the bruised skin until it heals," he tells me apologetically.

I turn my head, and I see the other two watching on with quiet fascination. Both are drinking their coffee and listening intently. Dayton doesn't even flinch when my eyes meet his. The girl, or woman, I guess, now that I can see her face, is probably somewhere between my and Kevin's age, so maybe late thirties, and she smiles sympathetically at me.

"That's okay, I was actually hoping to get a piercing," I tell him, and he beams at me.

"We can do that. Charity is our piercer, so you caught her at just the right time." He points to the girl who jumps down off the bed, her shirt still clasped against her naked top.

"Wrap me up, D, so I can help the girl. You can finish after," she tells Dayton, whose eyes haven't left me.

He startles slightly but quickly reaches for the plastic wrap and pulls off a long piece, taping it over the tattoo he was working on. The girl pulls her shirt back on, managing not to flash any of us during the process, then waves to me.

"Come into my lair." She chuckles, opening a door and gesturing inside. "Make yourself comfortable, and I'll grab the paperwork." She disappears, leaving me in the room on my own.

Shit, paperwork. I don't know what the piercing laws are here in Georgia. I'm assuming it's eighteen, and my fake ID says I'm seventeen and a half—ripe pickings for the traffickers, but illegal to get a piercing without my parents' or guardians' permission. Fuck it, hopefully they won't be too strict with the age. Maybe I can tell a good sob story and get some sympathy.

I'm biting my lip and looking around the room at the various posters of the different kinds of piercings I can get when Charity returns.

"All right, sweetie, we'll just get this filled out, and then we can talk about what you want to have done." She sits down in the chair and rolls it toward the bed, gesturing for me to take a seat.

"Um, so, I don't have parents to sign the form and, well, I'm pretty sure Mr. and Mrs. Standish won't sign it either," I tell her, biting my lip nervously, and she sighs.

"Do you have any ID?" she asks, her eyes softening.

I scramble around in my backpack and pull out my fake driver's license, handing it to her. I watch her scan it.

"You know what? We usually refuse on the spot, but you're only a few months away from eighteen, and you look like you could do with a little something for yourself. Let's just go ahead and put the date on here after your eighteenth birthday, and we'll hide it deep in the back of the filing cabinet. If anyone asks, it could take us six months to find it."

She scribbles a few things on the permission slip, putting the date of piercing the day after my fake eighteenth birthday. I make a note to come back and let them know that everything is okay and fill out my real details once this case is over. She's being so kind, and I have a feeling they don't often let things slide around here. The last thing I want is for them to get into trouble with any licensing authorities, though if she's part of the trafficking ring, she'll be in jail anyway, but a gut feeling tells me her and Kevin are not involved.

"Thank you so much, and you're right. I really

could use a pick-me-up. Life has certainly sucked recently." I mutter the last bit, but she doesn't miss it.

She passes me the paper to sign and pats my hand. "Alright, so let's make this happen," she says as I sign the papers, and then she whisks them off and shoves them in the back of an ancient filing cabinet she has on the far side of the room. "So what were you thinking about piercing?"

I look at all the posters showing the various piercings and what places on the body you can get them. There is some body modification stuff that makes me feel ill, and I must not be wearing much of a poker face because she giggles.

"We don't actually do that kind of thing here. It's just a display more than anything." She points out a picture of a woman with hooks in the skin on her back who's hanging from a rope in the ceiling.

"Is there a call for it?" I ask her, unable to hide my curiosity, and she shrugs.

"I've had a few inquiries, but when I explained that we don't do that kind of thing, they went in search of someone who would."

"But why?" I ask, opening my eyes wide and putting on the air of innocent schoolgirl.

"I actually don't know, but I know some people find sexual gratification from pain. There are rumors of a sex club here in town, but it's an exclusive invitation only thing, and Kevin and I haven't been together all that long to really experiment. Not to mention I'm a bit of a baby. Tattooing and piercing are about all the pain I'm interested in." Her cheeks have a slight blush as she admits this to me.

This is just what I need, a little segue that will allow me to ask a few more pertinent questions, and she just handed it to me on a silver platter.

CHAPTER 17

"So you haven't been working here long?" I ask, a little worried about her performing my piercing now, and she shakes her head quickly.

"Gosh no, I've been here for about two years, but Kevin was worried about our age difference, and it took me that long to wear him down."

"Well, congrats on wearing him down," I tell her, and she giggles again.

"What about you? Any love interests? I guess not with being new in town."

I shake my head and wrinkle my nose. "No, not at my school."

"Oh hey, Kevin's nephew goes to the high school. Ryland Turner. He's cute and nice. Maybe I could introduce you," she gushes, and it's my turn to laugh.

"Actually, I met him today, and you're right, he does seem nice," I reply neutrally. "But I'm like you, kind of like them a little more mature. Where would you suggest I hang out to find them?"

She leans against one of the cabinets on the wall. "Hmm, yes, I totally get what you're saying. There's a bar one street over with a dance club above it. I used to love going there when I was younger. I always met a lot of older wealthy men there. You wouldn't think our town would be a hot spot for night activity, but there was no shortage of men coming through that place."

Now if that doesn't scream red flag, I don't know what does. She's right, Summerville definitely shouldn't be a hotbed of nighttime activity. It's just a little too far away from any of the major cities for it to be worth the drive.

"Okay then, what about a belly button piercing? Guys love those." She points out the poster before opening up a side cabinet and grabbing a rack of sparkly bars. I could try and steer the conversation back to the club, but I think reconnaissance would probably be better than trying to get information secondhand.

Before she can bring them over, I shake my head. "No, I don't want anything that the Standishes are going to see."

She puts the rack back down and bites her own lip thoughtfully before shrugging. "Well, honey, we don't have a lot of choices then. I guess we could do your tongue, but they may notice it when you talk to them, though I think I have a clear bar we could use. The only other options are your nipples or down there." She points between my legs before gesturing to the relevant posters. "I mean, a VCH piercing is fun. It certainly spices up sex."

I read what a VCH piercing is. Oh shit, it goes through the hood of your clit. Well, the Standishes definitely won't see that.

"It's also quick to heal, unlike your nipples which could take ages." She pulls out another rack of bars. These ones are shorter and look like a slightly thicker gage than the belly ones. "I personally recommend something like this. The gem hangs nicely in the right spot for some really good stimulation." She pulls off one of the bars and offers it to me. I hold out my hand, and she drops it in my palm. It's a small, curved bar, but it's made of clear plastic. The top has a small teardrop shaped red gem hanging from it.

"Okay, let's do this, but can I get one with a purple gem?" I ask her, and she beams.

"Of course. Hop up onto the bed and drop your panties while I get set up. There's a sheet there if you want to pull it over your bottom half for comfort until I'm ready."

I do as she says while she rummages around in cupboards, pulling out sterile packages and putting them on the counter. She quickly snaps on some gloves and sprays something onto a bit of gauze. "Alright, honey, I just need to clean the area and mark it up, so just lean back and relax, and put your heels together for me, just like a Pap smear. I know it's not the most comfortable of things, but I promise I've done this a ton."

I lie back and put my hands behind my head. The same posters that are on the walls are on the ceiling, and I read about all the different piercings you can get. I kind of wish that I could get more, but at this moment in my career, it's just not possible.

Charity pulls up my skirt and wipes my mound with some cold antiseptic before grabbing a marker and the bar she plans on using, and then she fiddles around down there a little more. "You've got a nice sized hood, so this piercing isn't going to be a problem. Sorry, it's going to be a little uncomfortable. I have to put the receiving tube up there so when I poke the needle through, nothing else gets poked."

I feel her push a cold, lube-covered metal tube up and under my clit hood. It is uncomfortable but not really painful.

"Okay, you're just going to feel a little pinch. Take a deep breath in for me." I do as instructed, and there's a small pinch. "And breathe out. Good, all done. I just have to slip the jewelry in."

The door to the room suddenly bursts open, and both of us turn to look in shock.

"Charity, the school called. Deacon has fallen, and they think his arm is broken. They want you to take him to the hospital." Kevin is breathless, and Charity gasps in panic.

"Oh my god. Shit, I have to finish this." She looks helplessly between me and Kevin.

"Dayton can do it. D, takeover for Charity so that she can look after Deacon."

Kevin calls to my teammate, and I feel myself tense up. Shit, they don't know who he is to me. I don't really need another team member becoming intimate with my vagina today. I've already orgasmed twice on another team member. This is not how I wanted our temporary working relationship to go.

Charity must feel my reaction, because she pats my leg with her free hand, the other still holding the hollow needle sticking out of my clit hood. "Don't worry, D is very good at what he does and has about as much experience as I do at piercing."

I'm actually really curious about how she knows him so well. Her and Kevin's familiarity with him is not just from a few weeks' worth of knowing him. It's a long-term friendship, but now is not the time to ask about that.

Dayton appears in the doorway. "Yeah, of course I can. Go get your little man and give him a hug for me, and tell him that if he needs a cast, I'll draw him something cool on it." Dayton steps farther into the room and looks down. I guess he wasn't expecting to see my exposed vulva, because his mouth drops open in surprise before he quickly closes it.

"Thanks, D, you just need to thread the bar through and attach the ball on the end, and then she's good to go. Can you give her an aftercare sheet too?" Charity waits for him to snap on some gloves before she releases the receiving needle and steps away.

Dayton takes her place, and she hurries out, pulling the door closed behind her. There's an awkward silence as we just look at one another. I can't stand it any longer, so I break first.

"So, hi. This is a little awkward," I mutter, not meeting his eyes at all.

He grunts. "You think?"

"Just get it done, okay?" I snap, my body coiled tight with tension and nerves. I'm so freaking embarrassed, and it takes a lot to embarrass me. I've been embarrassed in front of my new team twice in the same day, and now I have this hot as fuck man leaning over my vag, fiddling with a very sensitive spot—a spot that has been aching for more since my last encounter with Team Bastards.

"Sorry, this is a little tricky. I'm not good with these because my fingers are big and the ball is so little." Dayton's hot breath washes across my bare mound, and I squeeze my eyes shut.

For fuck's sake, Kenzie, don't you dare get turned on.

I feel him slide the bar through the needle and pull it through, his gloved finger brushing across my clit as he tries to put the ball on the end of the bar. My clit starts to throb, and I clench my teeth and breathe shallowly. I don't want him to hear my reaction to him playing with my nether regions. His fingers brush against my sensitive nub over and over as he tries to get the small ball on the little thread at the end of the bar. My nipples tighten, and my eyes roll back into my head. This is fucking mortifying.

The harder he tries, the harder he pushes down on my clit. I wonder if the stalwart team leader is just as nervous as I am. I bet he didn't expect to ever be this up close and personal with my body. I turn my head and breathe from my nose, trying not to make any noise, but when I open my eyes, I get a good look at his crotch and discover he's rocking a pretty raging hard-on.

A moan slips out of my mouth, and Dayton freezes.

"Oh my god, I'm so sorry, but you keep brushing against my clit, and I'm only fucking human."

"It's okay." His voice is gruff. "I really am sorry. Do you mind if I keep trying? You've gotten this far, and if I don't get it on, we'll just have to remove it."

I sigh loudly and decide to be frank with him. "No, that's fine, but if I come while you're doing it, we will never talk about it again, and you won't say a word to your teammates," I tell him sternly, and he finally turns his head and looks at me. Holy shit. The heat and lust in his eyes is unexpected, and it causes a shiver to slide down my spine.

"Just let yourself go. Don't hold it back. If you come, we can clean you up and try again. Everything is so fucking slippery down here now, and I think that's why I'm having problems."

His fingertip slides across my clit deliberately this time, and I close my eyes and just sink into the sensation. He circles the swollen nub over and over, but it doesn't take me long. He's already primed me, and I clench my fists as I feel myself fall over the edge. I stifle the moan that wants to accompany the delicious explosion that rockets through my body, but I can't stop my toes from curling into the piercing bed or my fists from clenching the protective sheet that is lying over it. The orgasm is hard, but my body is coiled tight with tension, and it's not the most enjoyable release. Again, my pussy clenches around nothing. That's the third empty orgasm I've had, and I kind of wished I brought a vibrator with me so I could at least fuck that once I got into bed, but that's not going to happen, especially in a shared room.

I feel Dayton use a cloth to wipe over my clit, and with a few deft flicks of his fingers against my still sensitive clit, he finally screws the ball onto the end.

"All done," he says, turning his back to me and cleaning up the used equipment. He throws the receiving tube into a container for autoclaving and disposes of the needle in a sharps container. The rest of the stuff is disposed of in a bin. The tension in the room is so thick, I could cut it with a knife, but I think we've come to a silent agreement that we aren't even going to acknowledge what just happened.

"You can sit up when you feel like it and put your panties back on. If you meet me out front, I'll give you an aftercare leaflet and take your payment." Dayton leaves without a backward glance, and I feel a rush of heat on my cheeks.

Never in my whole career have I ever felt cheap about what I do. I made my peace with it a long time ago and have never been ashamed to use my body to solve a case or to trap a mark. In less than two hours, Team Bastards has succeeded in making me feel more embarrassed than any low-life scumbag ever has. I blow out a huge breath of air and sit up before straightening myself out. Putting on my poker face, I walk out into the main area with my backpack over my shoulder.

"That will be seventy," Dayton tells me while sliding a sheet of paper over the counter. "Here's the aftercare, but I'm sure you probably know how to take care of something like that anyway." He's still not looking at me.

I grab my wallet out of my backpack and pull out my card, tapping it onto the reader. It beeps, telling me my payment went through. I shove everything and the sheet back into my wallet before putting my hands on the counter and leaning forward.

"I need a team meeting. We all need to be on the same page, and I don't want any more surprises. Unknown factors make any job tricky, and we need to eliminate all the ones we possibly can. Imagine my surprise when I found out that one of my teachers, who I thought was a giant scumbag perv trolling his classes for premium pussy, is actually on the team, and he's been planted to look like he's an interested buyer. That should have been information I had. I'm guessing that Ryland is the other team member, but I'm not a hundred percent sure. What were you doing? Fucking testing me? Because if you're going to keep pulling that bullshit, I'm out. I came here to do a job, but I can do that job on my own. I don't need the seven of you. They obviously know who I am, so you know what? Fuck you. I don't need this shit." I'm fucking angry now. "I'm out. Good luck with it. Maybe you can convince them to take Miller, but he better be happy giving and receiving." I storm off.

I hear Dayton call my name, but I ignore it. I'm frustrated, both sexually and professionally, and I don't have time for this shit. This is why I love working alone. No gatekeeping bullshit, just me, myself, and I.

I exit the alleyway and look at my watch. Fuck, it's five, and I need to be back at the house by six. I might just have enough time to check out the bar Charity mentioned. I pull out my phone and google bars with dance clubs in Summerville and find what I hope is the one she was talking about. It's one street over from my location, so it must be the one. I head quickly in that direction, needing to get this done and then find the bus that will drop me back at the halfway home before dinner.

I guess I can claim that I got lost, since it's my first day and everything. Mrs. Standish seems strict, but not like a complete raging cow.

CHAPTER 18

The directions send me in the opposite way of where I started, and I take a left at the next intersection. There are a few larger restaurants, an arcade, and a movie theater along this street. I pass by all of them and find the bar I'm looking for—Life Lounge. I wonder what they mean by that. Maybe it's taking a break from your life. It's not very catchy if you ask me. The sign on the door says it opened a few minutes ago, and wouldn't you know it, there's a help wanted sign in the window. Perfect.

I push open one of the wooden doors and step into the dim room. There's quiet background music playing and the stale smell of beer and cigarettes. I scan the room, and it looks like a typical bar, with tables, booths, and a few screens showing hockey and football games. The room is empty except for a black man behind the bar who's drying glasses. I step farther into the room, and he lifts his head. Ah, so here's the last member of the team whom I actually know—Anders Brooks, aka Hot Chocolate.

He squints at me. I guess he can't make out details because of the dim lighting.

"Can I help you?" he asks, putting his cloth down and moving toward the end of the bar closest to me.

Behind him are shelves of bottles and a couple of flashy neon lights, and in front of him, a few beer taps are spread out down the bar in intervals. I move closer too, and I see his eyes widen when he finally figures out who I am. There's a slight inhalation of breath before he smiles.

"Hello, pretty lady, what can I do for you today?" he says in a flirty tone before sliding his eyes to the side. Now that I'm at the bar, I can see better, and I notice that at the end of the bar, the area opens up into a storeroom, and there's a man counting stock there. Right, so we're keeping to our covers.

"Oh, hey, I saw the help wanted sign in the window," I tell him.

"Well, you sure are pretty enough to work here, but your style..." He looks me up and down suggestively, and I see the other person start to pay attention at the other end. "Isn't really what we look for, but who knows, the patrons might dig the goth chick look for something different. Matt, we've got someone interested in the position." Anders's words seem to be loaded with more than what he's actually saying, so I need to pay attention.

A man holding a clipboard comes out of the stock-room. His lips purse as he looks me up and down. He's another member of the original Divinity of Morality Club, and I highly doubt that's a coincidence.

"How old are you?" he asks in a voice that sounds like he's been smoking two packs a day his whole life.

"Old enough," I reply hopefully, and he frowns. "Please. I just moved to town, and I really need this job," I plead when he doesn't seem inclined to give me the job. "I'll do anything, I just need to earn some money so when I graduate, I have something saved so I don't end up living on the street when the halfway house kicks me out." His eye twitches, and I see comprehension cross his face as he comes to a decision.

"I can pay you cash under the table if you're not legal, but if you get caught by the cops, I will tell them you produced fake documents saying you were legal. You will do everything I say without question, or you're gone, you hear me?" he asks, and I shrug.

"Of course, sure," I agree quickly.

"You will work during the week, five to eleven, which is when we close up, but don't expect to be home before early morning Friday and Saturday night. Is this going to be a problem?" he asks, and I wince.

"I'm not sure Mrs. Standish will allow me to work all hours on a Friday and Saturday night."

He waves a hand at me. "Don't worry about it. I'm good friends with Jim. I've had some of their kids work here before. I'll smooth it over with them, and as long as you go to church with them on Sunday, they won't care."

"Oh, thank goodness, because I really want the job."

His eyes narrow, and I can practically see the wheels turning in his head. "Well, good. Get over here and suck Anders's cock for him. He's been uptight and snappy this evening, and no one likes that in their bartenders. Let's get him right for when the patrons arrive."

Fuck my life. Seriously? Another encounter with a teammate?

Matt mistakes my pause for reluctance. "Or do you not want the job?"

"Fuck, man, do you think I can't get a girl to suck my dick by myself?" Anders grumbles, and Matt shrugs.

"You were talking about wanting more responsibility. How about you follow my instructions, and we can see about giving you another position?"

That conversation is laced with hidden meaning, and I can see Anders comprehend it as he reaches for his belt.

"Well, sure, who am I to argue about getting blown by a pretty girl." The sound of his belt buckle clanking is almost deafening to my ears as I bite my lip, feigning hesitation. I mean, I'm not all that thrilled about blowing my teammate, but I guess it could be worse. I could have been told to blow Matt himself.

"Well, come on. If you want the job, then you have to blow Anders or you can fuck off and find a job somewhere else, and I'll tell Martha that you propositioned me to get the position."

Holy fuck. How did it go from me applying for a job to him blackmailing me for it? What the fuck? I'm almost confused at the turn in conversation, but I drop my bag and move around to the business side of the bar. I look back at the door and raise an eyebrow. "What happens if someone comes in?" I ask, feigning nerves.

"No one should see you down on your knees, but you better make it a good one." Matt leans back on fridges that sit under the shelves of bottles, so I guess he's going to watch then.

Anders frowns. "What are you doing, man? You want to get a look at my dick?" he growls, and Matt doesn't even flinch.

"Sure, why not? I want to see what her lips look like wrapped around it. I bet she'll look so pretty at your feet. I bet she'll look even prettier choking on your cock. Make sure you make her cry. I love seeing tears run down their faces." Matt's tone is all monosyllabic, and I know serial killers who put more emotions into their voices. Hello, psychopath.

I can't put it off any longer. I get down on my knees, wincing as the mat on the ground digs into my bare skin, but I reach up and draw down the zipper on Anders's jeans and reach in. My eyes widen when I wrap my hand around his junk. It's fat, thick, and hard, and I'm worried I'm going to have trouble actually giving him a decent blow job. I prefer not to suck my marks' dicks since I find oral sex a little too intimate. That's not to say I won't do it, but I prefer to have sex than be up close and personal with my mouth.

Thankfully, Anders showers regularly, because his dick is not only long and thick, but clean. I run my tongue up and down his length before drawing back and spitting on it, getting it nice and wet. He grunts and reaches for my hair, pulling out the ponytail holder and letting it fall around my face. I feel a wave of gratitude as it hides me from Matt. I slowly slide his dick into my mouth, breathing through my nose. I bob on it, hollowing my cheeks and sucking hard before popping off again.

"Pull her hair back so I can see," Matt demands, and Anders pauses before sighing and threading his fingers through my hair. I look up at him, and his eyes are filled with a mixture of apology, regret, and no small amount of heat. Although he doesn't want it this way, he's still fucking enjoying it, so I may as well make the most of it and give him the best damn blow job he's ever had.

I reach up and cup his balls, rolling them around in my hand as I try to take his dick all the way down. It's long, and I have to work for it, but my nose finally nuzzles against his pubic bone.

"Holy fuck, look at that bitch. Hold her there. Yes,

that's it." Matt sounds excited as my eyes start to tear up and I try to pull away.

Anders's hands are gentle in my hair, but he keeps me in place a little longer before he allows me to pull back. I gasp for air when he finally lets go and I pull off.

"Oh yes, so pretty with those bruises and her tears. I think she's just perfect for the position. Don't you, Anders?" Matt taunts, and Anders grunts.

"Well, let's see if she'll swallow first." Anders's voice is husky and low as he pulls me back onto his dick.

"She fucking better if she knows what's good for her, but I bet those creamy tits would look fucking spectacular painted with our cum too."

My eyes widen as Matt reaches for his own zipper and pulls it down. Anders yanks on my hair and directs me back to his cock, and I go to town, praying that if I finish him then I won't have to do Matt next. I swallow down Anders's hot cock and get into a good rhythm that I know will have him coming. A voice on the other side of the bar startles me, but he just holds me in place.

"Hey, man, what can I get you?" Matt moves away from us. I guess he tucked his dick back in, but Anders doesn't let me pull away.

I feel his balls tighten in my hand, and all his muscles stiffen as he taps a finger against my head, warning me about what's coming—literally. My mouth floods with his cum, and I swallow it down as quickly as I can, but a little dribbles out the side.

Finally, he stops and pulls away, staring down at me with a look I can't decipher. I put a finger up to the crease of my lips and wipe away the bit of cum that trickled out, then I stick my finger into my mouth and suck it before winking at Anders, letting him know I'm fine.

His eyes widen before he growls, then he shoves his dick into his pants, zips them up, and refastens his belt before yanking me to my feet. I'm slightly dizzy from the rushed movement, and it takes me a moment to get my bearings. Matt is down at the other end, and as his customer heads to a booth, he returns to us.

"Did she swallow?" he demands, looking between us, and a sleazy smile stretches across Anders's lips.

"Like an alcoholic on a bender."

"Good. You start Saturday night. Give Anders your number so he can send you the roster, and make sure you do something about your face. My clients don't like bruises on girls unless they put them there." With that classy comment, he turns and goes back to the stockroom, picking up his clipboard on the way.

Anders reaches into his pocket and pulls out his phone, acting like we're exchanging numbers. "Fuck, I'm sorry," he whispers, but I hold up a hand.

"Not here," I hiss. "There were cameras at the school, so I don't doubt some are here too." He gives me a quick nod in understanding, and I smile and wave before leaving the bar. "I have to go, or I'll be late for dinner, but I'll see you Saturday," I call breezily, and when I see Matt watching me from the storeroom, I wave to him too before hurrying out of the bar.

I have exactly fifteen minutes to find the bus and get home. I don't think I'm going to be able to do it, and I can't imagine that's going to make me popular at the home. Hopefully Matt will call the Standishes and vouch for me.

CHAPTER 19

My run down the dirt driveway leaves me breathless and grasping at my sides as I push the door open that leads directly into the kitchen. The silence that greets me is deafening, and I feel all eyes on me in an instant. My own slide to Martha, who is frowning, her lips pursed with annoyance.

Before she can reprimand me, I quickly say, "I'm so sorry. I had a job interview and missed the right bus and had to catch the next one." I lean against the doorframe, trying to catch my breath. I'm not actually that winded, but I need to put on a good act, and yeah, my ribs do kind of ache. "The guy at the bar said he was going to call Mr. Standish and run it by him." I look hopefully at the man of the household, and his eyebrows rise in surprise.

"You got a job at Life Lounge?" He sounds surprised, and I frown.

"Yeah, I did. He said he's employed girls from your home before. Was he lying to me?" I bite my lip, pretending to be anxious, but James shakes his head.

"Oh, he has, I'm just surprised. He hasn't mentioned anything to me about interviewing you."

"Oh, then he hasn't called you yet? It was a last-minute thing. I went in after school today."

Martha huffs. "That man... You know I don't like our kids working for him," she snaps at James, and he shrugs.

"He pays under the table and doesn't question their age. There aren't a lot of options in this town. I'm sure Mackenzie is going to do just fine." He winks at me, and I have a feeling he knows the kind of interview I just went through. A shiver of disgust flows over me, but I hide it and beam at him.

"He wants me to work a couple afternoons a week and the weekends," I tell them, dropping my bag down and taking the last empty seat at the table between Will and Ty.

"But that means you won't be home for family dinner most nights." Martha sounds annoyed. "I'm not sure I'm happy about this. Out until all hours and parading around in that uniform? People are going to think the wrong thing about you, Mackenzie."

"Nonsense. They are going to assume she's doing everything she can to get a good start for the rest of her life. Leave her be, Martha. Matthew will take good care of her."

Martha sighs heavily. "Fine, but she will have to

come to church with us on Sundays and pray for the lord's forgiveness no matter how tired she is from working." Martha is firm in her desires, and James rolls his eyes good-naturedly.

"I'm not sure the lord sees bar keeping as a sin, but sure, if that will keep you happy. That's fine with you, isn't it?" He turns to me, and I look between them, quickly agreeing.

"Sure, of course."

"Fine, well, eat up, our dinner is getting cold because we waited for you." Martha gestures for people to start eating, and the teenagers who had been quiet up until now, eagerly waiting to hear the outcome of me being late, all start talking at once.

"Hey, maybe now that you're working there, Ty and I can get in." Will nudges me in the side.

"I highly doubt it. You two don't look old enough to get in," Cassie sneers across the table.

"Ouch, Cassie, I'm wounded." Ty playfully grabs at his chest before reaching for the breadbasket and tossing a roll onto his plate before handing it to me.

"Only whores work at places like that," Jessica hisses at me, speaking quietly enough that Martha, who is talking to the sisters about their day, doesn't hear.

"Oh burn, good one, Jess," I reply lightly. "I'm afraid you're going to have to find a new insult, because that one doesn't really hit hard. You think calling me a whore is hateful? The girl, who rumor has it, is quite open to spreading her own legs to get ahead? Pot meet kettle." I gesture between the two of us, and she scowls and huffs.

"At least I don't get paid for it. Not like you."

"Well then, you really aren't doing it right, are you?"

I can see from the corner of my eye that James, although eating, is listening intently to our conversation. Miller must notice as well.

"Hey, Mr. Standish, can you put in a good word for me when you speak to your friend? I need a job too, and I haven't had any luck trying to find one. Sounds like it might be a neat place to work."

James's eyes narrow, and he considers Miller's words. He finishes chewing his mouthful and then puts his fork down. "I'm sure I can speak to him. He's always looking for attractive staff to keep his patrons happy. No one wants ugly people serving them drinks."

"So why's Mac working there then? Why didn't you ever tell me to apply?" Jessica whines and flutters her eyelashes at him. "If Miller wants to work there, so do I."

"The interview process is pretty strict. I'm not sure if you would pass it, either of you," James says slowly, trying to discourage them.

I snort. I have no doubt that Jessica would have passed. She would have been on her knees to blow Anders in a second without hesitation. I still can't get a read on Miller, but would he have been asked for the same thing? I'm not sure.

"Well, you should at least give us a chance. I'm sure I can do anything Mac can do better." Jessica crosses her arms stubbornly, and James looks at Martha.

"Absolutely not. I will not have all of you working at the den of iniquity. All that loud music and gyrating bodies and the alcohol... No, just no. Jessica, as a member of the Divinity of Morality, it would be frowned upon for you to work somewhere like that. No, I will ask around and see if there is something more appropriate for a girl like you. You don't want to ruin your good standing you've worked so hard to achieve." Oh, fuck my life. Martha is obviously clueless of her niece and cohort's reputation. "Miller, you are welcome to apply, since I'm sure they can make use of a man like you."

I'm not sure how to take Martha's last comment or what she's implying. From the scowl on Miller's face, I guess nothing good. Hmm, I wonder what happened there. Last night, she was having a go at his tattoos, so I assume she doesn't approve of his style.

"Hmm, maybe. I'll talk to Matt. I'm sure he can find something for you, Miller," James assures him, and dinner conversation changes to more benign comments. After helping clean up, we are all dismissed to our rooms for homework.

I'm heading up the stairs and past the girls' room when an arm reaches out and yanks me inside. I stumble into the girls' room, and Sally quickly closes the door.

"Mac, you know that club you're working at is the one that is supposed to have the sex club underneath it, right?" Cassie hisses as the sisters look on, both of them wringing their hands in agitation.

"Really?" I ask, feigning surprise, but I'm excited to have my guess confirmed. "How do you know?"

The three girls exchange glances, and Cassie sits down on her bed. The twins both take a seat on the bottom bunk, leaving me a rolling chair.

"Sybil, the girl who used to live here, the one we were talking about last night..." Cassie trails off.

"The one you said had a modeling contract but disappeared before she made it to New York?" I ask, trying to remember the exact details.

"Yes. She had a job there, and, well, she told us things." Stephanie shudders, but I lean forward eagerly. Now we're getting somewhere.

"Like what?"

"Well, everything was okay to start with. She danced in one of those cage things on the weekends and ran drinks during the week." Cassie does all the talking as the sisters sit and listen, holding hands. "And she loved it. It was fun, and she made good tips, but then she was asked to serve at a special party. She was told it was a secret and forced to sign an NDA. At first, we didn't question it, but then she started to change. She withdrew into herself and would flinch at loud noises, and we finally had enough. We made her tell us what was going on. The party she was made to serve at was a sex party, and she had to be topless, and guests were allowed to touch her, but it was the depraved sex acts that were being performed that shocked her the most. The participants weren't always happy to be there, if you get what I'm saying, and this wasn't your normal BDSM club. Things were rough, and there was blood and punishments and screams. She was freaked out." Cassie's eyes are round and haunted like she's remembering the conversation all over again.

"We told her to go to the police, but she couldn't. The chief of police was one of the people at the party. They are supposed to wear masks, but his was knocked off during a particularly aggressive act, and she caught a glimpse of him," Sally says, taking over. "They also threatened her. They told her if she said anything to anyone, she would be the girl being used and abused next time, and then they would discard her like yesterday's trash, so she kept her mouth shut. It was only when she got her acceptance from the modeling agent and had an escape that she told us everything. She knew she was getting out."

"Except she didn't," I murmur, and tears form in Cassie's eyes.

"The last event she worked at wasn't actually a sex party. She came home and threw all of her things in a bag and made the decision to leave a week earlier than planned." Stephanie wraps her arm around her sister as she sobs loudly.

"What was it?" I ask, hanging onto every one of her words like it's the word of God.

"An auction. They were selling men and women to the highest bidder," Cassie tells me, shuddering. "You should stay away from that place. You don't want to end up missing like Sybil"

"What do you think happened to her?" I ask, and Cassie shrugs.

"I'm guessing she was sold to the highest bidder too."

"Is that what you think happened to the other foster kids also?" I ask, and Sally wipes away her tears.

"What else could have happened to them? Something is not right in this town. It's evil."

"Why didn't she try to tell anyone else?" I ask. "Maybe the governor or called in a tip to the FBI?"

"Because a girl she worked with tried to, and she was found dead, face down in a ditch outside of town. They blamed transient vagrants, and no one was ever charged, but it seemed like too much of a coincidence." Stephanie stands up and stretches.

"You better watch your back, Mac. Better yet, quit before you even start. You seem like a nice girl, too nice to be caught up in a place like that." Cassie sounds older than her young years, but I can tell by the haunted look in her eyes that she's putting on a brave facade.

I stand up and grab hold of the door handle. "Don't worry about me, girls. I can assure you, I know how to look after myself."

Sally just scoffs and looks at me with derision. "Sure, just don't come crying to us when you can't. I don't have the energy or the willpower to be friends with someone who is too stupid to live."

Whoa, the girl doesn't pull her punches. "Okay then, I won't bother you any longer." I pull the door open, and although the sisters are now blatantly ignoring me, Cassie's eyes are full of worry.

"Just be careful, Mac. Hopefully if Miller gets a job working there, you'll be protected."

I scoff. "Yeah, he wouldn't spit on me if I were on fire, so I doubt he'll have my back."

She tips her head to the side, and I feel like she's looking deep inside of me. "I wouldn't be so sure of that. His eyes tracked you at school today. It was like you were a black hole and he was being sucked in. I think you may be surprised."

"I don't need a man to watch my back, but I promise I will be careful. Who knows? I might be the key to unraveling their whole operation."

I can see that she doesn't believe me, but I've been as honest as I can afford to be. Time to cut my losses. I wave goodbye and pull the door closed behind me. Moving toward my room, I walk past the entrance to the attic, and again, I'm yanked into a room—or more correctly, up the stairs first.

"What the fuck?" I hiss at Miller when he finally releases his grip on my arm.

"What did you do? How did you get that job? Anders had a lot of trouble getting a position in there, yet you just walked in and instantly got one?" he demands harshly, and I shrug, feeling quite smug.

"Did you ask him?" I hedge, not sure if he actually knows or not. Anders should still be working, so I doubt he's had time to debrief his team.

"No." Miller shoves his hand through his hair, pushing his long bangs back off of his face. "He's still working, but Dayton sent a message. There's a team meeting tonight, and I'm supposed to bring you."

"About fucking time," I growl. "I had the delightful experience of learning that Maxwell Turner is also a member of Team Bastards today. I don't want any more surprises."

He's momentarily confused by me saying "Team Bastards," but he quickly recovers. "Fuck, you didn't blow his cover, did you?" He grabs hold of my arm again and stares down at me.

I yank myself free and shake my head, walking over to his window and pushing it up again to make sure it still slides smoothly.

"Fuck no, I didn't. I rode his cock like a good little slut and performed for the cameras." I feel him approach me and whirl so he can't grab me again, but before I can say anything, his mouth is on mine and his fingers are in my hair, yanking my head to get a better angle. He thrusts his tongue into my mouth and presses his hard body against mine, and I melt into him. Our kiss is like nothing I've ever experienced before. It's a tussle for domination, and he quickly overpowers me, owning me like I've never been owned before. I'm breathless and hanging onto him for dear life when he finally pulls away.

"Jessica was right, you are a whore," he sneers before pulling away from me and stalking to the opposite side of the room.

"No, Miller, I'm good at my fucking job. For your information, I would have happily fucked him to keep our covers, but he turned his chair and we faked it. That being said, I will never let something as stupid as someone else judging me prevent me from doing a job. Now how about you jump down off your high fucking horse? I get results, and when I am the one who breaks this ring wide open, I expect you to grovel at my feet in apology." I clench my hands into fists and refrain from smacking him.

"Not going to happen," he retorts over his shoulder, not even looking at me.

I guess he's ashamed of his lack of control. I have nothing to be embarrassed about. Sure, I melted into him like ice cream on hot pavement, but I also spent all afternoon being turned on and teased. Seriously, if he had thrown me on the bed and stripped me naked, I would have praised God. Pity he's such a judgmental ass, otherwise I might have suggested exactly that. Now I'm just going to have to suffer in silence, but from the look of the hard length in his jeans just before he pushed away, I'm not suffering alone.

"What time are we leaving?" I ask.

"Be up here just before eleven. Anders will pick us up on the way home from the bar."

"Tell him not to bother. I've got us covered," I tell Miller, heading back toward the stairs.

That finally gets him to turn and look at me in confusion. "Huh? How?"

"Don't you worry your pretty little head about it. You'll see later." I smile as his confusion turns to annoyance, and then I head downstairs, hoping that no one is at the bottom when I exit.

"Kenzie," Miller growls, but I ignore him, happy to be getting one over on him.

I hope he stews on his annoyance for the next couple of hours. That would make me very happy.

CHAPTER 20

"You know he's gay," Jessica says to me as I enter our room. She's sitting at the little desk on her side, doing what looks like homework, but she stops as I enter, and I frown at her.

"Who?" I ask, and she rolls her eyes and points at the ceiling.

"Miller, dummy. I heard two sets of feet up there, and it wasn't hard to put two and two together. Throwing yourself at him just seems desperate, and don't think we didn't see how friendly you were with Ryland today."

Oh shit, okay, that's not good. I didn't even consider that she could hear footsteps in this room.

"And I care because?" I ask her, unsure where she's going with this and almost certain after that kiss we just shared that she's lying, but I'm also kind of curious about why she's telling me this.

"Well, I wouldn't want you to get hurt," she threatens, and my mouth drops open in shock at her words before I can stop it. I sputter slightly, but she ignores me and continues. "He and Ryland are in each other's pockets all the time, it's just obvious, and Ryland has turned down all of Sophie's advances too. I mean, the two of them would be a complete power couple, just like Max and Stella are."

"Who?" I ask, completely confused by the crap that's coming from her mouth. My mind was whirling on all the information I discovered from the other three girls, and then it stuttered to a halt when Miller kissed me, so it's taking me a little more time to understand where she's going with all this.

"Mr. Turner and Ms. Standish, the French teacher, dummy. Apparently they are hot and heavy. Sophie says Stella thinks he's going to pop the question," Jessica says in a bored tone. "I think she's crazy. Mr. Turner has a wandering eye. I saw him checking you out today," she accuses, but I ignore that bit.

"So, apart from Miller turning you down and Ryland turning down Sophie, you have no other proof that they are gay? Fuck, maybe they just have good taste." I can't believe I'm defending that asshole, but I hate it when girls accuse a guy of being gay if they aren't interested. "Maybe they are just not that into you, Jessica. Have you ever thought of that?"

"Or maybe they are sucking each other's cocks and don't need us to do it," she sneers meanly, and I shake my head.

"I pity you. Why don't you go after Billy? He seems

like a sure thing," I retort, changing the subject, and her eyes narrow.

"Because even though Sophie doesn't want him, she doesn't want any of her friends looking at him either," Jessica grumbles, turning back to her homework. "Besides, I saw the bruises he used to leave on her. They looked a lot like yours, but she hid them better."

Huh, I don't know how to unpack any of what Jessica just said.

"Look, trust me. You don't want to get on Sophie's bad side, or a lot of the other kids at this school. She can be mean, and not just rich girl mean. Keep your head down, otherwise an accident might happen." Jessica is mumbling now, and her swing in attitude startles me. She started off defensive and fiery, and now she's in a shell.

"Are you okay, Jessica? Is there anything I can do?" I step toward her, and she picks up a pen off the desk as she shakes her head. My gaze zeros in on the ring of bruises around her wrist. I can see fingerprints, but they look too dainty to be from a male. "Did Sophie do this to you?" I ask, pointing at the bruises, and she puts her wrist in her lap.

"Just stay away from me and the popular group, if you know what's good for you. There are plans in the works for Miller, and you are just going to get in the way, and don't think I didn't notice how you didn't have your stockings on when you got home, you skank. If you get knocked up, Martha will kick you out quicker than you can say 'I'm pregnant,'" Jessica snaps before putting a pair of earbuds into her ears, telling me she's done talking.

I breathe out a big sigh and sit down on my bed, dropping my backpack at my feet. I wince slightly as I feel the slight pull of the ring between my legs. I've been able to ignore it up until now, since the small bite of pain is nothing compared to the rest of the aches and pains in my body, but now I feel it rub against my clit, which is a little sensitive and slippery after Miller's kiss. Nope, I'm not even going to think about that bipolar asshole.

I need a nap. I wonder if I can catch a couple of hours before we have to leave for the team meeting. Today has been a lot. I think I'm starting to work things out, or at least have an inkling thanks to the information from the girls, which was the most unexpected source. I'm not sure if Miller or the guys would have ever gotten that info, though it seems that Max and Anders may have an in with the possible bad guys.

I lean down and untie my boots, toeing them off before throwing myself backward on the bed and pulling a pillow over my head, blocking out the light. I'm feeling a little confused now. Martha didn't seem enthusiastic about me working at Life Lounge, but James did. Maybe I misjudged the woman, and she's not actually in on it. Maybe it's just James. That would explain why she tried to invite her kids back for Thanksgiving. I mean, if she knew that they had been trafficked, wouldn't she have just stayed quiet about it? There would have been no need to draw attention to the whole thing, unless she wasn't the one who did it. I just assumed, but what if it was one of the girls? It may have been the smartest and safest thing they ever did. I need to make sure it stays that way.

I'm feeling pretty pleased with myself as I allow my mind to drift off to sleep. I'm going to need to keep my wits about me over the coming days, but I hope we're one step closer to finding all those missing foster kids.

A deep rattling sound wakes me from my sleep, and I reach for the gun under my pillow. When my hand finds nothing but course sheets, I sit up, ready to fight off whatever woke me, but then I pause. It's quiet, and I think maybe I was dreaming when the loud sound comes again. It sounds like a hibernating bear has made itself comfortable in Jessica's bed.

"Holy fuck, I pity your future bed partners," I whisper as I pull my phone out of my pocket and look at the time. Crap, it's almost eleven. Miller better not have gone without me. I hurry, and as quietly as I can, I change my panties for fresh ones and put on a clean shirt before ditching the tartan skirt for a pair of skinny jeans. Riding the motorcycle with a skirt is just asking to get burnt. I pop some painkillers out of their packet and dry swallow them before grimacing. That's never fun, but my entire body aches something fierce this evening. I'd been good at keeping up with the painkillers, but I forgot to take them before I fell asleep, and I'm really paying for it now. Smothering a groan, I bend down to pick up my Docs and backpack and sneak out of the room. Jessica is sleeping so deeply she hasn't even stirred. Let's just hope it stays that way while I'm up in Miller's room.

I stick my head out to make sure the coast is clear. All the other bedroom doors are closed, so I sneak out of mine, pulling it shut behind me. The click of the latch is loud in the relative silence, but I'm sure no one heard it. I don't have to go far before I get to the landing to the attic. The door is cracked slightly, so I push it and hurry up the stairs. The lights are off in the room, but there's a bright glow on the bed. I can see Miller's scowling face illuminated by his phone.

"About time. I didn't think you were coming," he grumbles, climbing out of bed.

"Sorry, I had to wait for Jessica to be solidly asleep," I tell him. Yeah, I'm lying, but I'm not about to admit that I was sleeping. I'd never hear the end of it. I quickly pull on my shoes as he goes over and opens the window.

"It's just a step across to that thick branch, and then there's an easy climb down," he tells me, climbing up on the sill to show me. I throw my backpack over my shoulders and step up to watch his descent. "Just don't fuck it up, and I hope you know what you were talking about for transport, because I told Anders not to worry." Without waiting for me to reply, he ducks out and is gone.

I watch as he nimbly climbs down the tree without hesitation, showing he's done this a few times already. I wait for him to make it to the ground before I start my own climb. It's easy, but my ribs still pull slightly, and my new jewelry addition gives some surprising but not completely unpleasant friction in my skinny jeans. I jump to the ground with a soft "oof."

Miller grabs my arm to steady me. "Are you okay?" he asks, and although I can't see his face in the heavy shadows, I can hear a hint of worry. There's no way I'm going to admit what the issue is though.

"Ah, yeah, my ribs are still a little sore," I whisper quietly before shaking him off. I pull my phone out of my pocket and pull up the map with the pin my dad sent me. "Okay, this way."

I walk away from the house in the opposite direction of the driveway. Much like the woods that surround the school, this forest is fairly dense as well, and it takes me a while to forge a path to our destination, using our phones to light the way. Miller grumbles the whole time, but quickly shuts up once we arrive. Stashed next to a tree with a camo tarp over it is our transportation. I pull the tarp off, exposing a sleek, black Kawasaki Ninja 1000 with two helmets sitting on the seat and the keys in the ignition.

"Oh yes. Come to mama. Dad really knows how to

look after me." I grin ear to ear at the beautiful beast in front of me.

Miller whistles. "Now that is a bike. Dibs for driving." He leans forward to grab a helmet, but I shove him to the side and dive for one, throwing my leg over the bike before he even realizes what happened. "What the fuck?" He gapes at me, and I shrug.

"You snooze, you lose. Also, nobody drives my bike but me. You get to ride bitch." I pull the helmet over my head and flip the switch that turns on the helmet mic, blocking out whatever Miller is saying. From the look on his face, it's not good. I put my hands up to say that I can't hear him. He scowls and grabs the other helmet, shoving it onto his head, and the sound of him breathing heavily comes through the speakers in my helmet.

"I'm nobody's bitch," he growls but climbs on behind me and wraps his arms around my waist as I turn on the powerful machine. Thankfully, there's a small dirt trail that leads out of the forest, because this is no dirt bike. This is a pure, lean, mean road machine, and I wouldn't want to scratch it up going through the underbrush.

I pat his hand on my waist. "If you're a good boy, I might let you ride it some time," I coo into my microphone, and his hands clench, but he doesn't hurt me. "You are going to have to be the navigator, I have no idea where we are going."

"Go left at the end of the dirt road. It leads back

into town. Then head through a really run-down section that opens up to a rich neighborhood," he tells me as I drive slowly down the dirt track.

I don't think anyone would be able to hear the bike from the house, since it purrs beautifully, but I don't want to risk opening it up and waking the Standishes. I don't want them getting suspicious that someone is using this old path, then check it out and discover the bike. That would completely blow our cover.

"Oh yeah, I remember seeing it on the drive through town," I reply.

Miller snorts. "And I bet Martha pointed out Governor Turner's house, right?"

"Ah, yeah, she did and mentioned his two sons have come back to town." It all clicks into place. "Oh, I'm an idiot. I know that their last name is Turner, but now all the dots connect. Your team is here because their dad talked to mine."

"Yes, it was very easy to place both of them at the high school. Max and Ry didn't grow up here, and there's never been anything in the paper about them except that the governor has two sons. Creating back-stories about their return to their hometown to finish out Ryland's education after getting kicked out of a private school was easy, and Max is his guardian, so it was just as easy for him to get a job at the high school. All Jeff had to do was put in a good word for him, and the principal was thrilled to have Max teach at the school."

I turn left once we hit the blacktop and open up

the throttle. The bike jumps forward, and we fly down the road toward town. Miller whoops with joy, and I feel my own smile cross my lips. There's nothing better than feeling the wind against your body as the bike hugs the curves of the road, but I ease back once we enter the built-up area again. There's no point in getting a ticket, which would also blow our cover at this stage. The vibrations of the engine do nice things to my body, especially with the new ring between my legs and the feel of Miller's hard body wrapped around mine. I feel the need to squirm, but I don't want Miller to know that I'm turned on, so I grasp at a conversation to distract myself from my growing need.

"How do you guys explain the living arrangement? I'm assuming they all live together."

"Anders and Dayton are college friends of Max's who were looking for work, and Max suggested they come and stay with him. Lathan and Bishop are Governor Turner's two aides' sons, who are finishing their own schooling so they aren't dragged all over the country."

"And people believe that?" I ask, not hiding my skepticism.

"It's a small town, so of course they do." Miller's sarcasm is not hard to miss. "It would have been strange if we had moved them all in separately. This kind of town doesn't get that many new families all at once unless there's some big job opportunity that just opened up nearby, and there was nothing convenient for us to use."

Miller has been very forthcoming during the ride into town. It's almost like a switch was flipped inside his brain. I'm sure it won't last, but it makes for a more pleasant ride. The houses turn from dilapidated and dirt poor to middle class before changing into the upper end of the income scale. Miller points out a few more large properties on the way.

"That is Ted and June Standish's place. James's brother and his family."

"Sophie and Stella?" I ask flatly, looking at the antebellum style house.

"Yeah, Ted is in imports and exports, and he looks to be doing quite well for himself as opposed to James and Martha. It all seems like happy families on the surface, and they are all smiles at church every Sunday, but I sense some tension between the families. June and Martha particularly."

"Jealousy about status?" I ask, and I feel him shrug.

"I'm not sure. Ted came over to the house the week before we had our evaluation, and he and James had a heated argument, but I couldn't get close enough to hear what it was about. Martha kept us all upstairs in our rooms while it was going on."

"And you said Ted is in imports and exports?" I ask him, and I feel him nod his head, his helmet touching mine with the movement.

"Yes, he has ships coming and going from the wharf here in town all the time."

"Well, doesn't that seem awfully convenient. That

would certainly be a way to smuggle them out of the country."

We're quiet for the rest of the ride, both lost in our own thoughts. Is this a much bigger operation than we first considered? So far, my three main suspects are Ted and James Standish, and Matthew from the bar. He was entirely too interested in seeing if I would happily blow Anders to get the job. That's not normal, is it? I mean, I've never had a normal job, but surely people don't actually get away with that sort of thing. There is also the guidance counselor, Brock. The questions he asked me were beyond invasive, but that can't be how he speaks to all children, because there would be red flags galore by now. I have so many questions. Hopefully Team Bastards will be a bit more forthcoming face-to-face, otherwise I'm going to lose my shit. I'm achy, tired, and horny, which is not a good combination, so heaven help those men if they pull any of their bullshit tonight.

CHAPTER 21

I pull the bike up to the large mansion that Martha had pointed out to me as Governor Turner's home.

"Take it around the back," Miller says, gesturing at the driveway that curves around the large building. "There will be eyes on us even at this late hour. We don't need them seeing us get off the bike. It's better they assume it's some of the guys."

I do as he says, and a back light switches on as I pull the bike to a stop and we both get off. We remove our helmets and leave them on the seat before Miller leads the way past the pool to the back patio. There are curtains pulled across the large glass doors, but one is pushed far enough to the side to let us through. Standing there, looking sheepish, is Ryland Turner, confirming my guess that he's the last member of Team Bastards.

He waves and pushes the door open, gesturing for

us to come in. I stop in front of him, scowling, and he shrugs.

"Sorry. The others didn't want you to know, and we were outvoted. Both Max and I didn't think it was fair, but they wanted to test you." He sounds as annoyed as I feel, and I roll my eyes.

"What a load of misogynistic bullshit. No wonder you haven't had a permanent woman stay with your group, you're all a bunch of children." I push past him, and he shuts the door and pulls the curtain closed again.

I am in a lovely, open conservatory style room with lots of plants and greenery and a comfy looking sectional sofa. Sitting around it are the rest of the aforementioned Team Bastards. I gaze around the room, taking everyone in. Lathan smiles brightly and waves, and Bishop gives me a nod, but those are the only responses I get. Dayton, Anders, and Max won't even look at me.

Fuck my life, it's going to be a long night.

"Alright, let's get this shit all out in the open. Two of you gave me orgasms today, and I reciprocated for another. One wasn't strictly case related, but who cares? Get over yourselves. If that's what it takes to get the job done, well, we just suck it up and get over it. I will not have your issues making this difficult." I nudge my Doc Martins off and groan when my toes can breathe again. I love my boots, but I also love removing them.

The room explodes into noise as all of them get to

their feet and start yelling, but I just hold up a hand, and they fall silent. "Not to mention your bullshit gatekeeping crap you have going on. I still haven't received a full account of all of your talents, and I was shocked to discover Miller living at the same location I am and playing the same kind of role. All of this was sprung on me, not to mention the crap with those two." I point between the Turner brothers, who at least have the grace to look embarrassed. "I seriously thought he was one of the bad guys" —I point to Max — "and I was wondering whether you were in on it too." I shift my finger to Ryland.

"So your spy skills aren't so great after all then," Miller sneers sarcastically, and I flip him off.

"Fuck you, Miller. I bet I have information that none of you have yet."

"Hold up, who the fuck gave you orgasms today?" Lathan asks, all wide-eyed and unable to hide his amusement.

Ryland chuckles. "And I want to know who you gave an orgasm to." He looks accusingly at his teammates.

Both Max and Anders put their hands up sheep-ishly. Oh snap, I did give Max one while I was dry humping him. Well good, I don't feel so embarrassed after all.

"What the fuck?" Bishop demands. "When did this all happen? And why haven't you given us all the dirty details?"

Oh wow, okay, it looks like communication is

lacking within the team too, but Bishop seems more interested in hearing about how and not why.

"Calm down, Bish, we were waiting to share with the whole team once Anders returned. There was no point in going over it more than once." Dayton tries to placate his team member, but he just looks pissed. Yeah, it's not fun to be kept out of the loop, is it?

"Do either of you want a drink before we get started?" Max asks Miller and I politely, and I can see the others all have a beer in front of them.

"I'll have a beer. Thanks, Max." Miller's fucking mood swings are going to give me whiplash. He's so polite to his team member, which is the complete opposite of what he is to me.

"I'm fine, just a glass of water please," I tell him, and Max finally looks at me.

"Are you sure? I have wine and liquor if you don't want a beer."

I shake my head. "No, I'm good. I took a couple of my painkillers before I came, so I don't want to mix the two."

His eyes fill with worry. "Are you okay?"

I wave a hand and look around for somewhere to sit. "Yeah, I'm fine. I just ache, and it's been a long-ass day."

"Here, take my seat. It's the least I can do after springing this afternoon on you." Max moves from the large recliner he was sitting in.

"Thanks, I won't argue with you this time," I say gratefully, placing my phone and bike keys on the little table next to the chair. When I sink down, he leans over me and pushes a switch on the side of the chair. The footrest lifts up, and the back slides backward, but I'm too busy inhaling Max's scent to pay attention. Holy fuck, he smells so good, and my mind goes back to our little dry humping session from this afternoon. That does not help the ache that built inside my body on the ride here.

He stands back up and stares down at me, looking pleased. "I'll just go and get the drinks, and then we can get started." He turns and leaves, and I realize everyone is staring at me.

Lathan is still grinning, and of course Miller is scowling, but Bishop, Anders, and Dayton are all frowning. Before I can ask what the fuck their problem is, Ryland takes a seat at my feet, grabbing one and giving it a squeeze.

"It's nice to finally meet you properly. Kenzie, right?" Ryland's thumb pushes right into my arch, and it feels so fucking good, a moan of pleasure escapes my mouth before I can stop it. He freezes, and his eyes widen minutely.

I grimace. "Sorry, my feet are sore, and that felt amazing. Yes, Kenzie is right, but let's stick to Mac for now because we don't want to fuck up at school or somewhere important."

"Okay, cool. So how was your first day? What did Mr. Marshall want with you?" Ryland keeps rubbing my feet, and my eyes just about roll back in my head.

I try to pull my foot out of his hands, but he just holds on tight.

"Relax, I'm just helping out a team member, one who's hurting. I would do this for any of them."

Lathan snorts. "Like fuck you would rub any of our feet."

Ryland flips him off. "That's because your feet stink. I rub Miller's." He points at the surly member of the group, and I feel my eyebrows jump in surprise. Miller just grunts and crosses his arms defensively. "And if anyone else asked, I would."

Bishop chuckles. "I'll remember that next time my feet hurt." Ryland winces slightly but shrugs in acceptance as Max returns with a beer in one hand and a large glass of ice water in the other.

"Here we go." He passes the beer to Miller, who takes it with a grunt of thanks, before placing the water on a small table next to my chair. Max takes a seat on the sofa with the others, while Miller leans against the wall. "Okay, shall we get started?"

Lathan jumps up and moves over to the coffee table, then he sits down at it and opens up the laptop he has there. "I'll take notes so we can gather all the information into one spot, and then I can keep Percy apprised of the situation." He pushes his glasses up his nose before swiping the hair that had fallen across his forehead out of the way. I want to grin, because he's so fucking adorably nerdy, but I push that urge deep down.

"So who is the team lead?" I ask, pointing between

Dayton and Max. "During the meeting when I first met you, I could have sworn Dayton was, but now that I see you all together, I'm not so sure."

"You mean the meeting where you were posing as your dad's secretary?" Bishop retorts, and I guess he has a point. "Max and Rhy weren't even there, so you know what they say about assuming."

"Yeah, yeah, fine, so who is it?"

Dayton shrugs, still not looking at me. "Neither of us, really. We work so well as a team that we don't really need any one person in charge, but if we had to name someone, it would be Max."

"And Dayton if I'm not available," Max adds.

"They both have big daddy energy, and we all look to them for guidance," Ryland jokes, winking at me, and I chuckle at his playfulness. I hadn't expected that from him.

"Enough of that shit," Miller snaps, and Ryland looks at him in surprise.

"Jesus, what bug got up your butt?" he teases, and Miller just growls.

"I think that might be me, but I have no idea why," I tell him.

"It's because you intimidate him," Lathan says, his fingers flying across his keyboard. "Your skills exceed his own, which doesn't happen very often. That, and he doesn't cope well with change."

"Shut your fucking mouth, Lathan. She does not intimidate me," Miller snaps at him, but Lathan doesn't turn away from his screen.

"Dude, it must be like looking into a mirror. You're both crazy talented, blunt, and not afraid to use what God gave you to get the job done. No wonder you're freaked out."

Anders chuckles, pointing between us. "Two fucking peas in a pod. Miller wouldn't have flinched either if Matthew had told him to get down on his knees and suck my cock. Thankfully for me, you were the one who applied and not him, because as much as I love the guy, there is no way I want him bobbing up and down on my cock, and Matthew would have made him do it too. He likes well-rounded individuals working for him, if you get what I'm saying."

Well, there is my confirmation that Miller will do what it takes to get the job done.

"How long have you all been together as a team?" I ask. It's something I've been dying to know, because they all seem comfortable with one another, except Bishop. He's quieter, and when he speaks, there's an edge of aggression to it. He doesn't seem to gel with the team as well as all the others.

"Dayton, Anders, and I have been a team since we were eighteen," Max explains.

"How old are you now?"

"We're all twenty-six," Anders answers.

"And what about the others?" I look at the individuals I'm asking about.

"Miller, Lathan, and Rhy all joined when they turned eighteen, and they are all twenty-two," Dayton replies.

"So the same age as me, cool. But what about you?" I turn to the last man in the room, and he shrugs uncomfortably.

"I've been with the team for six months." Before I can ask about this, he goes on. "Okay, can we just cut the chitchat crap and get on with the meeting? I'm tired, and I have an early start with the football team in the morning." Bishop yawns and stretches.

"You're joining the football team?" I ask, trying to sit up, but Ryland holds my foot tightly, so I sit back, huffing my annoyance, and he winks at me.

"Yeah, we need someone in with those guys," Max replies. "Billy's dad is the chief of police, and we think he might be in with the ring."

"He is," I interject, and Max frowns.

"How do you know this?"

"I'll tell you in a second after you share what you know first," I counter, and after holding my gaze for a moment, he nods.

"Okay. So we're going to stage an argument between the guys, and Bish also spoke to the coach yesterday about joining. She seemed pleased, but the team will make his life hell unless he looks like he's cutting ties with us." Ryland takes over, not even pausing in his fabulous foot rub that is turning me to jelly.

"Shall we get on with exchanging information? It's getting late, and Miller and Ken—Mac can't be caught out of the house," Anders suggests.

"Yeah, and I share a room with Jessica. I don't

doubt she won't blab if she wakes and finds me gone, especially if she checks your room. She already heard me up there earlier," I tell Miller.

"How about we get you some sedatives in case you need to leave again? You can slip it into something," Anders offers, getting up and disappearing the same way that Max had gone before. I'm assuming it's the kitchen.

"Anders is our medic, so he'll get you what you need," Max explains.

Dayton has been pretty quiet this whole time, and I can't stand the tension that's radiating off of him. I'm about to tell him to chill the fuck out, but Anders returns with a package.

"There are some needles in there, but I'm not sure if that will work. How heavily does she sleep? Would she be able to sleep through the pinch?" he asks, passing me the package, and I giggle, remembering the bear-like sounds she was emitting.

"Yeah, I'm almost certain she would, but I can cover it up anyway. I'll just slap her and tell her I saw a spider. Most girls would be relieved, even if they were woken up when you killed it."

"Smart." Lathan stops what he's doing to beam at me. I shoot him a wink, and he blushes slightly before looking back at the screen. Damn it, he's so stinking cute, I just want to eat him up.

"There are also some pills too. Crack them open and tip the powder into drinks or food," Anders suggests.

"Yup, I know the deal, thanks," I assure him and place it on the side table with my phone and keys. "Okay, let's do this debrief. You tell me what you've got, and I'll tell you what I've discovered so far. Sound good?" I suggest now that everyone is sitting again.

"You first," Miller sneers, obviously wanting to keep the upper hand, but I don't care. I'm pretty pleased with what I've done today.

"Okay, so this is what I've discovered."

CHAPTER 22

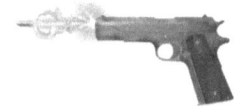

I tell them all about my meeting with the counselor. None of them are surprised to hear the outcome, but they did have a chuckle about my dad putting solicitation in my file.

"Well, it seems to have worked, so it's not a bad thing," Anders points out.

"Yes, we think Brock Marshall is a recruiter. He interviews all the new kids that come into the school, but he seems to have two different spiels—one for the regular kids, and then the one he gives foster kids. He also works at a couple of the other schools in the area as well, so he really does have a large target area," Dayton says, finally speaking up, but he doesn't look at me.

"And then I overheard a conversation that Mr. Marshall had with none other than Mr. Turner. Seriously, you sounded like the biggest fucking creeper," I tell Max, and he grimaces.

"You heard that, did you? Yeah, I've made it very clear that I like young girls and that I wouldn't be opposed to having a young girl permanently in my life, but because of my dad's position, it might not look good. Brock has hinted that he may be able to make something like that happen. I've also made it clear that I have particular tastes in the hopes that I might get an invite to the sex club that we think is operating in the area. Brock thinks it's great to have something on Governor Turner's son. Apparently my dad was invited back when he went to high school here, but he didn't like some of their practices and left. He never thought anything else about it until someone brought all the missing foster children to his attention."

"It's the Divinity of Morality Club, isn't it?" I ask, and his eyebrows jump in surprise.

"Yes, it is. How did you figure that out?"

"Anyone who preaches abstinence and is as judgy as that is suspicious as fuck," I reply, and the whole team laughs.

"Yeah, you're not wrong, and there is no abstinence, it's just all hidden under a thin layer of respectability."

"No, I was propositioned three times today by three different girls. One of them stuck their hand directly down my pants and felt me up." Bish should look upset about this, but instead he looks proud.

"You didn't accept any of their advances, did you?" I ask him, and he frowns.

"And why shouldn't I? They are all legal." Oh my

fuck. I look at Max and Dayton, who are both scowling at Bishop. "It also effectively sells my cover. I'm not suspicious, unlike those three fucks. None of them are showing interest in any of the girls. That's just not right, and people are starting to talk."

"Yeah, but we're also here to work, not to get our rocks off. You can do it during your own time," Dayton tells Bishop, who shrugs.

"Why not do both at the same time?" I can feel the tension ratchet up in the room again, so I jump in and redirect the conversation. They obviously have a few issues within their team dynamic, and that's none of my business, but I am for sure going to call my dad and ask him about it at the first opportunity.

"Jessica was telling me today that you are hot and heavy with Stella Standish," I say to Max.

Ryland snorts and swaps sides so he can rub my other foot. "She wishes."

"Stella has been asking me out, but I've managed to put her off until now. If her parents are involved, though, it might not hurt to have an in there too."

"Okay, let me tell you about the rest of my day, and then you can tell me everything you know."

Max blushes slightly because he knows what's coming next, but he nods his head in agreement.

"So I was sent to Max's office after school so I could catch up with what I missed out on in class. That was Brock's idea, right?"

Max nods. "Yes, I'm certain he was testing both of us. I discovered the cameras in my office when I first started. I wasn't sure what they were there for, but I guess they were used today."

"And are you sure they couldn't see what was going on?" I ask.

"I can guarantee they couldn't see. Look." Lathan turns his laptop around, showing me the screen, and I watch as I step into Max's office. "I hacked the feed when we discovered them, and Max and I did some messing around in case we ever needed to hide anything from the camera. The mic still picks everything up, but watch. When he turns his chair, you can't see anything." Everyone crowds in so they can see the laptop. Miller even pushes off the wall and stands behind my chair, resting his hands on the headrest.

We all watch the scene between Max and me, and Lathan is right. Once Max turns his chair, we can't see anything. I watch as I take off my panties and slide onto his lap, but after that it's just me grinding on his lap. We can see me, and I applaud my facial expressions, but it really wasn't that hard considering what he was doing to me. The room falls silent, and the sounds of Max's filthy words and my moans can be heard. The tension ratchets up even higher, and Ryland's hand tightens on my foot. I orgasm, and Lathan chuckles.

"Well, I guess that explains one of the orgasms."

We watch as Max grabs me and shoves me down. We can't see me anymore, but it's obvious what I'm supposed to be doing. I hadn't realized it because I was distracted by the pain in my knees, but he turned his chair enough that we can see my head bobbing up and down on his lap. Luckily I kept up the act instead of just sitting there. No wonder he forced my head down.

We hear the rest of the filthy words come out of his mouth, and he groans again, pretending to come, or so I thought.

"And that explains Max's orgasm." Lathan ticks off two on his fingers.

"You came?" I ask him, sounding surprised and feeling a little relieved that it wasn't just me.

"Yes, honey. There's only so much dry humping a man can take, and with someone as gorgeous as you bouncing on my lap, well, I'm only human." Max doesn't sound embarrassed at all. Finally, someone who doesn't look at me like I'm a whore. Lathan pauses the video as Max starts telling me to get up and get out.

"Well, it was certainly a good show," Bishop remarks, sitting back down and adjusting himself.

Max scowls at him. "It did the job. Not five minutes after she left, Brock was knocking on my door. He asked how the meeting went, but I could tell he had been watching the camera by how excited he was. He suggested that if I played my cards right, I could probably wrangle an invitation to an exclusive club, but that was all he said."

"The sex club?" Miller asks, and Max shrugs.

"Hopefully."

"Now this is the sex club that is under the bar you

work at, right?" I point at Anders, and he nods.

"Yes, we think that's where it's at."

"Well, the foster kids I live with all but confirmed it," I tell them, and Dayton and Max exchange a look before turning to stare at Miller.

"Hey, don't look at me. I've tried to talk to them, but they all seem a little wary of me. They've taken to Mac like a duck to water," he grumbles, and the others all turn to look at me.

"It's because Jessica is up his ass. The rest of them are afraid of upsetting her."

"So what did you find out, Mac?" Dayton leans forward, showing real interest. Huh, maybe he got the bug out of his ass. Hopefully it doesn't return when we get to the part where he gave me a nice big O.

"One of the missing foster kids told the girls all about working at the bar. Warts and all. She confirmed she worked for private parties held beneath the club and that it was a sex club, but she said they do nasty, depraved shit. It scared the hell out of her, but she was stuck for the time being. She also mentioned that the chief of police is definitely a member of the club. Then they held an auction, but by then, she had received her modeling contract and was leaving, so she packed up and left town."

"And disappeared," Lathan says, his fingers flying across the keyboard. "That would be Sybil Cross. Her modeling contract was legit. Her photo appears in the lineup for one of the top talent agencies in New York. As far as we know, they are on the up and up."

"So she worked for the bar that the two of you are now employed at, right? You have some suspicions about Matthew Stewart, the owner, don't you, Anders?" Dayton leans back, relaxing a little. He seems to have really calmed down now that we're talking about the case. I guess it probably helps that we skipped over the bit where he gave me an orgasm.

"Yes, he's been shifty and very wary from the start. It's only in the last week or two that I've been able to get him to open up a bit, but I deliberately got caught watching some pretty sketchy shit on my phone for him to become that way, and I can't thank you enough, Mac. I think that blow job secured me an invite to tend bar next time they run the sex club."

"That would explain the orgasm that you gave Anders then." Lathan and Ryland chuckle, and I shoot them a wink.

"And you called me out on my activities. Jesus, you're practically a whore," Bishop grumbles, but before I can defend myself, a surprising voice jumps in.

"Shut your fucking mouth, Bishop, before I fucking shut it for you. Mac was securing both her and Ander's cover. You were just trying to get your dick wet." Miller has stepped closer to where Bishop is sitting.

Bishop slowly gets to his feet, not backing down in the face of Miller's fury. "Listen, you fucking prick. Just because you get your dick sucked on a regular basis doesn't mean the rest of us do. I haven't been laid since we got to this miserable town, and I've had enough. I'm bored and tired, and I need a break. I don't know how this team can work nonstop for so long. It's too much. And now we've got this bitch saddled on us, another one whose only use is to spread her legs, and we can't even say anything because she's the damn director's precious daughter."

Everything in the room comes to a standstill in the face of all of that hostility. I slowly drag my foot out of Ryland's hand while lowering the footrest on the recliner. I get to my feet, and his attention turns from Miller to me.

He holds his hand up in a placating gesture. "Hey, you know I'm right. You're only useful because you've got a great rack and you obviously have mad blow job skills. Anders hasn't looked so relaxed in ages."

I look him up and down and shake my head. "Really? Is that why you were wearing my boot print on your temple for a few days?" I ask quietly, wishing I had tucked my gun into the back of my jeans before we left, but I left all of my weapons at the home. It was my mistake, thinking that I could trust this team.

"That was a lucky shot, and you know it," he sneers, and before I can answer, Dayton does.

"No, it wasn't. She far outclassed you during that fight. I saw all of it. So how about you sit your ass down and shut your misogynistic piece of crap mouth before I make you?"

Bishop scoffs. "This team is a joke. I see how you all fawn over her. She's working her pussy magic on all of you, and you're going to end up fighting over her.

She will destroy this team, mark my words. I want a transfer."

"You mean she'll achieve what you have been trying to do all along," Ryland comments, joining the fight now, and he is not happy. "I'd rather work with her than you any day."

"Sit down, you faggot. Nobody asked you. You're only on this team because your brother leads it." Bishop doesn't pull his punches, and I see Lathan and Miller take a step toward him, but Anders and Dayton move between them. The mild-mannered sexy nerd looks like he's ready to rip Bishop's head off, and forget about Miller, because if looks could kill, then Bishop would be six feet under.

Oh my god. Why didn't Dad warn me that this team was on the verge of imploding? Or does he not know about any of this? This team should have been pulled from active duty until they had gotten their dynamics sorted out. This is a shit show, and for once in my life, I'm fucking speechless.

"No, you're a fucking joke. You've been through five teams in the last year and a half. I think you need to face the fact that you're the problem, not any of them, so do as Dayton said and sit your ass down before we all make you. I suggest you don't open your mouth again for the rest of the meeting." There is no disguising the violence in Max's tone.

Bishop sits down abruptly, obeying him, and a shiver of desire runs down my spine. Fuck, that was hot. He really does have big daddy energy, both of them do. I would fan myself, but that would only add fuel to Bishop's fire, and I won't give him the satisfaction.

"Do you think I care what you have to say about me? Do you believe that I'm some fragile, shattered girl who's going to give a fuck about the opinion of a dude who is so insecure he's hitting on highschoolers? Please, bitch, you are nothing. Not only am I Phantom, with many captures and kills under my belt, but I'm fucking Princess Kensington Watson. You are nothing but a gnat on my windshield, a blip on my radar."

His scowl drops, and his eyebrows rise as a smirk creeps across his face. "And imagine if the tabloids found out what darling Princess Kensington was really like."

Did that fucker just threaten me? Because that's a surefire way to end up dead.

"Hey, dude, that is not cool. You can't go around saying shit like that." Lathan holds up his hands, trying to be the peacekeeper. "Why don't we all take a moment to breathe, and then we can get on with the debrief. We've all been working really hard, and I think maybe everyone is a little tired. Let's just relax."

Everyone moves back to their corners of the room, so to speak, as I lower myself back in my recliner. I don't take my eyes off the asshole who is causing so much trouble. He doesn't know it yet, but he basically just secured his transfer to some outpost in Siberia or his death. I guess it depends on how generous Dad is feeling when I speak to him.

CHAPTER 23

The tension in the room is thick, but I've never let that stop me before, so I just start talking. "Okay, so we've discussed me being wary of the Divinity of Morality Club and how lots of the key players from the original one seem to be connected, or in the very least suspicious as fuck." I start ticking them off on my fingers.

"There are the Standishes, both sets, though I'm starting to think that maybe it's just the men. Martha is so freaking rigid, she was in a small panic when she heard I was working at Life Lounge."

"Wait until you meet June at church on Sunday. She's even more uptight," Ryland chimes in, trying to help break the tension that fills the room. I smile at him gratefully, and he pats my foot but doesn't go back to rubbing it.

"Then we have Brock the counselor, and Matthew

the bar owner, who are both skeevy and questionable as fuck. I wonder how many girls and boys have had to blow him to get jobs. Was that your first blow job?" I whip my head around to stare at Anders, who quickly puts his hands up.

"Yes, shit, I promise, and I would have refused you too, but he's been watching me so closely I haven't been able to snoop around. I thought that would at least get me an in with him and secure you a job."

"Yeah, yeah, it's fine. I'm not upset. I came into this job knowing I'd have to use my body to get it done. I hadn't expected to blow my teammate on the first day out, but hey, at least it got rid of all that awkward tension between us," I joke, and Anders grins at me.

"It sure did," Bishop scoffs.

"Okay, and back to the list. I also popped into Inkubus today to check out Kevin Turner. He was in the Divinity of Morality Club too, so I wanted to put out feelers on him."

"Uncle Kevin? You think he's in on it?" Ryland asks, sounding surprised, and I raise an eyebrow.

"Well, don't you? I'm assuming that's why Dayton is working there."

Max shakes his head. "No, actually. Dayton regularly does guest spots at Kevin's studio when we have downtime, so his cover was actually organic. Kevin has heard the rumors but hasn't been able to score himself an invite, despite being a member of the Raging Scorpion MC. None of the members have been invited mostly because I think they are scared of Uncle Kevin going to my dad, but he is the only tattoo studio and piercing place in town, and they do get some odd requests."

I shudder when I think about what Charity told me. "Ah, yeah, Charity was telling me about some of it before she had to leave for an emergency mid-piercing."

"You got a piercing?" Miller asks, sounding surprised and interested, and nonaggressive for the first time since I've known him. "I didn't see one."

I feel myself blush, and I want to punch myself in the tit. *Jesus, Kenz, get your shit together.* "Ah, yeah, I got it in a place where the Standishes wouldn't see it."

"So belly button then?" Miller smirks. "How very cheerleader of you." I know he's laughing at me, so I flip him off.

"No," Dayton grunts, and everyone turns to look at him.

"Oh yeah? And how do you know where she got pierced?" Anders asks, crossing his arms and raising an eyebrow.

I start to giggle as he shifts uncomfortably. "Because Dayton had to take over when Charity left, and she'd only gotten as far as putting the needle through. He had to put the bar in."

"So nipple then if you got a bar," Ryland guesses, and I shrug.

"No. Lower."

His eyes widen, and his gaze drops to my pussy. "Oh!"

"Yeah, and he really had a hard time getting that little ball onto the end of the bar." I meet Dayton's eyes, and I can feel the heat between us, even though he's sitting on the other side of the room.

"Whore!" Bishop coughs into his hand, and Max makes a fist and pounds it into his face. Bishop's eyes roll back in his head, and he's out like a light.

"He really can't take a hit, can he?" I say conversationally.

"The guy is a grade A pussy. Are you going to tell your dad about this?" Max replies, shaking out his hand.

"Yeah, I'm going to have to. That crack about telling everyone what Princess Kensington is like is too much of a threat. He can't be left with that kind of knowledge without learning the consequences."

"Fucking hell, that fucking cunt." Miller picks something up, and I think he's going to throw it, but Anders jumps up and grabs it out of his hand.

"Not here, man. Jeff loves his things, and he's kindly letting us stay here, so let's not destroy them."

Lathan gestures to his computer. "Shall we get the director on a chat so we can all talk to him about it? It will probably be best if we tell him about our issues first."

"Yeah, that sounds good." I grab my phone and look at the time. "He should still be awake."

Lathan presses a few buttons, and the screen starts making the calling sound.

"You know, I had no idea my dad was the handler

for another team, and I'd never heard of you before all this. Why is that? I've tested lots of teams over the years, except yours."

Before anyone can answer, Dad does. Lathan situates the screen in front of the sofa so that Dayton, Max, and an unconscious Bishop can be seen. Anders and Miller slide in behind, and Ryland scoots over on the floor, sliding in next to Lathan who has moved back slightly so Dad can see everyone.

"Hi, guys, what's up? And why the fuck is Bishop unconscious?" Dad starts breezily, but we can hear his concern by the end.

"Because he was mouthing off and went too far this time." Max takes charge, running a hand through his short curls and grimacing. "I'm sorry, Percy, but this isn't working. We really did try, I promise. Even Miller made an effort, but he just doesn't want to be a team player."

I hear my dad sigh. "What did he do this time?"

I climb down onto the floor and crawl into the picture, wiggling my body between Lathan's and Ryland's, who both chuckle at my antics.

"Oh, Kenzie love? Well, this is a nice surprise, and none of you have killed each other yet. That warms my heart," my dad jokes, but I can tell he is really relieved.

"Hey, Dad. Bishop is a giant dick. Not only is he messing around with the girls in the high school, but he threatened to out Princess Kensington."

"And he called her a whore," Miller grinds out from between clenched teeth.

Wow, he really took exception to me being called a whore. I wonder if we are more alike than I thought. I see Dad's eyes widen at Miller's fury.

"Hey, Miller, buddy, it's okay. I'm sure Kenzie wasn't all that upset about it. Right, baby?"

"Pfft, I've been called worse," I agree with Dad, and he beams at me.

"Doesn't make it right." Miller grabs hold of the back of the sofa, and I hear some fabric rip.

Dad's smile drops, and he frowns at Miller. "Hey, why don't you go cool down?" Dad suggests, and I have an idea.

"Why don't you take the bike for a spin? That should help, and when I'm done with this conversation, we'll get going, okay?" I propose, pointing at the keys on the little side table, and I see all the tension leak out of his body.

"Yeah, thanks, I will." He doesn't say goodbye to anyone, just grabs the keys and leaves.

"How did you know that would work?" When I turn to look at Ryland, his mouth is dropped open in shock.

"I didn't," I tell him, and Dad chuckles.

"It's because they are so alike, it's frightening. She often rides a bike to calm her down when she gets worked up." I flip my dad off, but he's not wrong.

"See? I called it," Lathan gloats, nudging me in the side, and I push back, a feeling of warmth rushing through me. Holy crap, what is that? Am I getting slightly attached to this bunch of assholes? Nope, time to reactivate lonely island mode.

"Please, I'm not an angry asshole like he is," I argue, and Dad tips his head to the side and studies me closely. I refrain from wiggling under his penetrating stare, but it's a close call.

"No, but you have your own insecurities."

Damn it. Dad always sees right through me. He sighs and runs his hand through his hair, rubbing the other one across his face. I actually pay attention, noticing my dad is in a T-shirt and that I can see our lounge room in the background. He looks pretty tired, and I don't like it. I can't remember the last time he and Mom went on vacation. Maybe once I get home, I can convince them to leave for a while.

"Okay, let's get back to the subject at hand. Bishop is causing problems and threatening to cause more. We'll have to recall him and reassign him... again. Do you think he will tank this case for you?" Dad asks, sounding weary. "He knows you were his last resort. I can't believe he wouldn't try."

"I just don't think he's cut out to be a team player. He'd be better off being a ghost like Kenzie. He's too arrogant and self-involved to work well with a team," Dayton suggests, and I turn to look at him, raising an eyebrow, and he sputters slightly. "Ah, not that I'm saying you're anything like that." He tries to backpedal quickly, and Max and Anders move away slightly so as not to get in the line of fire. "I mean, so far we seem to be working well together, don't we?"

It's his turn to raise an eyebrow, and I can't believe it, but I think he may be referring to the incident this afternoon, when we did work pretty damn well together. There's a mischievous glint in his eyes, and I'm taken aback. I didn't think he had it in him. Dayton has been standoffish and cool toward me, so I wonder what has brought about this change in behavior. Or is he finally starting to understand that I can be a valuable asset?

"He is intimidated by Kenzie, and to be honest, I don't think he would tank this case, but I think he would definitely out Kenzie. That would all but ensure that she would no longer be able to work for MITHOS." Lathan pulls off his glasses and cleans them with his shirt. When he lifts it, I can see smooth abs, and I snap my mouth closed so no drool leaks out.

Jesus, Kenzie, get it together.

Dad swears a blue streak, and I hear my mother in the background. "Percy, what is it? Is everything okay?" My mother appears on the screen, and her smile lights up her face. "Ah, there are my favorite people." Then she notices me sitting in front, and her smile gets even bigger. "Oh, and my baby girl! It warms a mother's heart to see you all together. Is it going well?" she asks, and we all respond with various affirmations, but then her gaze falls on the unconscious Bishop. "What is wrong with him?" She looks around and frowns. "And where is my Miller?"

Her Miller? What the actual fuck?

"Miller is cooling off, and Bishop is having an

enforced rest," Max explains to her. "You look beautiful, as always, Sadie."

His compliment distracts her slightly, and she smiles at him. "Oh, my handsome boy, I missed you when you did not come home with the others. You too, Ryland."

"Okay, back the truck up. What is going on here? How are you all so familiar with each other and I have never heard of this team?" I'm annoyed and ready to get to the bottom of at least this one mystery. No one was very forthcoming the last time I asked.

"Every time Team Basilisk has been home, they have stayed with us due to not having their own house until recently. Coincidentally, this occurred when you were off on assignments," Dad says, rubbing his chin, and I can tell he's not telling me the complete truth.

I glare at him, and he and Mom exchange a look, and then he sighs and drops his hand.

"Fine, I deliberately kept you apart until now. I had always intended for you to join their team, but none of you were ready yet. I thought it would be better to keep you apart until the time was right. Look, none of you are getting any younger, and, well, Kenzie, won't it be nice to have someone else in your life other than just us and Katie?"

My mouth drops open, and I stare at my parents in shock. Are they actually matchmaking? Are they trying to set me up with the whole team, or do they have a particular member in mind?

"No. We are not even going there today," I tell

them, shaking my head and waving a finger. I can't believe what I am hearing. "We are going to worry about that problem first" —I stab my finger at Bishop — "then we are going to solve this case, and only then will we discuss whatever this is that you two are scheming," I growl at my parents, who don't even have the grace to look embarrassed. In fact, my mother crosses her arms and tips her head at me like she's daring me to try her. No, not going there, and if I have to catch the next flight to Jordan and ask for asylum from my grandpa just to escape her schemes, I will. She will not get the best of me.

"Ryland, honey, why don't you go see if Miller is okay?" Mom ignores me and speaks to the guy next to me.

"Pfft, he's fine, he has my bike." I brush off her concerns, and her gaze turns frosty, even as Ryland quickly gets up to do as instructed. He disappears out the back curtain-covered door.

"Did you just question me, Kensington?" My mother adopts her imperial princess voice, and I roll my eyes.

"You bet your ass I did," I retort, and the simultaneous intake of shocked breath from the men behind me reassures me that they have also been on the end of her moods a time or two before and have learned to tread very carefully. "What are you going to do all the way from over there?"

"I would be very careful right now, young lady. I know what is best for my boys, and if I say Miller needs to be checked on, then I know what is best. Do not think that because you are so far away from me that you are immune to my punishments. How about I never make you your favorite mac and cheese ever again?" The guys groan, and Lathan drops his head onto my shoulder.

"Please, no, Kenzie. Please, just trust that your mother knows best," he pleads, and I feel a hand on my other shoulder, squeezing it tight.

"We will all make your life a living hell if we never get her mac and cheese again, I swear." Anders's threat sounds real, and I chuckle quietly. They just gave me ammunition.

"Please, I know that recipe inside and out. We don't need her," I tell them, adding fuel to the fire. My mom screeches and stomps her foot. "Uh-uh, that wasn't very princess-like behavior, now was it?" I tease, and my dad groans before pulling my mom onto his lap and whispering in her ear. The frown quickly turns to a giggle. I gag not so quietly at their PDA, and my pretty, refined, princess of a mother flips me the bird.

"I can't wait until it's my turn to tease you for PDA," she says, getting back to her feet. "Now I'll leave you to talk work stuff, but you better make sure Miller's okay. Tell him I want a phone call tomorrow, or I will worry."

"I'll tell him, Sadie," Dayton assures her, and she waves goodbye before leaving the screen.

"Okay, Kenz, you head home," my dad instructs,

"and if one of you guys will give him a shake or a slap, we'll deal with Bishop."

"Are you sure, Dad? I can just pop him here and now and be done with it," I offer, and I feel the guys surrounding me freeze in shock. Whoops, were they not on the same wavelength as me?

CHAPTER 24

"What the fuck, Mac?" Anders growls, and I shrug.

"Look, you guys can't deny that you thought the same thing. If he's a liability to this case and especially to me, then there aren't really many options. I am not ready to be outed and forcibly retired, and he's the one who threatened me, not the other way around. If he had done that when we were alone, and I'd had my gun, then I probably would have eliminated him instantly."

The guys explode into protests and shouts, but Dad quickly shuts it down with a piercing whistle. "Look, guys, she's not wrong. He knows too much. Apart from my sending him somewhere with no communication or locking him up for the rest of his life, there aren't many options, and if I can't find a suitable solution for all of us, then we may need to consider other measures."

When our agents retire, most of them happily go on and lead normal lives, keeping their past a secret. The other option, if they decide not to pursue active duty, is to become trainers or admin. Most of our agents work well into middle age, since there's nothing that says you need to retire as long as you pass all fitness and skill requirements.

"But death is a bit extreme, isn't it?" Lathan sounds subdued, and I don't like that.

I reach out and take hold of his hand, giving it a little squeeze. "Yes, but don't forget that if he outs me as Phantom, my life is in danger too, and if he goes further and outs MITHOS as a whole, then all of our lives and those of every agent working for us here and across the world is in danger."

"We don't use it unless it's a last resort," Dad adds, looking grave.

"And how many times has it been done?" Max asks. There's no judgment, just curiosity. He seems to understand the gravity of the situation.

"In the time MITHOS has been active, there have only been five, and each one of them had gone rogue and been seduced by illegal activities," Dad replies, sharing classified information with them.

"They'd gone to the dark side. It doesn't seem like Bishop is there yet, but we do need to keep an eye on him." I give Lathan's hand one more squeeze before reaching for my boots, putting them back on, and standing up. "Okay, I'm out. Love you, Dad, and I will see you guys at school in the morning. I don't work a shift at the bar until Saturday night, so I guess I'll see you when I see you." I aim the last bit at Anders and Dayton.

"Be careful, Mac, these guys don't fuck around," Dayton warns.

"I'll be fine. Oh, Dad, Miller will need a tracker implanted in him too just in case."

Dad nods. "Good thinking. I'll have one overnighted to you, and Anders can insert it."

"Okay, well, see you." I wave awkwardly and hurry out the back door and straight into a scene that could have come directly from my wildest fantasies. Ryland has Miller backed up against a nearby garden shed, his hand in his hair as he tilts Miller's head so he can get the best angle as they exchange a scorching kiss.

Oh my lord. Now wouldn't it be fun to be the meat in that sandwich? I fan myself and clear my throat slightly. I don't want them to be pissed at me because they were too busy making out to hear me open and close the door.

I watch them stiffen, but they don't pull apart. They just break the kiss and turn to look at me, staring at me with intense gazes. I know they are trying to judge how I feel about their relationship, but they aren't going to find any disgust from me. Nope, if they look too closely, they will find the exact opposite, and I'm not sure if I'm ready for them to see that, but I don't look away. I wouldn't want them to mistake my hesitation for disdain.

"Ah, hi." I wave, and Ryland smirks, but Miller

doesn't take his eyes away from mine. "Are you ready to go?" I ask him.

Ryland releases him and steps back a little. "He's ready. Be careful sneaking back in. We don't want you to get caught."

Ryland walks past me, but just when I think he's going to pass, he stops and grabs the back of my neck, resting his forehead against mine. "He's okay, but watch him for me, will you? He's a little volatile," he murmurs quietly, and a shiver runs down my spine. Ryland puts off some daddy dom energy too, and inner me is squealing with excitement.

"He's an asshole," I hedge, not wanting to give in so quickly, and his hand tightens slightly.

"Yes, but he's my asshole, and I don't want anything to happen to him. He gets reckless when he's mad, and I don't want him to do anything stupid. You can help me with that, can't you? You'll go straight home, right?" Gone is the affable teenager he portrayed this morning, and in his place is a grown man who knows how to get what he wants.

I roll my eyes, trying to play off that I'm not affected by any of this, even if that's so not true, but I have an idea brewing, and it's one that I'm going to have to think about a little longer before sharing with the team. "Fine, but if he's a dick, I can't guarantee he won't be unharmed. I might just kick him off the bike and leave him in my dust."

His lips curve into another smirk. "That's okay. Sometimes he needs to be punished." With a light brush of his lips against mine, he disappears back into the house.

My fingers come up to my lips as I blink in surprise. A quiet chuckle has me looking over at Miller, who is still leaning against the garden shed.

"Ryland is a quiet force of nature. You don't know he's after you until you're caught firmly in his web. You better watch out. He has his eye on you." He pushes off the shed and starts walking in the direction of the bike, which is parked in the driveway.

"What do you mean by that?" I ask, hurrying after him, but by the time I get to him, he's already shoved the helmet on his head and thrown his leg over the bike. I guess it's my turn to ride bitch, and Miller doesn't answer my question or share how he feels about his... boyfriend hitting on me.

The ride home is quiet. My body is wrapped around his, and my hands rest against his sculpted abs. I lean my head against his back, both of us lost in our own thoughts—mine swirling between the case, Bishop's threats, and Ryland's last comments to me. I'm assuming he and Miller are a couple, so how does Miller feel about Ryland sort of kissing me? Is he pissed? Is that why he's been quiet all the way home? I couldn't believe it when he stood up for me against Bishop. Miller has been nothing but antagonistic, so I'd have thought he would have taken Bishop's side. Yet not only did he defend me, but he got mad enough that he wanted to damage Bishop. Maybe he's not as indifferent to me as he pretends.

We bump down the dirt access road, returning the bike to the bushes we found it in. Together, we pull the tarp back over it, concealing it from any potential eyes.

We start the short trek back to the house. I take a deep breath, about to talk to him about what just happened, but he hurries ahead of me. I can't talk too loudly because I don't want to get caught, and I guess he's not ready to talk to me. He's back to his previous state of hating on Mac. It's fine, I don't need or want his friendship or approval anyway.

When I get to the tree, he's already halfway up it, so I wait for him to enter the house before making my own climb. It's not as easy as it was on the way down, and my boots slip a couple of times, but I finally make it to the window. I climb in, and Miller is already in his bed, his back to me and his covers pulled up over his head.

"Shut the window," I hear him mumble, and I do as he asks. It slides into place quietly, and I leave without saying another word to him. I can certainly take a hint.

Tiptoeing down the stairs, I crack the door open at the bottom to make sure no one is in the hallway. It's all clear, thankfully. It would have been hard to explain why I am dressed like I am instead of being in pj's. I hurry to my shared bedroom, and just like before, Jessica is fast asleep, the rattling sounds of her snoring loud in the quiet room. Fuck, I'm never going to be able to get back to sleep with that sound.

I remove my boots and jeans and pull my bra off

from under my shirt, but I leave that and my undies on, before climbing into bed. I roll over and pull the blankets high up over my ear in an attempt to block out the noise. My thoughts turn to the conversation that I'm assuming is still happening over at the governor's house. I wonder what options Dad will give Bishop. Hopefully, I will get a quiet moment to ask one of the guys about it at school tomorrow.

I think about how everyone reacted to learning about all the orgasms today, and I guess I'm a little surprised that no one was more upset about it. I thought with the way the team had originally reacted to learning about me using my body to get information that there would be more disgust, but they all seemed strangely okay with it, apart from Bishop.

I wish I had a chance to talk one-on-one with each of the people involved in said orgasms just to make sure that they were okay and to assure them I was too. They are all sexy men, so I can guarantee it was no hardship for me, even the one that wasn't strictly business. Seeing the sharp, sedate Dayton flustered more than made it worth it, and discovering this evening that maybe he's not as straightlaced as I thought was a nice surprise. Although I still don't want to join their team, I think I'm going to enjoy working with them even if it is temporary. Maybe Mom and Dad were both partly right. It would be nice to have some more friends.

Jessica makes a weird sound, and I pull the blankets back to check on her, but she's just rolling over. It looks like it's quite the process, and she flings back her covers, hauls her body over, and then pulls the covers back up. I don't think she actually wakes, but the snoring does cease now that she is on her side. She snuffles a bit then settles. I go to pull my blankets back up, but there's a strange sound coming from her now. I strain my ears to listen and feel a smile spread across my lips when I recognize what she's doing. She's humming in her sleep. It's not one long continuous song, but little brief hums almost like musical sighing. It's kind of cute and much more preferable to the grizzly bear sounds she was making previously.

I roll back over and close my eyes. Her humming is actually soothing in the quiet room, and I find myself drifting quickly to sleep.

The next morning is much like the first. We have breakfast together and then walk down the drive to the bus. Miller has gone back to ignoring me, and despite Jessica's somewhat kind warning the night before, she does nothing but glare at me with disdain, so it's business as usual. The same car as yesterday pulls up, and the passenger side window lowers. Lathan smiles at me but speaks to Miller, offering him a ride again. The sun isn't in a weird spot today, and I can see Ryland in the driver's side. He stares at me while everyone else is distracted by the others. He slowly lowers his glasses and winks at me before raising them again. Damn, the Turner brothers have some potent energy, and I find myself wanting to lean into it.

I need to kick myself in the ass. I do not need anyone else, I've been on my own for years. I'm a self-sufficient, confident woman who needs no man, but there's a small, albeit tiny, part of me that yearns to be taken within their fold, to be spoiled and looked after for once in my life. If anyone asked, though, I would shoot myself in the foot before I would admit it.

I turn my back on the car as Miller and Jessica climb in once more. I don't catch sight of Bishop, but then he did say he had an early start with the football team, so maybe they dropped him off before. I need to corner one of them discreetly and ask what the outcome of their conversation was when we left. Miller won't be able to ask in the car because Jessica is with them. Lathan waves a cheery goodbye, and the tires kick up dirt as they pull out of the bus stop.

"Why didn't you go with them? I'm sure they would have made room for you too. Lathan seems really friendly, maybe you could have sat on his lap," Cassie teases, nudging me in the side.

"I'm not here to make friends. I'm going to work hard, graduate, and blow this popsicle stand," I tell her. "I don't have time for schoolyard drama."

She frowns. "Yeah, well, let's just hope schoolyard drama is all you have to worry about. You be careful at that job of yours. You may find out you've bitten off more than you can chew."

The bus arrives, and before long, we're at school. The guys take off in one direction, leaving me to walk with the three girls, but as we traverse the front steps, there's more attention on me today than there was yesterday. People are talking and whispering and pointing.

"What did you do?" Sally asks, glaring at me. I guess she's still not over her bad mood from yesterday.

"Nothing that I know of," I tell her, grabbing a nearby kid by the arm. He's probably a senior like me, but he smells like weed and has greasy hair. He's wearing tight black skinny jeans and a Pantera T-shirt. "What is going on?" I ask him, and he does a double take before looking me up and down.

"How much?" he asks, raising an eyebrow cockily, and my frown deepens.

"Huh? How much for what?"

"Well, I always wanted to try anal, so how about that?"

"I'm sorry, but what did you say?" I ask, my tone turning deadly, and the guy blanches when my hand tightens on his arm.

"Well, aren't you a whore? I saw an advertisement that says you'd put out for minimal cash, which works for me because I'm broke."

I grind my teeth together as Cassie asks, "Where did you see that?"

"It's on the school noticeboard with a mug shot from when you were arrested. So how about it?"

I release the guy.

"Fuck off, Gary," Stephanie sneers at him. "You know that's just some bullshit prank."

Cassie grabs my arm and tows me up the steps as I catalog how many ways I can kill someone quietly and efficiently to calm myself down.

The noise escalates when we enter, but I ignore everything. Cassie stops in front of the noticeboard, which just so happens to be outside the French class-room next to the trophy cabinet that I was checking out yesterday.

"Oh my god," Sally screeches. "It is you." Sure enough, there is a mug shot of me, followed by a flier advertising my services. All three girls look at me. Stephanie and Cassie look concerned, but Sally snickers.

"Well, I guess you'll fit right in at the club then." She turns her back and flounces off in a fairly good impression of Jessica. I'm not here to make friends, but it hurt that she automatically believed it.

"That's not right, is it?" Stephanie asks quietly, and because of my cover, I have to play this a certain way.

"I was forced to do it at my last home. If I didn't, they would have pimped out the younger kids as well," I murmur, looking down at the floor and shuffling my feet nervously.

"Oh, you poor thing." Cassie yanks me in for a hug, and I stumble into her as Stephanie crowds in at the same time. "It's okay. We've all had to do things we aren't proud of to get by, but how did they find out?"

I grit my teeth, and when I hear a peal of laughter, I look up and find Sophie and her cohorts laughing and pointing. Jessica is with them, but the boys are nowhere to be seen. The football guys and Bishop are though, and they are all laughing as well.

"I have a good idea who it might have come from. Sophie's sister is part of the faculty, isn't she?" I fist my hands and start marching in their direction, acting how I think a tough as nails foster kid might act, but Cassie leaps after me, hauling me to a stop.

"Don't do it, Mac. Sophie is untouchable. You will get suspended or worse, expelled, and then you're screwed."

"So I'm supposed to let this violation of my privacy go?" I ask, feigning anger.

"Yup, even if you do complain to the principal, he won't care. You're just another foster kid with no parents to scam donations out of. You are worth next to nothing in his eyes. Just ignore it, it will go away eventually."

This fucking sucks. I can't believe these kids get no support. There is so much wrong with all of this. I wonder if Princess Sadeen is looking for a new cause to support, because the foster system is certainly a worthy one. I will speak to her about it next time I see her.

"Fine," I grind out and turn my back.

"Hey, Mac, I hear you're an expert at sucking cock,

how about giving this one a go?" I whirl back around, and Bishop is cupping his junk as everyone else around him laughs.

"I do like to suck cock, but in order for it to be enjoyable for both of us, I would need to find it first, and I don't have a magnifying glass handy, so you're out of luck," I call back, flipping him off.

He scowls, but I don't have time for his shit. I need to get ready for class, or I'm sure Ms. Standish will find some excuse to call me out over something. I'm done with this whole assignment. The quicker we can get it wrapped up, the quicker I can return to my life. Killing bad guys on a regular basis is more fun than this shit.

CHAPTER 25

French is awful. Stella Standish is a massive cunt, and she and Sophie twitter annoyingly throughout the whole class. She manages not to teach anything for the whole lesson, instead just tossing innuendos and sly remarks in my direction the whole time, so I stick my earbuds in and listen to music.

"Am I boring you, Mademoiselle Walsh?" she asks, pulling one of the buds out of my ears. I hadn't heard her approach because I'm channeling my anger by listening to the German rock band Rammstein. Their music is so delightfully German, and I'm fluent, so it's fun to listen to.

I snatch my earbuds out of my ears. "No, but I'm not sure you have the ability to teach me anything new, and since you seem to be using today to throw catty, useless remarks in my direction, I don't see the need to listen to your pettiness. I'm sorry you're stuck in a dead-end town with no prospects. It must be very demoralizing for you knowing you'll probably go nowhere, but hey, you might marry a man who won't put on fifty pounds six months after the wedding, and you might have two children who won't be complete shits, but I wouldn't hold your breath for too long." I say all of that in French, and the class falls silent as they try to figure out what I just said, but Stella is obviously fluent, because she understood it all, and she screeches and stomps her foot.

"You will not talk to me like that." She slams her hand down on my desk.

I slowly get to my feet, my eyes locked on her, and my gaze turns cold like it does when I'm dealing with one of my targets. "How about you shut your damn trap about my past then? You are supposed to be the adult in this class and advocating for my rights, but instead, you join in the bullying. You are no better than my johns, but at least they paid me for the privilege of fucking me over."

I pick up my backpack and walk out of the classroom, not even flinching when she yells at me to come back. I don't notice what direction I'm going in, I just know that if I don't leave, I will do something that might jeopardize the case, and we can't have that.

I wander aimlessly until I find myself in front of Max's office. I consider knocking, but I'm still debating whether or not I should when the door opens. "Ah, Ms. Walsh, just the person I wanted to see. Why don't you come in?" The smile he gives me is false and slightly sleazy, and I am instantly on alert.

The two of us have to be careful. I'm not sure how I'd forgotten about the damn cameras in his room. We wouldn't be able to have a conversation anyway, so I need to find one of the other guys to get the information on my dad's dealings with Bishop. I'm still voting for offing the asshole. Maybe he was the one who told everyone about my supposed record. Did I mention that last night? I can't remember.

"Ah, sorry, sir, I was lost... I didn't mean to disturb you," I murmur, backing away and shaking my head.

"Oh, come now, you look like you've had a hard morning. Why don't you come in and tell me all about it?" His eyes implore me to go with what he's saying. I guess he received more instructions, so I step into his room. I don't even get a chance to put my bag down before he has me pinned up against the wall.

"I'm sorry. They want to see more. They were pissed that everything was blocked by the chair yesterday," he hisses into my ear as he yanks my head to the side and bites down on my neck. "I promise that I would want to do this to you anyway, and I'll try to make it feel good, even if what I'm saying is horrible. I respect you and think you are amazing." He brushes a little kiss against my cheek before he bites down again. I cry out, the bite just a little bit this side of painful, but my nipples pebble and my clit throbs. He starts talking louder for the cameras.

"Oh yes, a little pain slut. I do like my girls to react

so prettily," Max growls. "I'm not sure what you've done to me, but I haven't been able to stop thinking about your pussy all night. I even told my brother all about how tight and wet it was."

I widen my eyes as he pulls away and bite my lip nervously. "Do you think maybe your brother would like to join us?" I ask him, not holding his gaze, and he chuckles darkly.

"Oh, you little slut. My brother has his eye on someone, but he may be persuaded to join us. I bet he'd love to try out your ass, but imagine my surprise when my roommate told me all about the slutty bitch who blew him for a job interview yesterday. Normally I don't like to share my pets, but the thought of watching my brother and friend defile you makes me fucking hard."

A shiver runs down my spine that I don't even have to fake as I feel my panties grow damp with excitement. I can't deny that all of that sounds fucking good to me too. Jesus, what is wrong with me? Could it possibly be because none of these guys are my marks, and I'm actually enjoying it and want more?

"But those kinds of things require permission from your master, and because you didn't get it, I will have to punish you." He grabs me by the hair and drags me over to his desk, where he sweeps everything off before pushing me down. I struggle a little, and his hand loosens in my hair so I can put on a good show without it hurting me. He pushes my legs apart with his feet so I'm now bent obscenely over his desk.

"Oh please, sir, no. I'm so sorry. I didn't think I had a choice," I plead as he lifts my skirt up and runs his hand over my thong-clad ass. I don't have stockings on today.

"Look at this!" I squeak as a sharp slap hits my left cheek. "Wearing a thong so that anyone could see it if a breeze happened to blow that slutty little skirt upwards. You are mine," he growls and slaps my right cheek. "No one sees this ass unless I give you permission, do you understand?"

"Ye... Yes, sir," I stutter out, squirming all over the top of his desk. I feel him crouch and run his hands down my thighs to my calves before he buries his face in my pussy from behind and inhales deeply.

"Oh yes, you're all wet and ready for me. I knew you would be perfect for me, you obedient, dirty little girl." He reaches up and peels my panties down. This time when he shoves his face against me, his tongue brushes against my clit, and I moan loudly, not having to fake anything for the camera this time. It's only the slightest brush, but it's enough to have me gushing.

"So wet and ready for me. You're such a responsive girl, just how I like it. How about I fuck you with my fat cock and ease that ache inside you?" he asks as he pulls back and stands up, slapping my ass once again on each cheek.

"Yes, oh yes, please, sir. I ache so badly," I cry out, turning my head so the camera can see the tears streaming down my face. I'm sure that will keep the perverts happy.

I hear him open the buckle on his belt before his slacks fall to the ground. I try to reach back to grab him, but he slaps my hand away. "Hold onto the desk while I ruin your pussy for any other man."

I feel him run his thick, hot cock head through the wet mess of my pussy. He rubs it up and down, brushing against the clit ring I got yesterday, which sends a sharp but not unpleasant sensation through my body. Without any warning, he thrusts it deep, slapping my ass at the same time, and I scream. Although I'm dripping with need, he is long and thick, and I was not prepped for any kind of intrusion like that.

"Yes," he hisses through gritted teeth. "Just like I remembered. Your pussy must be made for me." He gives me all of five seconds to adjust before he starts pounding away. Within two strokes, the pain has eased, and my eyes roll back in my head at the feel of him. His hands come up and around to cup my breasts through my shirt as he leans his whole body on mine, driving into me furiously.

"Oh my god, sir, you're so big and thick and long. Harder, please."

He does as I ask, and the whole desk starts to move across the carpeted floor. "My little slut likes it rough. Such a good little whore," he praises, and I grow even closer to my orgasm. Do I have a praise kink? I guess I've never heard those kinds of things before.

"More please, I'm so close," I beg him. My clit is banging against the desk, and the ring is doing a damn good job of taking care of what my fingers would normally do.

Max tugs my head to the side and bites my earlobe, whispering, "You really do feel amazing, hot and tight and gripping my dick like your pussy was made for it."

Oh my lord. Whispery, kind Max is just as sexy as dirty, dominating Max, and I explode. I moan and mutter words of praise as my body rides the exquisite wave of pleasure Max wrings from me. He keeps going for a little longer before he pulls out and comes all over my ass.

"Look at your ass covered in my cum. There's no chance of knocking up a slutty bitch that way." His words are nasty for the camera, and I feel a twinge of regret, but then I come to my senses as he steps away and tosses a couple of tissues at me. "Clean yourself up, and I don't want to hear about you giving anyone else sexual favors without permission from me. Your hot little mouth might come in handy. I'm trying to establish myself in this town, and using someone like you to bestow special favors might win me some points."

I debate my response. Do I want to appear submissive and mild, or do I need to fight back so that they feel the need to tame me? I think the latter would be more appealing to the assholes who run this ring.

"Like hell," I spit out, grabbing the tissues and cleaning up the mess Max made as I whirl on him. "Who do you think you are? I am not going to be your little toy to pass around. You can kiss my ass. I just wanted to pass my history class, not become your slave." I throw the tissues at him as he redresses himself before bending down to pick up my panties, but he's quicker than I am, and he grabs them and shoves them into his pocket.

"We'll see about that. You better watch your mouth, girl, or I'll make sure you can't talk back to me." Max's eyes are cold as he sneers at me, and a shiver runs down my spine. I hope the cameras take it for fear, but really, it's admiration. This guy is so good at his job, and if I didn't know better, I would say he was definitely a perverted sex freak. I mean, he may be, but at least he's on the good side of things.

"Fuck you, Mr. Turner." I flip him off and hurry toward the door, bending down to grab my bag on the way. I feel a cool breeze wash over my pussy, and I roll my eyes where the camera can't see. Oh, for fuck's sake, I need to be careful today. Turning the lock, I open the door just as the bell rings.

Seriously? What stupid luck is this? Kids spill out of the classrooms, and I get quite a few looks as I walk down the corridor to the girls' bathroom. I know I look freshly fucked. It couldn't be avoided with the way his hands were in my hair. The whispers are not quiet, and I hear "slut" and "whore" hurled in my direction before I push into the bathroom and the door closes behind me.

Thankfully, there is no one else in here at the moment, and I work quickly to put myself back together. I fix up my hair, taking the band off my wrist and putting it into a messy bun, then I wash my face and get rid of the makeup smears. Lastly, I grab a paper towel and wet it before rubbing it over my ass to make sure none of Max's cum is left on it. I wince as the rough paper scrapes against my skin. My poor ass is tender from his hand, but I'm pretty sure it's clean now. I use another bit of paper towel and do the same thing to my pussy before flushing it all down one of the toilets.

I look mostly put back together except for the lack of panties. I don't even have a spare pair in my backpack because I don't get my period, thanks to the IUD I have so I don't end up accidentally pregnant. Now I have to go sit in his class with my sore, bare ass pressed against those damn chairs. He didn't do me any favors. I think I'm going to blow off the rest of the day. It's not like it's hard to sneak off campus, and hopefully Max will cover for me somehow, though anyone who watched that scene with Max won't find it weird if I leave. I'll just pretend to be upset.

I pull out my phone and send Lathan a message. Somehow his number ended up in my phone at some stage last night. He's under his own name, because if anyone finds it, it won't seem suspicious due to us being classmates. I let him know I'm leaving for the day. I'm going to go see Dayton and find out if he can update me on the conversation with Bishop.

Me: I'm out. Going to see Asian Hottie for an update. I can't take high school drama today.

Lathan: Are you okay? Brock leaked your records

to all of the faculty, and of course Stella shared it at dinner with her family last night. Sophie is responsible for the notice on the message board.

Me: Yes, I'm annoyed, but whatever. Want to speak to Asian Hottie about Latino Lovely and what the boss had to say.

Lathan: You want company?

Me: Nah, I'm good.

He sends me a thumbs-up emoji, and I shove my phone back into my bag since there's no place in my skirt to keep it. I wish women's clothes designers would put more pockets in dresses and skirts. When I leave the bathroom, the corridor is empty once more with everyone having transitioned to their next class, so it's as simple as can be for me to stroll out and away from the school and toward the center of town. I'm done playing a highschooler. If there is anything this job has done, it has assured me that I would not have enjoyed attending a real high school. I would have been expelled for violence within weeks.

My heart skips with excitement at the idea of seeing Dayton. I mean, I really need to speak to him about what Bishop's decision was, but I also kind of just want to say hi and maybe clear the air a little more after yesterday. I can't believe I'm about to admit this, but it's not awful working with them now that they have pulled their heads out of their asses and we are starting to work as a team—not that I would ever say that out loud. If we can get Bishop to keep his shit together, we may have this wrapped up in a week or two, but do I want to be done with Team Basilisk so quickly? I won't be upset if the job drags out either. The more I get to know them, the more I enjoy it, and having sex with gorgeous men for my job is no hardship at all. The fact that they are sweet about it is a bonus. In the past, anyone I had sex with wasn't in the know, so I was treated all kinds of ways. Max and Anders have both been so kind and respectful, and it's a nice change.

I wear a smile on my face and walk with a skip in my step as I make my way toward Inkubus. There is quite a breeze today, though, so I have one hand on my skirt so I don't accidentally flash a driver and cause an accident. That wouldn't be very good for my cover.

CHAPTER 26

LATHAN

I frown at the conversation that just took place on my phone. Mac just texted me to tell me she was leaving for the day. I don't know how, but she seemed shaken and not as confident as she usually is. I guess that kind of attention can be tiring regardless of how tough you are, even if none of it's real.

The door to the classroom bangs open, and Max stomps in. He's pissed, and he confirms it when he snaps at everyone to get out their books. What is up his ass now? He left early this morning, and none of us have had a chance to talk to him yet. He was not happy about the outcome of last night's meeting with Percy, and I'm almost certain he followed Bishop to school and kept an eye on him at football training. Bishop has become a huge problem, and as team lead, he doesn't want Bishop to fuck everything up for all of us, not to mention Kenzie. The world would come crashing down around us if he outed her as an international spy and assassin, not to mention we would all be out of a job if he also announced to the world that MITHOS was a covert black ops outfit and not the exclusive college it's portrayed as to the public.

I try to catch Max's eye, but he won't look in our direction at all. He just turns around and starts spouting off dates and facts, telling us to make notes on them.

I lean over and ask Ry, "Hey, what's up with Max?"

Ry's lips are pursed, and he's watching his brother very carefully. "I have no idea, but whatever it is, I don't think it's anything good," he replies. Miller turns his head to listen in to what we're saying while still taking notes. I'm not sure why he bothers, since none of us are going to be here long enough to fail or pass, and we know all this shit anyway.

"I just got a text from Mac. She bailed for the day," I tell them, and this has Miller turning around to join the conversation.

"Maybe something happened between them again?" he suggests without judgment in his tone.

"You may be right. Max was pissed that we weren't allowed to share our identities with her yesterday. You jackasses wanting to test her really made things awkward for him. You know he has the hardest job in this mission."

Bishop leans back on his chair, two legs floating in the air. "Bullshit. He gets to tap her sweet ass. I wouldn't mind swapping spots with him." He doesn't speak all that quietly, and people turn around to stare and whisper amongst themselves, but that all suddenly dies off, and I turn my glare away from my asshole team member and back to the front where our team leader is fucking frosty.

"Did you have something to add, Mr. Ramirez?" Max's tone says *don't fuck with me*, but of course Bishop doesn't care. He lets his chair drop down and then casually stands up.

"I was just telling your brother that he should try out the whore who's advertising on the noticeboard, that way he can really get a feel for whether he likes boys or girls without having to worry about any unnecessary attachments. It's just a transaction, and I've heard she can suck a golf ball through a garden hose. I bet she does some nasty things too. I love me a nasty bitch, they can be so creative."

My mouth drops open in shock. I can't fucking believe he just said that. He's really taking his role a bit far.

"You shut your fucking mouth," Miller shouts and leaps at him. Yes, we choreographed a fight between them, but it wasn't supposed to be until lunch. Bishop just got personal, even though none of the surrounding students know that Miller and Ryland are lovers.

They have been my best friends for years. We were all in the same MITHOS class, and Miller and Ryland got together halfway through our initial year of training and have been together since. The rest of our team doesn't care, and we're happy they have each other to turn to when they need comfort, but Bishop has been clearly homophobic since he joined our team, which is only one of his problems. I can't wait to see the back of him after this assignment. It can't come soon enough.

Miller and Bishop are wrestling, knocking over chairs, and trying to throw punches. Luckily for Bishop, Miller doesn't connect solidly, otherwise he'd be knocked out much like last night. The stupid asshole has a glass jaw. By the time MITHOS discovered that, he was already through training and assigned to a team.

Ry and I jump in and try to separate them, but it's not easy.

"Enough!" Max shouts over the crowd that's egging on the two combatants. He strides in and gets between them. His nice clothes are deceiving, but Max is built, and he manages to yank the two apart, shoving them in opposite directions.

"Sit," he tells Miller, shoving him at his desk. "And you get out," he tells Bishop, pointing at the door. "I will not tolerate that kind of behavior in my classroom, nor will I tolerate bullying." He looks around the room. "If I find out who put that flier up of Ms. Walsh, they will be spending every Saturday in detention with me for the next month."

"Whatever," Bishop sneers and walks out. Billy, the quarterback and the son of the chief of police, looks at him with interest. Despite the fight being real, I guess it did what was necessary.

Billy stands up. "Ah, hey, can I get a pass? I need to speak to the coach about the game next weekend," he asks Max as we try to right some of the tables the guys knocked over.

"Fine, go." Max seems distracted, which works in Billy's favor, but I can guarantee he's not. They are just playing into our hands.

I planted a camera in the guys' locker room this morning, so hopefully that's where they are both headed and I can catch some of the conversation on it. If Bishop is still doing his job, he will steer the conversation in the right direction.

Billy leaves, and Max returns to teaching, but everyone keeps throwing side glances at Miller and Ryland. Sophie and her minions, Lucy and Michelle, whisper back and forth to each other, wearing frowns of disappointment on their faces, before they all turn and look at me. Fuck, that's not good. They think Ry and Miller are no longer options, so they are turning their attention to me. I do not want that. I glance at Ry who just shrugs.

"I could kiss you, too, if you want so they lose interest," he offers with a smirk, and I shake my head.

"No thanks," I reply quickly. "I'm not sure I'm that desperate yet." He flips me off, still smirking, before leaning closer to whisper to me.

"I'm pretty sure I know a pretty goth girl who would help you out if you asked nicely."

I'm momentarily confused before it occurs to me that he's talking about Kenzie. "Ah, um, but..." I stutter, and he just keeps grinning that stupid grin that makes me want to hit him.

"Don't deny it, dude. You like her. We all do. She's hot, feisty, smart, and fucking good at her job. Percy has no idea how right she is for our team, or maybe he does and that's why he forced the issue. I don't know about you, but I don't want to let her go after this, and I'm pretty sure my brother feels the same way if his pissy mood has anything to do with her."

He looks at Max who has continued with class now that the disturbance is over.

I frown at my friend. "You like her too? But what about Miller?" I ask, unsure where he's going with this.

He shrugs. "You know we like girls too, we just haven't found one that fits in with our team yet—one who would be interested in sharing with all of us and wouldn't be upset sharing me with Miller—but I think that search is over now."

"Miller hates her," I argue, and he scoffs.

"He does not. He just thinks he has to so he doesn't upset me. I will set him straight eventually, but it's amusing to watch the two of them dance around one another."

Ryland chuckles, and I just roll my eyes when I consider what he just said. He's right, Kenzie is all of those things, and I am incredibly attracted to her, but I hadn't hoped to start anything because I know she wants to return to her ghost status once we're done here. Maybe we just need to persuade her that Team Basilisk, minus Bishop, really is a better choice in the long run, and it would be fun trying to convince her of this.

"Okay, I'm in," I whisper to my friend, who just nods.

"Good. There's a party tomorrow night at the shack. I want you to convince Mac that you need her to keep the other girls off your back. Ask her to make out with you."

"Isn't that a little dishonest?" I ask him, and he just raises an unimpressed eyebrow at me.

"Would you rather have to put out to one of them?" He nods in the girls' direction, and when I look at the three of them, they giggle and wave flirtishly.

"Fuck no," I grumble, turning back to him.

"There you go. Mac will be fine with it, and I saw her looking at you last night. Trust me, she wants you."

Just then, Miller nudges him on his other side, so he turns his back to me, leaving me to ponder what he just said. Okay, I can get on board with the plan—anything that will keep those high school leeches away from me and help convince Mac we're the team for her.

I scribble down a couple of notes, so it looks like I actually care about what Max is saying, but mostly I think about the party tomorrow night and feel a sense of anticipation. I'd been dreading it because I spent the last one fighting off teenage girls, and let me tell you, these kids are not backward in coming forward. There was practically an orgy going on in one of the back rooms, and more drugs and alcohol than I've ever seen at a high school party. Knowing Mac is going to be there is a huge relief, and it has me looking forward to it immensely.

School seemed to drag, and I didn't see Bishop again. Apparently, he was training with the football team who had been given leave for an extra practice to help integrate the new team member.

We didn't get a chance to speak to Max either, because he had a staff meeting at lunchtime. When the bell rings at the end of the day, I get Ryland to drop me off at home so I can go through the footage from school. I make myself a coffee, and I'm just sitting down on the sofa when Max slams through the back glass door, throwing his briefcase onto the floor and himself down on the couch, and puts his arm over his eyes with a groan.

"Are you okay?" I ask him, and he remains silent. I start to worry, but he finally answers without removing his arm from his face.

"No, not really. I feel fucking dirty. This assignment is eating away at me. I'm not sure how Mac does it all the time."

"What happened?" I inquire, and he finally drops his arm and sits up, resting his head back to look at the ceiling.

"Brock was lying in wait when I arrived at school this morning. He said that while his associates were happy with seeing me seduce a teenager, they were disappointed that there wasn't more to watch. They wanted to see more, so I bent Mac over my desk and fucked her for the camera. I was rough. I spanked her ass, and I forced myself inside her, all things that I'm sure would get the people on the other side of the camera off."

"Was Mac okay? Is that why she left school early today?" This gets his attention, and he sits up and looks at me.

"She left school early? I wondered why she wasn't in our class, but then Bishop acted up, and I forgot about it."

"Yeah, she sent me a message just before I had history with you. She bailed from French with Stella, who was treating her abysmally, but not before handing Stella her ass," I tell him, and he nods.

"That must have been why she was at my door. All I wanted to do was gather her in my arms and hold her tight. Even though the stuff is not true, and we all know it, it's still no fun being whispered about no matter how thick your skin is, and Mac has never had to deal with high school bullies. She's been a lone wolf for so long, I'm not sure if she knows how to deal with any of this shit. Instead, all I could do was throw her around and violate her in front of the cameras." Max is pissed. Although I know he is dominant in the bedroom, he's also a big softy, and it can't be easy for him to degrade a woman like that. There's a definite line between consensual domination and abuse, and he never crosses it. No wonder he feels dirty.

"Was she okay?" I ask, and he's quiet for a moment.

"Yeah, she orgasmed, so I think she was fine," he replies.

"Did she fake it?" I ask, and he scowls at me.

"I think I would know the difference. No, she did not."

"What about you?"

"Yeah, I did a big finish all over her ass for the fucking pervs, and then I made her leave without underwear, her ass red with my handprints."

My cock started to grow hard when he began talking about fucking Kenzie, but that sealed the deal. It's now uncomfortably hard and pushing against my zipper.

"Where did she go?" Max asks, getting to his feet and picking up his briefcase as I distract myself from thoughts of Mac by opening my laptop and pulling up the footage of the locker room.

"To see Dayton. She said she wanted to get the downlow on the Bishop situation and didn't want to ask at school since there were cameras everywhere," I tell him, and he nods and disappears upstairs, I assume to get changed.

I sit and watch the footage from the locker room, my mouth falling open in shock at what I discover. "Holy crap," I whisper.

"What?" Anders is standing nearby in a pair of sweats.

"Hey, are you off today?" I ask him, and he shakes his head.

"No, I have the evening shift, so I start at five. What are you watching?" he asks, nodding at my laptop.

"Something I think you're all going to want to see. Can you call Max down? I'll call Ry and Miller and tell them to come home. I want you all to see this before Bishop gets here."

"What about Dayton?" Anders asks, and I consider the question.

"Yeah, call him too. I think Mac is with him. Get them both to come, they need to see it also."

CHAPTER 27

DAYTON

"Thank you so much for taking over that piercing yesterday, man," Kevin says as he washes his hands and sets up his station for his first tattoo of the morning.

I don't have any clients booked in today, but I do have a couple of sketches I want to draw up, so I flick on the light for my drawing box.

"Poor Deacon was distraught, but he calmed down as soon as his mom got there," Kevin says affectionately, and I study the man who could also be my uncle. I've spent so much time working for and with him. He's the one who gave me a chance to start tattooing when Max showed him my art.

"You really like her, don't you?" I ask, and he nods.

"Yeah, man, she's kind and sweet and loving. She's

had it rough. Her deadbeat ex is a piece of shit. I just hope you can arrest him once you make all the arrests associated with the ring." Kevin knows all about why we're here. This town has been plagued by this group for a long time. His MC tried to keep things safe, but the traffickers wait until the kids leave town and nab them on their way to their destination. They have foiled him at every turn, which is why he went to his brother and asked for help.

Charity's ex is the coast guard captain, a member of the original Divinity of Morality group, and how we think they are trafficking these teenagers out of the country. Well, actually, we think that Ted Standish is doing it in his shipping containers, but we think the coast guard is conveniently turning a blind eye when they leave port, the same as the customs inspectors.

"We will do our best. Hopefully now that we have an in with both Max and Anders, things will move smoother."

"And that pretty goth girl from yesterday." He smirks. "The one whose clit piercing you had to finish. She's the new temporary member of your team."

"How do you know that?" I ask him, surprised that he knows about Kensington. No one apart from our team and Percy should have that knowledge.

Kevin shrugs. "Percy asked Jeff to ask me to watch out for her."

My eyes widen in surprise, and Kevin chuckles.

"She may be a ghost operative and a deadly

weapon, but she's still his kid, and she took quite a beating at your hands. She looked terrible yesterday, and it's been almost a week since it happened. Poor girl looks rough, but she's putting on a brave face so she can get on with the mission, and that shows just how tough she is, but I saw Charity once after her piece of shit ex Isaac beat her black and blue, and she wasn't able to move for weeks. The fact that Kenzie is not only up but also working undercover is a testament to her professionalism, but parents worry."

A lump of guilt settles in my stomach. It's my fault that she looks that way. I was the one who basically shoved her down a flight of stairs. I'm not sure how I'm ever going to make it up to her. Then yesterday, there was the whole piercing debacle. Fuck my life, I'm an idiot. I was all fumbling fingers. I almost swallowed my tongue when I realized where she had gotten pierced, and I failed to keep it professional when I couldn't get the ball on. Giving her an orgasm was the highlight of my day. I closed up after she left and went home and rubbed one out to the memory of the sounds she made. I just wished it was wanted and not forced on her through necessity. I could barely look at her last night even though she didn't seem at all concerned about it. I guess when you're a honeytrap, you get used to those kinds of things.

Thinking about her using her body to trap her marks makes me angry, so I turn my back on Kevin so he can't see the swirling thoughts in my eyes.

"Don't worry, we'll take care of her," I assure him gruffly, and he chuckles.

"I think that's what Percy is counting on."

Kevin's customer comes in then, so our chat ends. "Hey, Dayton, I didn't know you were back in town." I whirl my chair around and find Timothy Slater. He's Kevin's best friend, and he and his wife Rebecca own the Mug Shot Diner.

I get up and shake hands with him. I really like him and his wife, and they have provided me with many a home-cooked meal whenever I've been in Summerville working for Kevin.

"Tim, good to see you. Yeah, with Max moving back to work at the high school, I thought I'd tag along and see if I could pick up some work."

"You guys looking to settle down and put down some roots? It's about time you started thinking about your future and not drifting from place to place." Timothy is not in the know like Kevin. He just thinks we're flighty young adults trying to avoid any responsibilities. He's not mean about it, he just thinks we should do more with our lives. "I was proud of Max when Jeff told me he would be working at the school and seeing Ryland through his final year. I can't say I was surprised when I heard he'd been expelled from his last school. Kind of reminds me of his uncle," Tim jokes, and Kevin smiles, rolling his eyes playfully.

"I wasn't expelled," he counters, and Tim shakes his head.

"No, but you saw the inside of detention more than your own home."

They get on with putting his stencil on, and I turn back to my own work.

I once asked how no one knew that Ryland was too old for high school. It seems weird that their hometown doesn't know the real ages of the governor's sons. Max explained that his dad moved away before they were born, and he wasn't really friends with anyone back in town except his brother. When his parents passed and left them the house, Jeff bought out Kevin's share and started spending time here occasionally, but he never brought his sons.

By then, Max had joined MITHOS, and Ryland had every intention of following in his brother's footsteps. Both boys faded from the public eye when they started attending the school, and Jeff had the MITHOS nerd herd clear all information about them off the internet, and any records were destroyed. The world forgot about the governor's sons. Even now, they are only well-known here. Once we leave, any record of them will be scrubbed, and they will fade into the memories of the townsfolk like we do at any assignment. They may talk about the governor and his sons occasionally, but Jeff will probably sell the house here, and Kevin is talking about moving his tattoo studio elsewhere. He's had enough of this small town as well. He said it was time for a change of pace, but that depends on if he can convince Charity to leave with him.

I'm not sure how long I'm lost in my thoughts, but

when the bell above the door rings, my back screams in protest as I sit up straight. I must have been drawing longer than I thought to have been so seized up.

"Hello, pretty lady, how is that piercing today?" I hear Kevin ask with a smile in his voice.

I swivel my chair around and come face-to-face with my obsession. Mac is biting her lip and looking between Kevin and Tim.

"Ah, hi. I was wondering if I could talk to someone about a tattoo." She seems nervous, and Kevin smiles while Tim frowns.

"Shouldn't you be in school?" he asks, and Kevin's smile morphs to a scowl.

"Jesus, man, stop trying to chase off my clients. If the lady wants a tattoo, then let her get one. How about my man Dayton here takes you into the piercing room for a consultation? That way the old fuddy-duddy won't make you nervous." Kevin is a saint, obviously guessing Mac is here to talk to me.

I get up from my seat and wave my hand at the room.

Mac smiles at Kevin. "Thank you," she says before hurrying through the store and brushing past me to get into the room. She smells like sex and my best friend's cologne, and I feel my cock harden as I wonder what she and Max got up to this morning. Tim wasn't wrong with her needing to be in school. What rattled this experienced agent so much that she blew it off to come here?

She doesn't take a seat, she just paces back and

forth across the room. I wait it out, knowing she will tell me what's wrong as soon as she calms down.

"This fucking town needs to be burned to the ground, and all the fucked up people in it should be fed to the sharks," she explodes loudly. Not even twenty seconds later, I hear Kevin switch the radio on in the parlor, the loud music hopefully blocking out the sound of our voices. This time when she whirls around, her skirt lifts up, exposing a rosy red ass with large handprints on it. Ahh, so that's why she's not taking a seat.

"Want to talk about it?" I ask, smirking at her, and she growls, seeing where my eyes are, and smacks me on the arm.

"Stop it. Max was cornered by Brock this morning. The people behind the camera were not happy about the lack of visual sex yesterday and demanded that he rectify that if he wanted an invite into the supersecret sex club." She screws up her nose. "I swear if anyone gives me an excuse to go trigger happy, I will lay waste to the people involved." She cocks her head to the side and looks me straight in the eye. "Can't I just kill them all off? That would solve everyone's problems."

The little minx is out for blood, and it's so fucking sexy, but I don't get a chance to comment before she's pacing back and forth again.

"This town is so... Ugh! Dayton, if I don't get out of here even for a moment to breathe, I will kill someone, and it won't be pretty." Her chest is heaving now, and she's tugging at her hair.

"Hey, hey," I murmur quietly to her, grabbing her hands and stopping her from hurting herself. "Look at me," I demand, holding her wrists, and that seems to snap her out of her fury.

She looks up at me, and I watch as her pupils dilate. I am starting to get a handle on Ms. Kensington Watson. Despite all of her bravado and unquestionable skills at being an agent, she secretly wants someone to take care of her, and she seems to react positively to firm control.

"I have you now. Take a breath in through your mouth and out through your nose." She does as instructed, and I talk her through a couple more breaths until I feel her heart rate settle under my fingers. "Okay, good. Now, I have an idea. Come on, I'll take you somewhere. You can blow off some steam and get away from this town. It does have a habit of closing in on you, and I can't imagine the high school is any better."

I open the door to the consultation room, and Kevin and Tim look up. "Are you done?" Kevin sounds surprised, and I shrug.

"No, but Mac isn't completely sure what she wants, and I thought a drive to help her clear her mind might help her process. Plus, I'm hungry, and thinking on an empty stomach is not fun, so I'm taking her to lunch."

Kevin smirks at me. "Yeah, okay, you player," he mutters, putting on a good show for Tim. I just wink, and Tim grunts, looking at Mac warily when she exits the room behind me. Now I know Tim is Kevin's best friend, and he seems like a standup guy, but we haven't been able to get a good read on him yet as far as the case goes. He is one of the original members of the club, both he and his wife. They seem to be on the up and up, but so do a lot of the other residents of this town.

We wave goodbye, and I feel their eyes on us as I drag Mac out the back door and to my car. Mac admires the classic American muscle car as I open the door to the 1974 Pontiac Firebird Trans-Am, helping her in. Before she sits, I reach over and grab a gym towel off the back seat and lay it down for her. Her eyebrows jump in surprise, and she looks at me questioningly.

I just smirk. "Your skirt flew up before, and I saw the red handprints on it. This might make the ride a little more comfortable."

Her eyes narrow, and she glares but sits down gingerly. I close the door behind her and hurry around to the driver's side. I start the car and leave the lot, heading past her foster home and in the direction of some hot springs that are a favorite of mine whenever I'm in town. At this time of day, they should be empty with all the teens still in school. I stop by Subway, running in to grab us some subs and drinks, before continuing on our way. Mac's eyes close not long into the trip, and I decide to keep my thoughts to myself so she can get some rest. It was a late night with the team meeting, and I'm sure she needs the rest. After all, she's still healing from the damage I did to her.

I turn the radio on low. An easy listening country channel floods the car, and I tap my finger along to the beat.

"I did not picture you as a country music fan." Mac's voice is low and husky as she turns her head to look at me.

I don't take my eyes off the road as I shrug. "My parents were obsessed with it for some reason," I reply.

"What nationality makes up Dayton Wexley?" she asks, closing her eyes again. "It's not a very Asian name."

"My parents are of Korean descent, but they are third generation American, born and bred. My great-grandfather was stationed here during the Korean War as a liaison to the Americans, and he married my great-grandma, who was also here for the same reason, and neither of them left."

"Ah, but that doesn't explain the slight accent," she says, and I'm impressed she can hear it. Not many do.

"My family ensured that we were bilingual. Korean was spoken at home, and I guess we all have a touch of the accent from my grandparents."

"Do you still see them, and do they know what you do?" she asks quietly, and I guess it's only fair. I know everything about her family—hell, they are practically my own.

"Yes, I do still see them, and no, they think I am a

traveling tattoo artist. They know that I'm friends with Anders and Max, and we kind of played up Max as being a bored rich kid. It's a good cover, as you know, and they never question where I am in the world. It's safer that they don't know, and neither do my four siblings."

"Four? Oh wow, that must have been fun growing up." A wistful smile spreads across her face, but her eyes stay closed.

I snort my disagreement. "Ah, no. I was the youngest of five, and the rest were girls. I assure you it was hell."

She chuckles. "Oh no, was poor little Dayton used as a doll by his big sisters?"

"Constantly," I grumble as I turn off the main highway and drive my precious car down a gravel access road. The locals have made it wider over the years, but I still take care with my car. I pull into a small parking area and turn the engine off. She opens her eyes and looks around.

"Where are we?" she asks, and I pat her knee.

"It's a surprise. Come on, it's a short hike." I grab our subs and drinks before climbing out, and then I get my duffle bag from the trunk. I shove the food and drinks inside and put it over my shoulder. When I get back to the front, she's waiting for me.

"Will I need my backpack?" she asks, and I shake my head.

"Nope, I have everything. Come on." I grab her hand and tow her up the path toward the springs.

She allows me to, which is just one more tick to the *wants to be looked after* box. If she didn't, then she would have yanked her hand out of mine, but she just sighs and follows along like a lamb. This isn't what I thought our newest team member would be like, but she's starting to feel comfortable enough with us to let her guard down, and I'm going to make the most of it.

CHAPTER 28

It's nice letting Dayton take charge. Not having to think about where we're going or what we're doing is blissful. I just let go of everything that is happening on the case and ask him some personal questions. Sometimes I need to do that, otherwise all the bad in the world gets to me, and I have a mini breakdown, which was where I was headed, but he could see that and just took charge and distracted me.

The vegetation on either side of the path is thick like much of the vegetation in this area. I guess there's no shortage of water in this part of the world. The path opens up to a pool of steaming blue water, and Dayton drops his bag onto the ground before bending down to unzip it. He pulls out a blanket and shakes it, and I chuckle.

"You just happened to have a picnic blanket in the back of your car?"

He frowns and looks down at it before looking back at me. "Yeah, sure. Don't most people?"

Well, that's a good question actually. Do they? I have no clue what normal people are like.

He bends down and rummages around in his bag again before standing up and holding out a pistol and a magazine. "Here, why don't you blow off some steam?"

I feel a smile spread across my lips as I take the magazine and jam it into the gun. There are a few bottles and cans lying about, and Dayton gathers them all and sets them up on a log about sixty-five feet away. I'm practically itching to fire the gun, but I wait until he returns to my side.

"Sorry, I don't have any ear protection," he apologizes, and I wave him off with my free hand.

"It won't be too bad out here anyway."

He stands next to me as I blow out a huge breath of air, trying to center myself, and let all the chaos float away. All it's going to do is make me tense, and then my aim will be off.

"How about we make this interesting?" I suggest to Dayton, and I see him grin out of the corner of my eye.

"What do you suggest?" he asks, sounding curious, and I shrug.

"How about I get to drive your car back if I hit them all?" I wonder if he's going to be funny about his admittedly beautiful classic car.

"Okay," he agrees easily, and I frown, wondering what the catch is.

Turning, I raise an eyebrow. "And if I miss?" I'm interested to hear what he wants from this game.

"A kiss for every one you miss." My mouth drops open in surprise before I can stop it, and he chuckles. "But that shouldn't be a problem for you, right?" he teases, and I turn back to the lineup.

The asshole knows what he's doing, because while I was coolly confident I would hit them all before, he now has me slightly rattled. Does he really want me to kiss him, or was it just to throw me off my game? It fucking worked, and he may very well end up claiming those kisses.

I close my eyes and let all the background crap drift away. It's not a huge distance, and one that I've easily done before. Shit, I hit Dad from three times this distance, but I had a scope and there was no pressure. This is a whole different kettle of fish now that there are stakes involved, and I kind of hope I miss. I would love to know what it's like to kiss this quietly confident, brooding man. Is he a slow smolder burning beneath the surface, or will he ignite like a flash fire and burn me to the core with his passion?

I open my eyes and fire the first three rounds. *Ping, ping, ping.* I easily take down the first three cans, and they fly off, lost in the vegetation behind the log. Next is a bottle, and I frown.

"I don't want to spread glass everywhere," I tell him. "That will just make this spot dangerous for anyone else who uses it."

"Well, I guess that counts as your first miss, so I

get one kiss." I scowl at him before turning back to the log. There are two more glass bottles and two more cans.

"You set me up," I grumble as he shoves his hands into the pockets of his jeans and grins. I pick off the last two cans, but there are still three glass bottles standing that I refuse to hit.

"Look at that. I guess that means I get three kisses, and you don't get to drive my car."

Growling, I empty the last four bullets from the magazine into a large tree farther back from the glass targets. Wood slivers fly through the air as the bullets strike the large trunk, and I hear Dayton chuckle next to me. The slide clicks open, telling me the magazine is spent, and I drop my hand and shove the gun back at the sneaky bastard.

"Yeah, yeah, chuckles, laugh it up, but let the record show, you cheated. Though I'm not sure I'm surprised. You cheated when you tripped me down the stairs too. You fight dirty." I poke him in the chest as he takes the gun out of my other hand. His eyes sparkle with light and amusement, and it almost takes my breath away. This side of Dayton is sexy and seductive, and wow, it's so unexpected

He grabs my hand and tows me back to the picnic blanket, where he shoves the now empty gun into his bag before pulling out two towels.

"Food or swim first?" he asks, and I debate my options. If I eat first—depending on what's on the subs—it will affect how good the kiss is. I have no idea if they have onions on them or not. If we swim first, though, I can probably get my kisses in then.

"Swim," I answer, and a slow smile spreads across his lips.

"Sounds good." He strips off his shirt, and I'm momentarily pectomized. Whoa. The man has well-defined pecs, and across his right shoulder and over his chest is a bright blue and green Chinese dragon tattoo. There's another one that wraps around his left waist, just under his left pec, moving toward his back, but this one is red. On his right hip, just where his pants sit, I can see another dragon head, this one yellow, and I guess the rest of the body is on Dayton's back. They are stunning, and I'm mesmerized by them because with every movement, it looks like they are undulating across his body. I never expected so much color in a tattoo on this man, but I guess I shouldn't judge a book by its cover. I reach out before I can stop myself and trace a finger over the dragon on his chest. He stops moving and allows me to.

"Why dragons?" I ask, and he shrugs.

"Chinese dragons were adopted by a lot of Asian cultures. They are a Buddhist representation of the seasons and compass directions. I'm not sure why, I've just always been fascinated with them."

I consider what I know about Buddhism and Chinese dragons. "Five of them, if I remember correctly."

He nods. "I have the black and white ones on my legs."

I step back from him and gesture for him to continue taking off his clothes. He rolls his eyes playfully but complies, stripping off his jeans. Now, he's only wearing a tight pair of black boxer briefs, and I feel saliva pool in my mouth. Holy shit, the man is cut. I twirl my finger, asking him to spin, and he holds his hands out and does so with a grin on his face.

I allow my eyes to devour his body, taking in the two other dragons he has. There is one on each thigh, looking at one another across his groin. I desperately want to trace them with my tongue, but that would not be appropriate right now. Maybe one day—a girl can only hope. He finishes his twirl and faces me again.

"Well?" he asks, and I grin.

"I like your dragons," I tell him, and he grins before putting his hands on his hips.

"Okay, your turn."

I go to comply but freeze. I have no underwear on. How did I forget about that? I grimace.

"What's wrong?" he asks, losing all playfulness as he steps toward me with concern in his eyes. "Are you okay?"

I shrug. "Yeah, but I just remembered I have no panties on." It takes a moment for my words to sink in, and when they do, his eyes heat with more than amusement.

"Well, it's not like I haven't seen it before," he offers, and I stare at him for a moment before giggling.

"Yeah, I guess you're right. Am I allowed to get it

wet?" I didn't think about my piercing, and I can't remember what the aftercare instructions say.

"Yeah, the hot spring will be fine, but I'd avoid spas and pools for a few days. Too many chemicals and an abundance of people."

He turns and walks to the hot springs, stepping down the gently sloping bank and into the water. I think he's giving me some privacy to get naked, which I appreciate, but it's really not necessary. I'm not even sure why I hesitated before. I'm not shy, and I regularly get naked and fuck strangers for work. Shit, I still have the sticky residue of Max's cum on my ass cheeks, but this is something different. It's not work, it's my private life, and I'm not sure how to navigate this, so I appreciate the gesture.

I strip down, tossing my clothes onto the picnic blanket, and grab the towels before hurrying after him. I throw the towels on the bank and sprint into the water, creating a large splash that drenches Dayton's back before I dive down. The water is warm and feels amazing, and I groan as I surface. This was just what I needed.

I lose track of time as we splash around, kicking up water and play fighting. My body still aches in places, but the water is helping soothe some of that.

I grab him by the shoulders and push him under. When he comes up, his playful smile is gone, and in its place is something exciting—something that promises he's about to get his own back tenfold. He dives for me, and I turn and try to swim away, but he grabs my ankle and tugs me under.

Spluttering, I fight my way back to the surface, pushing my hair out of my face. When I open my eyes, I find Dayton just in front of me, his expression etched with desire. Sure, I'm no stranger to seeing that look in men's eyes. I keep my body fit and tight, the perfect trap for a male, but seeing desire in the eyes of someone I'm not being paid to kill or capture is a new thing for me. Yes, I've seen it before when I've gallivanted around, playing up my Princess Kensington cover, but I have never seen it in the eyes of someone I reciprocate desire for. I've never had the time or the urge to have a relationship outside of work. It's frowned upon, and how would I explain why I disappear for long periods of time?

Seeing it in the eyes of this man is intoxicating, and I feel a shiver flow down my spine as he reaches for me.

I've kept my body below the water, almost shy to show him anything else, and he doesn't force the issue. His eyes don't even drop away from mine as he pulls my body to his so that he's holding me pressed against him, my legs wrapped around his waist. Without saying anything, he leans in and presses a kiss to my mouth. It's short and sweet, and when he pulls back, he studies me closely, checking to make sure I'm okay. He must realize that I am more than perfect with this arrangement, because I thread my fingers through the back of his hair and pull him down to meet my mouth. This time the kiss is the exact opposite of the last one. It's long and languid, with drugging strokes of his tongue, and he owns my mouth. I meet him stroke for stroke as I squirm, rubbing my clit ring against his hard abs and creating a delicious friction between the two of us. I drop my hand to reach for his cock, but he grabs it, stopping me, and pulls away. When I blink at him in surprise, he rests his forehead against mine.

"I want to take this slow. I have a feeling you've never had slow before, and I want to enjoy making out with you in the hot springs. Nothing more today. I want to build up the anticipation and court you in a way that you've never had." His voice is husky and low, and it does things to my insides, which makes my stomach roll and purr. As much as I like his sentiment, I'm not sure we are in the same place. Does he want me to be his girlfriend and for us to be an exclusive item? Because in my line of work, that's never going to happen, not to mention what I have to do for this job.

"I've fucked Max and blown Anders in the span of less than twenty-four hours, not to mention Ry brushed a kiss across my lips that confused me, and I am ridiculously attracted to Nerdy Sexy."

"Who?" he asks, looking confused, and it's freaking adorable.

"Oh, Lathan." The confusion clears, and he chuckles. "So I'm not sure exactly what's happening here, but if you want something exclusive, I can't offer that to you, nor do I think I want to."

He is quick to respond this time. "Oh no, that's not what I'm asking for. I can't ever give you that either. My first priority is my team, and where they go, I go. I also have a feeling that all of them feel something toward you too. No, I was just asking if you would give me a chance when and if you can also. No pressure, no commitments, just fun."

A wave of relief washes over me, and I smile brightly at him. "I can totally be down with that. This has been really nice. It's kind of a first real date for me, even if I am naked."

He looks stunned at that, but before he can answer, his phone starts ringing, and he groans. "That's Anders's ringtone. Fuck, what crappy timing."

I unwrap my legs from his waist, my body brushing against his thick length as I lower my feet to the bottom of the pool. He reluctantly pulls away and hurries out of the water to get it before it stops ringing. I wrap my arms around my body. The water is warm, but the loss of his hardness against my body leaves me feeling bereft for some reason.

"Yeah?" I listen to Dayton's side of the conversation. "What now?" he asks, looking back at me before sighing. "Yeah, okay, we'll be there in thirty minutes." He pauses while Anders talks. "What? No, I'm not at work." He pauses again before huffing. "No. I'll tell you later." He hangs up and grimaces.

"Lathan needs us back at the house. He has something he wants us to see." He picks up both towels and quickly rubs himself dry before wrapping it around his waist. He holds the other one out for me without averting his eyes, clearly throwing me a challenge.

While I may not be experienced with real boyfriend-girlfriend flirting, I can straight up nail a seduction, so without breaking eye contact, I walk out of the water like Jane Fonda in *Barbarella*, except X-rated. I have to say I admire his willpower. His eyes don't drop from mine until the very last second, when he wraps the towel around my body and helps me dry off. It's sweet, and I love being taken care of. Who'd have thought it? Maybe my mom and dad were right, and I don't want to be an island anymore, but there is no way I'm ever going to tell them they were right, and shit this could all go sideways anyway. I know there are a lot of teams who have poly relationships within their team. It's not easy to be a spy, and it makes sense. I just never thought it would be in the cards for me, and I'm not sure if that's what Team Basilisk wants either. Also, to be honest, I am not attracted to Bishop whatsoever, so if he stays with the team, it's a nonissue anyway, so I better not overthink this until I find out where they stand with him.

"But I owe you a kiss," I remind him, disappointed our time here is done, but hopefully we can do it again another time after we take care of the sex trafficking ring.

"I'm saving it for when I really need it," he jokes, passing me both of the subs we haven't had a chance to eat. I hang onto my towel with one hand while reaching for the sandwiches. He makes quick work of gathering all our things together before ushering me back down the path to the car.

"I promise that you don't have to save it. There are plenty more if you want them," I tell him as he unlocks the car, shoving everything into the back seat. I climb inside the passenger seat, amused that I'm still only wrapped in a towel. I rest the subs on my lap and put on my seat belt. He does the same, starting the car and heading back down the little track.

"Well, that's good to know. Hey, can you unwrap my sub for me? I can't do it and shift at the same time." I do as he asks, pulling back the top part of the wrapper so he can eat it one-handed once he's moved through the gears.

"I wonder what Lathan has to tell us," I muse out loud while eating my own lunch during the drive back to the governor's mansion.

"I'm not sure, but it didn't sound good."

CHAPTER 29

ANDERS

I hang up my cell with a frown.

"Did you reach them?" Lathan asks from the sofa, drawing my attention.

"Ah, yeah, they'll be half an hour," I answer, and Max grunts.

"Where are they? Inkubus isn't thirty minutes away."

I shrug. "Dayton wouldn't say. Listen, I'm just going to run upstairs and get ready for work. I'll have to leave soon, and I don't want to miss out on whatever it is you have to tell us."

Without waiting for an answer, I haul ass upstairs, thinking about my conversation with my teammate. Dayton sounded strange. I'm dying to know where he and Mac were. Dayton is probably the quietest of the group, which really isn't hard since we are a fairly exuberant bunch, but he's always been happy observing. It's what makes him such a great second-in-command. He just knows what to do and when to do it because he's so detail oriented. I was surprised when I discovered he was one of the guys who had given Mac an orgasm the other day, and it wasn't even mission related. The poor guy must have been so flustered, he just said fuck it and let it all hang out. Sometimes Dayton needs to be ripped out of his own head, and I bet trying to put Mac's clit ring in had been just the kick in the pants he needed. He'd been so wary of her.

One, she's Percy's daughter, and he has the utmost respect for our boss, but two, he almost killed her when he tripped her down the stairs, and he hasn't been sure how to deal with it. He's never been comfortable hurting women, even when they are the bad guys. Hey, I get it I'd probably be the same if I had four doting big sisters.

Now, Mac is a conundrum that I never saw coming. You could have knocked me over with a feather when Matthew told her she had to get down on her knees and blow me to get the job. I mean, I knew that's the kind of behavior we had expected of him, but I never thought I'd be on the receiving end. Then, she just smiled and got down on her knees and gave me the best blow job of my life, hands down. Fuck, it took all my training not to flinch when she did, and then I thought about my grandmother naked so I didn't blow my load too quickly. Her mouth was hot and wet, and the way she took me back into her throat and swallowed around my cock was mind-blowing. She could even take a bit of rough treatment. She looked so pretty with tears leaking out because it was my dick that was doing that to her.

I open the door to my room, stride straight over to my en suite shower, and turn it on before stripping. Taking my rock-hard dick in my hand, I run my fist up and down, stroking it as I think about her on her knees in front of me again. It doesn't take long until I feel the tingling sensation in my spine, and my butt cheeks tighten as I splatter cum over the wall of the shower. I groan as I imagine Mac swallowing it all down again, licking her lips and scooping up the drop she missed like it was her favorite flavor.

I swear I almost got down and begged her to join our team there and then, and again when she turned up at the team meeting, her hair mussed from the bike helmet and her cheeks flushed with the exhilaration of the ride. It was a gut punch seeing her in her tight little jeans, completely unperturbed by what she has to do to work the mission. It was sexy as fuck. She owns her shit, and I am so here for it. This is the girl we need in our group, one who is comfortable in her skin and comfortable with us to do what needs to be done. We've had girls who came home and cried because they'd been felt up by a mark and had to allow it so they didn't blow the case. They never lasted very long. They always picked a favorite and tried to play us against one another. We won't stand for that, and we quickly sent them packing. But not Mac. Nope. She calls us on our shit and doesn't apologize for being the best agent she can be. I completely respect that.

I see how my teammates look at her, each and every one of them, and even Miller is fascinated with her, though I'm almost certain Bishop's fascination isn't good. I'm convinced he would gain a sick sense of satisfaction over ruining her career, and I won't allow that to happen. Although I acted as shocked as everyone else, I'm secretly on Mac's side in the opinion that we should get rid of him permanently. He is going to be a problem.

What's not going to be a problem is sharing this girl between us. We just have to convince her we're the right fit and that she wouldn't be better off without us after all.

I wash my body and quickly jump out when I hear the rumble of Dayton's Trans-Am drive around to the back of the mansion. I hurry and dress so I can be downstairs when they walk in.

I know I'm not quick enough when I hear Max shout, "Why the fuck are you both wearing towels? And please tell me you have something under that."

I walk into the conservatory and lean against the doorframe, watching on in amusement. Max's dominant energy is suffocating the room, and I see Mac's eyes narrow, so I just stand back and wait for the fireworks. This is going to be fun.

"Hey, Max, calm down." Dayton holds his hands up, trying to calm our easily riled friend, but he stubbornly crosses his arms and waits for an explanation.

I see the exact moment when Mac loses her shit. She raises an eyebrow and calmly releases her hold on the large towel wrapped around her body. The room is so quiet that the sound of the towel hitting the floor thunders in my ears, or maybe it's all the blood rushing from my body and into my dick at the sight of her beautiful, naked body completely unadorned aside from the sparkly bar in the hood of her clit.

"Fuck me," Lathan mutters, swiping a hand across his mouth. I'm almost certain he's checking for drool, and I quickly do the same.

"Mac," Dayton scolds and hurries to lift her towel up and around her, but she holds up a hand.

"Dayton, stop. I may be willing to play along with daddy dominant over there while we are in front of the cameras for the mission, but I will not be told what I can and can't do during my off time. If I want to go swimming naked with Dayton, I will, and if I want to have a gang bang with Miller, Ry, and Lathan, I will. If I want to get down on my knees and blow Anders every morning before school, I will, and nothing you or anyone else says will change this."

"You had an orgy with Ry and the guys?" Max asks, turning his glare on Lathan, who jumps to his feet, his laptop sliding to the ground.

"No, we..." Lathan tries to defend himself, but Mac shushes him, and he shuts his mouth.

"It doesn't matter if we did or not, Maxwell, because you don't own me," she growls. "And as enjoyable as you bending me over your desk was today, it was a part of the job. I can separate the two, can you?"

Before he can answer, Miller and Ry walk up the back path the same way Dayton and Mac had come. The moment they see Mac naked, they stop dead in their tracks. Ryland's eyes widen before he smirks with amusement, but Miller scowls and stomps into the house.

"What the fuck is going on? Put some fucking clothes on, Mac, nobody wants to see you naked." Miller glares at her, and if I wasn't watching closely, I wouldn't have noticed her flinch, but I did, and I want to punch Miller in the head.

All of his hate is fake, but she doesn't know that. He just doesn't deal well with change, and he lashes out. Not to mention he didn't think Sadie and Kensington were close. Mac looks like an airhead to the general public, and Miller and Sadie are particularly close. She's the mother he always wished he'd had, not the abusive piece of crap that was his reality, and I guess he thinks maybe he's going to be replaced in Sadie's life.

"Actually, I was thinking what a delightful surprise it was to arrive home to." Ryland comes in behind Miller and closes the door before striding up to Mac, pulling her into his arms, and kissing her soundly on the lips. "Hi, honey, I'm home. Shall we fuck to celebrate?"

Mac is so flustered by Ry's attention and words, she's speechless, which gives Max the opportunity he was waiting for. "No, you will not. You can have your turn later." He snatches up the towel Mac dropped and drapes it around her before gathering her up in his arms and striding away. "I will find Mac some clothes. Be ready to debrief in ten minutes, Lathan." He disappears with a protesting Mac in his arms, Dayton following behind them.

"I'm just going to get changed myself," he tells us with a wave.

I start to chuckle as I make my way farther into the room. "Well, that was certainly fun." I drop down onto the sofa and watch as Lathan adjusts himself before picking up his laptop and sitting back down. "You okay there, Lath?" I ask, curious to see what our tech man has to say.

"Ah, yeah, wow. Mac certainly isn't going to put up with anyone's crap, is she?" He sits down again and slides his glasses off his nose, cleaning them before putting them back onto his face.

"No, and are you okay with that?" I ask, interested in his opinion, but before he can answer, Miller grabs Ry by the arm.

"What the fuck was that?" he demands, and Lath and I pause to watch the lovers' spat. Ry is so fucking laid back, I have no idea how he deals with all of Miller's intensity and angst.

Ry shrugs Miller off, and his affable smile drops as he arches one eyebrow at his boyfriend, and just like that, Miller backs off. Seriously, their dynamic is fucking fascinating, but the Turner boys are both dominant men, and learning Miller was mostly submissive with a praise kink was certainly a shock to me. I'm used to it now, but I certainly wouldn't have called it when we first saw them in action at MITHOS and were deciding if we wanted to add them to the team or not. In their professional lives, they are both incredible agents without many shortcomings, but their personal dynamic is the complete opposite of what I thought it would be.

"What? Wouldn't you like her to be the meat in our sandwich?" Ry steps toward Miller, backing him up to the wall. "Imagine her husky voice being the one to tell you you're a good boy and how much she likes it when you please her." Ry's voice drops, and I watch Miller shudder and swallow.

"Well, shit, that just got uncomfortable for all of us. Thanks for that." I break the sexual tension in the room, and I hear Lathan release a sigh of relief. Ryland just flips me off and doesn't take his eyes off of his boyfriend. They are whispering now, and I can see it's still heated, but that's for them to sort out.

Lathan and I ignore them while his fingers run absently across the keyboard. "How long do you think they'll be?" he asks, looking up at the ceiling like he can see through the plaster.

"Who knows? I guess it depends on how long they fight for or if they have hate sex," I tell him, and he grins.

"Who do you think will win? My money is on Mac.

I bet she has him groveling for forgiveness before they even return downstairs."

I sit up and hold out my hand. "I'll take that bet. No way Daddy Max is going to let her get away with that behavior. I bet he has her over his knee as we speak, and her ass will be too sore to sit on when they return."

"Agreed. What are the stakes?"

"Loser cleans the team's primary weapons and fills all the spare magazines."

Lathan grumbles but agrees, just as shouting can be heard from upstairs.

CHAPTER 30

MAXWELL

I struggle to hang onto the thrashing, furious woman in my arms, but her defiance triggers something in me that insists she can't speak to me like that. Having her bent over my desk this morning and her responding so beautifully to my over-bearing nature, despite it being for the cameras, was pure fire for me. I have never had a sub who responded to me like she did. She practically melted under my touch, and although it was supposed to be an act for the cameras, I'm almost certain I saw the real Kens-ington Walsh, one who has had to be in such tight control in every aspect of her life and career that being able to let go like that was freeing for her—or that's how she responded anyway.

She is such an enigma to me. When the guys returned after being recalled by Percy, there was tension in them that I wasn't expecting. Usually, visiting Percy and Sadie eases some of the hardness in my team. Sadie lavishes us with love and home-cooked food, and Percy treats us all like the sons he never had. This time, though, he sprung a team assessment on them by faking a supposed hit. Not only did he fake his death, but it turns out the hitman was a girl *and* his daughter, and it was all a setup.

Ry and I couldn't believe our ears when they told us she was Phantom, one of MITHOS's ghost operatives who was responsible for the hits of some of the nastiest characters the agency has been tasked to get rid of. Each and every one of them was shaken. Lathan was completely intrigued and fascinated, and I thought he was rocking a small crush. Dayton was harboring some serious guilt for what he did to her, and when I saw her, I wasn't surprised. Miller, our resident asshole, was feeling some major hate for her, but it was misplaced because she didn't actually kill her own father. And Bishop? Well, he was seething. He didn't come out and say it, but I could tell he was not happy that we were getting a new member so soon after he joined the team. The chip on his shoulder just got bigger, and I knew he was a train that was about to derail. The only one not affected was Anders, so he was the one I questioned. His response surprised me.

"She's the one, Max. She will fill the hole we so desperately need filled," he said, and then he walked away.

The rest of the team decided that we weren't going

to share that Ry and I were also placed at the school. It was a stupid test that Bishop suggested, and Miller agreed with him for the first time ever. That all went to shit when the first interaction I had with her was a test on me. I made it no secret around town that I am a dominant looking for a submissive, but I also let people overhear me chatting to Anders at his place of employment when I said I liked nothing better than to have a girl at my beck and call, a slave. The network must work quickly, because no more than a few days later, Brock approached me, telling me they had a good candidate coming into the foster home here— someone who had been arrested for prostitution. Imagine my surprise when that turned out to be Kensington Watson. The guys hadn't warned me about the tidy little package she was. Her goth persona stood out amongst the Barbie doll clones that the rest of this town emulated.

Not only that, but I was also stunned when she played along that first time in my office. I considered just letting her fuck me, but that would have been unethical, so I whispered to her who I was. I saw the brief disappointment in her eyes, and I felt like banging on my chest like Tarzan because she was attracted to me, but she just rolled with it and produced such a great performance that I came in my pants just from her grinding on top of me.

I throw her down on the bed and stare at her as she glares at me. I can see she's fuming. The towel is barely covering the interesting parts, and I can't get the thought of the clit ring out of my mind. I just want to lean down and take it into my mouth and give it a good tug. Pain and pleasure are such close companions, and I know how to ride the line perfectly.

"What the fuck, Mac?" I demand, and she scrambles around, getting up on her knees. The towel falls to the bed, exposing her gorgeous breasts with mouth-wateringly pink nipples to my view.

She puts her hands on her hips. "What, Maxwell? What is your fucking problem?" She doesn't back down, and I feel a thrill from the challenge.

When she defiantly dropped that towel, proving to me that I, in fact, did not get a say in her choices, it was like a match to gasoline. Something inside of me lit on fire, and I saw red. It wasn't because she was naked, and it wasn't because she was swimming that way with my teammate—I was actually thrilled that she and Dayton had sorted out their differences—it was because she wasn't buckling under my demands, and she stood up for herself. Our team needs someone who can do that, someone who won't wilt under the pressure we will put on them when we demand that she be shared between us. It's the only way this will work.

"Just because I fucked you doesn't mean you own me," she says again, and I sigh, sitting down on the bed before pulling her into my lap. She tumbles, a yelp of surprise escaping her, and her arms circle my neck to steady herself.

"No, I know, and believe me, I am beyond thrilled that you and Dayton are friends."

She cocks her head to the side, not embarrassed at all about being naked in my lap. I run my hand up and down her thigh soothingly, my fingertips brushing against the round globes of her ass that I itch to make a pretty red with my palm again.

"I'm sorry, I was just surprised, and it's been one hell of a day," I murmur, "and I took my frustration out on you. I didn't want the first time we had sex to be something that will be used as jacking off material for a group of disgusting men."

Her frown changes into a brilliant smile, and she smacks a kiss against my lips, startling me. "Yeah, but it was pretty fucking amazing sex, and I bet they are so fucking jealous of you right now." Her response and change in attitude has me blinking and practically suffering from whiplash.

"That's it?" I ask, and she shrugs.

"Yeah. I mean, I get it. Missions fuck with my head too, and we all need to blow off steam. If you need to yell at me occasionally, that's fine, as long as you're willing to listen to my side of whatever your problem is. I also hear that hate sex is pretty awesome, not to mention makeup sex."

With that statement, the little minx slides off my lap and heads over to my drawers. Pulling open the top one, she rummages around before pulling out a pair of my boxer briefs. She bends over and pulls them up, and I get a mouthwatering view of the pussy I got to taste this morning. I need to get my mouth on it again, but we really need to talk about everything that has happened with the case since we last saw her.

She pulls open the next drawer and rifles through it, obviously not finding what she wants, so she closes it and pulls the next one open. "You know, I think you should be pulling for your brother to become a member of the club as well. Tell them he's interested in Miller. That way we'll get two chances at being kidnapped, not just me."

Out of the third drawer, she pulls out one of my old MITHOS T-shirts. Smiling with pleasure, she tugs it over her head, and her delectable body is now covered from head to toe in my clothing. My cock throbs inside my pants, and as much as I would like to strip them off her, I get a huge rush out of seeing my clothes on her too.

"Does this house have a basement?" she asks randomly, and I nod, frowning.

"Yeah, it does. Why?"

"Maybe you can ask around about getting it reno-vated. Maybe as another bedroom with bars and locks on the doors to make it known that you are both serious about wanting a pet. Hopefully they will have their next auction soon. It's been a while since the last group went missing, and we have no idea if they are still here in the country or if they were auctioned off and sent wherever."

"Lathan has found proof of the temporary auction site, but there are no results, and it doesn't become active until a day before the auction," I explain. "That's when they put up their product range, so to speak. He's monitoring it twenty-four seven, but so far there has been no movement."

"I think their next move will be inviting you to the club. I'm dying to poke around Life Lounge to see if we can find evidence of it."

"Anders hasn't found anything yet, but there are cameras everywhere, and Matthew barely ever leaves. Hopefully between the two of you, you can find something." I stand up and hold out a hand. "Come on, Lathan has something he wants us to see, and we need to do it before Bishop returns."

She allows me to guide her back downstairs. "What was the outcome of the rest of the meeting?" she asks me, unable to hide her curiosity, and I detect a hint of concern as well. I don't blame her, since she was the one who was threatened by that asshole.

"Your father made a promise to Bishop that if he could keep his shit together for the rest of this assignment, then he would give him a trial run as a ghost operative." I feel her hand tighten in mine, and when I look back at her, she's scowling. "You don't like that idea?"

"There are only four of us for a reason, and Bishop is the exact opposite of us. He has an arrogant chip on his shoulder, can't work well with others, and is most definitely not a team player. Even with our ghost status, we still rely on a team of anonymous people to help us with our duties. We also follow instructions and look out for one another. The ghosts are a tight-knit family. We give each other the support a team gives one another, even if it's from the other side of the world. I could call any one of them, and they'd be here if I needed them. There is no way I would ever trust Bishop, and the rest of them are going to ask me about him, and I won't lie. I can't believe Dad is giving in to him."

I stop on the stairs and turn around to face her. She stops a step above me, and it puts her at the perfect height for me to nuzzle her breasts if I wanted to. "I'm not sure if your dad will follow through. I think it was a ploy to get him to keep his head down for the rest of the mission."

She shrugs and looks doubtful. "Yeah, but short of retiring him permanently, what other options does Dad have? Bishop is a loose cannon, and I have no idea how he even made it through the psych eval, let alone the physical with that glass jaw. Dad's going to have to go back and look at his evaluator and follow up on any other agents that person approved to make sure he's the only liability to slip through the cracks."

"We will keep an eye on him, I promise. In fact, that's why we're here. Lathan got some footage of them in the locker room after I kicked him out of my class, and Billy followed him out with a bullshit excuse."

"Alright, let's go and see what Nerdy Sexy has for us, but I'm not ruling out popping Bishop if he becomes problematic," she warns me as I spin around.

The guys and I actually discussed that this

morning after Bishop left before I followed him. We have all come around to Mac's way of thinking. It was just a shock to hear her say it out loud last night, but she is right, and he is way too much of a loose cannon. We just have to bide our time by feeding his ego, and hopefully the promise of ghost status and all the perks that come with it will satisfy him for now.

"Finally," Lathan grumbles as we enter the room. The other six are all there with beers and sodas in front of them. There is a spare beer for me, and one of each type for Kenzie to choose from. She gives Dayton a kiss on the cheek when she selects the soda.

"We need to make this quick. It's getting late, and Mac can't be late again. Martha almost had a meltdown last night," Miller warns, crossing his arms. He is sitting apart from Ry, which is telling.

Usually the two of them are glued to each other in private during a mission. Miller's anxiety levels sometimes get the better of him, and Ry soothes all his rough edges. I guess they are fighting over something, and I can pretty much guarantee it's the beautiful woman in the room. My brother is such a shit stirrer. I know he loves his partner, but they have also wanted a female in their relationship for a while. While I'm not sure forcing Miller to accept Kenzie is the way to get what he wants, it's certainly amusing seeing Miller flounder. Lathan was so right when he said that Kenzie and Miller are similar. Even though he has his personal issues, he is an amazing fucking agent who isn't afraid to do anything to get the job done.

"This is what I caught on camera today. Bishop doesn't know they are there." Lathan presses a key, and a video starts playing.

We gather around so we can all see the screen, much like last night, but Mac and I are behind the couch, and she bumps my hip before leaning against me, getting comfortable. I throw an arm around her shoulders, marveling at how right this all feels. It's kind of natural, and Mac seems to feel it too, even though when the guys returned, they told us she didn't want this any more than we did. It's good to see we can admit we were wrong.

We watch as Bishop slams into the locker room, picks up a football helmet, and throws it against one of the lockers. "Fucking slut whore," he shouts, and Mac snorts.

"Is he talking about me? Man, I really have put a bug up his ass about something. Has he treated all the female agents you tried like that?"

"We've only had one try since he's been with us, and no, they were fucking like rabbits," Anders says dryly, not taking his eyes off the footage.

"It does seem a little extreme to me." My brother leans in. "He's really losing his shit. Did anything happen between the two of you?" he asks Mac, who quickly shakes her head.

"No, unless you count me dropping him during your test," she replies, and Dayton nods slowly.

"You know, that may be enough. He's misogynistic, and his ego is fragile enough for him to be upset about being beaten by a girl."

He slams around the locker room, really taking out his aggression on the equipment. Not five minutes later, Billy follows him in. "Hey, are you okay?" My eyebrows jump at Billy's concern, and I see Bishop react the same way.

"What the fuck do you care?"

"Well, you seem to be wound up, and I hate to see my football player like that. It doesn't work on the field if we're all blocked, if you know what I mean." Billy is vague, and I see Bishop shake his head.

"No, I don't know what you mean."

"Well, there seems to be some pent-up tension within you. You obviously don't like the family you are staying with. I was just going to offer you an outlet for some of that aggression."

Bishop stops slinging stuff around and tilts his head. "I would have thought you would want aggression on the football field."

Billy grins. "Well, yeah, but not this kind. Your mind isn't on the game. What would you say if I offered you a little way to blow off some steam so you could get rid of some of your tension and focus on winning?" He's vague, but Bishop takes the offer.

"I'd say I was listening."

"There's a party on Friday night, and we have something that can make the girls very friendly. If you wanted to take your anger out on the new goth girl, well, I can guarantee she'll cooperate, and no one will think anything of it because she's literally a whore. You just have to make sure you dispose of the body when you're done."

"Holy fuck!" The whisper slips out as we wait for Bishop's reaction.

He thinks about it for a moment. We can see him running it over in his head before a smile slips across his lips. "It sounds like you may have the answer to all my needs." He holds out his hand, and they shake. Lathan turns the video off.

"Does anyone else get the feeling that Bishop wasn't acting?" Dayton asks slowly after a moment of digesting what we just saw.

"I do." Mac puts her hand up and wrinkles her nose. "I can't believe that asshole. Now I have to worry about date rape on top of kidnapping and sex trafficking."

"We won't let it get that far," I assure her, "and let's wait until he gets home. If he tells us about it, then he's still fully involved in this mission, and if he doesn't, then we know he's gone rogue and he will have to be dealt with."

"Dibs." Mac's and Miller's voices mix together as they both volunteer to make sure a rogue agent gets put down.

"Let's just wait. I still have my doubts. This may be another angle he's decided to work, because date rape drugs sound like something a sex trafficking ring may have a hand in. Billy is looking like another link," I tell them.

"That's no surprise considering who his dad is. I'm going to do a little search of the county morgues to see how many other rape victims turn up. It sounds like the football team has quite the scam going on." Lathan's fingers fly across his trusty keyboard.

"Hey, Dayton, can you grab your bag out of the car? I need to get dressed again so I can get home for dinner. I also kind of don't want to be here when Bishop gets home. I'm not sure I could look him in the eye without killing him," Mac requests.

Dayton gets up and grabs his duffle bag that he left next to the door and hands her a pile of clothes. She doesn't even wait to strip and put the old ones back on. The room is silent as we're mesmerized by Mac, but we quickly snap out of it when she picks up my shirt and hands it to me.

"I'm keeping the underwear for now. Alright, I'm ready," she announces.

"Good thinking. Take Miller with you. I can hear his teeth grinding from here." Ryland grabs his boyfriend's hand and squeezes it. "You can't kill him, okay? We need to see how this plays out first. Just because you don't like him doesn't mean he's gone bad."

Miller grunts and stands up. "Fine, you can drive us home, that way we won't be late." He gestures to himself and Mac, and I see both hers and Ry's eyebrows jump in surprise, but my brother quickly scrambles to his feet. "I'll get my keys."

"Be careful tomorrow night. Neither Anders,

Dayton, nor I can be there. It's highschoolers only," I warn Mac, and she blows me a playful raspberry.

"I'll be fine. Trust me. I have somewhat of a tolerance to date rape drugs even if he does manage to slip one into my drink, but let me know which side of the scale he decides to fall on, because I want to be prepared, and I need to advise Dad. If he doesn't tell you, Dad will put out a termination order on him. Even if I wasn't the one he planned to betray, when you betray an agent, and you betray everything MITHOS stands for."

The room falls into a contemplative silence as we wait for Ry to return. When he does, they quickly leave. Mac waves to us all and gives us a saucy wink. I look around the room as the door closes behind them, happy to see that the remaining members of my team look just as smitten by the princess as I am. This is going to work. We just need to deal with Bishop and this assignment, and then we can work on convincing her to stay.

CHAPTER 31

The ride home is quiet. Ry's car is lovely and lush, and I settle into the leather back seat while he and Miller talk quietly during the drive. I think about what I just saw, and while I am disappointed, I'm not surprised. I saw that coming a mile away. It doesn't happen often, but when an agent goes off the rails, it's usually in a spectacular way. I'll wait and see if he shares that conversation with his team, but I very much doubt he will. Bishop is out for my blood. I could see the manic light in his eyes when Billy gave him a solution to his supposed problem.

I'm actually incredibly surprised that he didn't blow the rest of the case. I guess there's still a small piece of goodness left in him that wants to save the kids being taken, but is it enough to keep him from a bullet? Only the next twenty-four hours will tell.

Ryland drops Miller and me at the end of the driveway, and we both walk up it together in silence. It's not uncomfortable, and there's still an underlying tension between us, but it's nothing like what I have with Bishop. I just need to leave Miller be and let him work out his own issues. Who am I to force him to face them?

Martha is at the sink when the two of us walk in. "Ah, good, you're on time today. Go wash up, and Mac, can you please come back down and help me with dinner?"

I smile at her and do as she asks. Miller and I separate at his door without a word, but I'm okay with that. We both have shit on our minds. I dump my backpack in the bedroom, which is empty of Jessica, and return to the kitchen.

"Where is everyone?" I ask Martha as I start to peel the carrots she pointed at.

"Jessica is at cheerleading practice, and I asked the rest to give us some space." Martha sighs and turns to look at me. "I heard what happened at school today. Are you okay?" I blink at her for a couple of moments, surprised by the compassion I'm receiving from this woman. She's been fairly distant since I arrived, and this feels like a one-eighty.

I shrug but don't answer, instead looking down at the carrot peels. "Ah, yeah, I guess."

She places her hand on my arm, stopping me, and I look up. "I know life before us wasn't easy, but I want you to know I'm here for you if you ever need to talk. I called the principal and complained, but he said that without any evidence, he can't punish anyone."

I feel my eyebrows jump. I hadn't expected Martha to care. "It's whatever." I shrug and look away from her.

"We've all had to do something we're not proud of to get by. If you work hard and get good grades, you can make something of yourself. Okay?"

I nod, and she passes me some potatoes.

"Here, can you peel some of these? I want to make some mashed potatoes to go with the chicken and beans."

I take the offered vegetables, and we work in a comfortable silence. I run over everything that I've learned today in my head. I'm pleased with how things are going. Sometimes it can take me weeks before I discover anything that can help me with a mission. Working with a team does have its advantages. They are not bad on the eyes either. This temporary arrangement is working out better than I could have ever imagined. I'm also really looking forward to my first shift at Life Lounge on Saturday. Hopefully I can do some snooping and find evidence of the sex club.

The next day is much like the previous one. I'm teased and bullied by a majority of the student body, but the classes go quickly, and before I know it, it's time to head home again. I didn't expect to see Miller, but to my surprise, he and Jessica are on the bus back to the foster home with me and the younger teens.

Cassie chuckles at my surprise. "With the party tonight, Miller and Jessica will be model students and do their homework and assist with dinner. They usually ply Martha with a glass or two of wine so she sleeps extra heavily and doesn't hear them sneak out."

"Are you guys going to come to it as well?" I ask, and Cassie screws up her nose.

"No thanks, that's not our kind of scene."

The sisters chime in their agreement.

"You be careful, Mac, weird things happen at those parties too. I've heard of date rape, and one girl even turned up dead in a field after one of those parties," Stephanie hisses quietly. Thankfully the noise of the bus covers our conversation nicely.

"And the town just turns a blind eye to all of this?" I shake my head, still unable to understand adults not giving a shit.

"The Divinity of Morality Club contains some high-powered town officials—the police chief, pastor, school counselor, business owners, and even the coast guard captain. I even heard someone whispering at work that the mayor has used their clubs. If anyone who is not actually in it uses their club, then it has to be the ultimate blackmail material if you have a family or are respected in town." Sally has a point, and she seems to be talking to me again, or at least a little less frosty.

The conversation stops as we arrive home. Sure enough, the girls are right, and Miller and Jessica seem to have this coordinated dance they play with Martha who is thrilled to have their attention. They make her sit and put her feet up and pour her a glass of wine while telling her that she is overdue for some spoiling. She just twitters at their attention and gladly accepts it, putting on some asinine reality show while Miller and Jessica take over dinner. I just shake my head and go upstairs. They obviously have a plan, and who am I to interrupt it?

"Oh, Mac, dear," Martha calls out to me, and I stop on the first step. "Fridays are very casual around here. James has his weekly poker night and won't be home until late, and the kids tend to take turns cooking, giving me a break."

"Okay, thanks for letting me know. I'll just put my stuff upstairs and go see what's happening in the kitchen."

Dinner is a noisy but fun affair. Even Jessica puts her hostility away as we all make our own burgers and wait for the fryer to make the fries golden and crispy. We all join Martha in the lounge for a movie afterward. It's one I've seen before about a boy wizard, but it's fun, and we turn it into a game, saying all the famous lines from it. Jessica and Miller keep filling Martha's glass with wine, so by the time the movie wraps up, she's snoring. Sally shakes her awake, and she and Stephanie help her to her room, while Jessica hurries upstairs. We leave the boys to watch the next movie in the series, and Cassie stays with them. Miller stops me before I can enter my room.

"Martha will be out like a light, so when we leave, we can go down the front stairs. James won't be back until late, but we will have to climb up the tree when we come home. Ry is going to pick us up at the end of the driveway in about half an hour. Make sure you're ready. We can't take the bike because Jessica will ask questions."

"Okay, see you soon," I tell him. He looks like he's going to say more, but he snaps his mouth shut and runs up the stairs to the attic without looking backward.

Jessica has on a pair of skinny jeans and a cute top, and she is sitting on her bed, pulling on her shoes, when I walk into the room. She looks up at me and studies me closely before sighing.

"Shit, I'm only telling you this because you look like a pathetic mess. Be careful who you take a drink from or get cornered by. Some of them aren't very nice, and they don't like to hear the word no." With that, she grabs her little bag of makeup and goes out to our shared bathroom, leaving me to get dressed in peace.

Well, maybe Jessica isn't so bad after all. She didn't need to say anything. Maybe she's just trying to fit in, and in this cesspool of a town, I guess being an asshole is what works.

I hurry and get ready, wearing a pair of skinny jeans, a long-sleeved, fitted top, and my faithful combat boots. I pull my long black hair into a ponytail, and when Jessica returns, I take my own turn to put my makeup on. Before long, we're all walking down the driveway to wait for Ryland. Jessica's arm is in Millers, and she's talking excitedly about who's going to be at the party.

I listen absently, more focused on my first shift at the bar tomorrow night, though I should probably get my head in the game. To my surprise, Bishop came home and told the team about Billy's offer, but not that it was directed at me. He kept that to himself, substituting some random girl instead. That pretty much sealed his fate. They told him to go along with the plan in case it was a test from Billy, and that it might be another lead for the ring. He has to be getting his drugs from somewhere, and he might help facilitate the kidnappings. We want Billy to trust Bishop. Bishop also said Billy hinted at being able to get easy and free pussy whenever he wanted, and he didn't have to work for it like you did with high school chicks.

Ryland's car is waiting for us at the end of the drive, so we hurry up. When we get there, I slide into the back with Jessica, and Miller gets into the front.

"Hey there." Ry turns around to smile at us. "You ready to have some fun?" He's looking at me, but it's Jessica who replies.

"So ready."

I don't think Ryland means the kind of fun that Jessica thinks he does.

"Come on, we're going to be late," Miller grumbles, back to his surly self. The guy gives me whiplash. I must remember to ask Ryland if he feels the same way.

In the dark, I kind of lose track of where we are, but we pass the school and drive around the oval at the back. There is a parking lot back there, and about a dozen cars sit in the lot. Ryland pulls into a spot, and we get out before he presses the button to lock his expensive car.

"Don't people realize there's a party going on?" I ask, surveying all the cars. Miller and Jessica have started walking toward the woods, but Ryland hangs back and walks with me.

He shakes his head. "Mostly yes, but they don't care. It's another one of those weird, small, tight-knit community things. The adults pretend they don't know and never attended such a thing when they were in high school, and the teenagers pretend the adults don't know and they are being sneaky."

"So Martha and James know we're sneaking out?" I ask, and he shakes his head.

"James probably does, but I doubt Martha would be okay with her foster kids going to this kind of party, or at least that's the impression I get. Martha is a good, church going citizen, and she frowns at lewd and animalistic behavior. There is a circle of women who have typical, judgmental, small-town mentalities."

We're quiet as we walk a little farther. I can hear the faint echo of music, the throbbing bass loud in the silence of the woods.

"Hey, can you do me a favor?" Ryland asks. "Michelle and Lucy have their eye on Lathan. He's freaking out because he's a nice guy and he hates to let people down. If you could latch onto him, maybe be seen making out with him, then they might leave him alone."

I stop and raise an eyebrow. "Are you pimping me out?" I ask dryly, and his mouth drops open, and he shakes his head vehemently.

"Fuck no, I just don't want Lathan to be put in an awkward position and blow the case. I wasn't suggesting anything." He sounds stressed, so I decide to let him off the hook.

I chuckle and nudge him with my hip. "I'm just fucking with you. Of course I'll help Nerdy Sexy. It's no hardship."

Ryland glares at me in the low light. Thankfully the moon is bright above us so we can at least see each other and where we're going on this path. He steps toward me, but Miller's voice interrupts whatever he was going to say.

"Hurry the fuck up," he grouches.

"You will keep," Ryland promises me, and then he grabs my hand, hurrying after the other two.

The party is in full swing when we reach the clearing and the abandoned ranger's house—not that it looks all that abandoned now. There are party lights strung up on the verandah and lots of seating for everyone. The fire pit in the middle of the clearing is blazing brightly, music is pumping out of some speakers set up on either side of the patio, and there are people everywhere. I recognize some from school, and there are others that are unfamiliar and quite a few who look like they may be college-aged kids.

Jessica leaves Miller, spying her friends on the other side of the bonfire, and she quickly hurries over to join them. Miller waits for Ryland and me to catch up as Lathan and Bishop approach us. Lathan looks relieved, and Bishop just seems bored, but he quickly smiles when he sees me looking at him.

"I feel like we got off on the wrong foot. Here, I grabbed you a drink." He holds it out, and I can feel a ton of eyes on me, not just the ones in the immediate circle.

Internally, I roll my eyes. Shit, I haven't even been here five minutes, and he's already trying to get rid of me. Instead, I smile brightly and take it.

"Thanks. Now who wants to dance with me?" I ask without taking a sip of my drink.

CHAPTER 32

"**L**athan will." Surprisingly, it's Miller who shoves Lathan at me. Nerdy Sexy stumbles, not expecting the shove, but he quickly recovers.

"Absolutely, let's go." He takes me by my drink free hand and drags me over to the crowd of partying kids and the makeshift dance floor. He pulls me into his arms, and I wrap my empty hand behind his neck. "Pretend to take a drink, Bishop is watching," he whispers in my ear, and I throw my head back and laugh before pressing the bottle to my closed mouth and pretending to swallow. "What an asshole. He just smiled when you did that. I want to kill him myself."

"Is he still looking?" I ask as Lathan sways our bodies in time to the music. He's a pretty damn good dancer, and I'm getting into it.

"No, Billy just called him away."

"Good." I sidestep us until we're on the opposite side of the dancing crowd. Once we reach the edge, I tip the drink into the bushes. "In ten minutes, you and I are going to stumble inside the house, and we're going to find a room where we are going to make out like crazy. That way, Bishop or any of his new cronies can't corner me, thinking I'm drugged, and I won't have to injure anyone and blow our case. After about half an hour of that, I will pretend to pass out, and you can ask Ry to borrow his car so you can take me home."

I watch him swallow, but he quickly nods his agreement.

"Great. Now pucker up, there's someone heading in our direction, and she seems to be on a mission for your ass." I can see Michelle over his shoulder. Her eyes are narrowed on us, and she is pushing her way through the crowd.

Lathan goes to look, but I just grab the back of his head and pull his mouth down to mine. I run my tongue along the seam of his lips, and he quickly opens, allowing me entry. Our tongues tangle, and he tastes like the same sweet beverage that Bishop tried to get me to drink. Hopefully his was drug free though. His arms tighten around me, pulling me closer to his body as he takes control of the kiss. It's perfect—perfect pressure, perfect amount of tongue, perfect amount of nipping and sucking—and I find myself dazed and seduced when a hand yanks me away from him.

"Listen here, you whore. We don't want sluts like you ruining all the good men in this town," she sneers, and I slap at her hand. "Why don't you go back from whatever hovel you crawled out of?"

"Aww, poor baby. Can't find a man of your own, so you have to try to steal ones who are already taken?"

"Taken?" she screeches. "He's not your boyfriend."

I scoff. "No, why would I want to tie myself down? But he is my Mr. Right Now, and I like them a little shy and nerdy, so why don't you run off so I can corrupt him a little? You can have him when I'm done. I'm sure you'll even thank me. I'll teach him things you could never have dreamed of."

She lifts her hand to slap me, but I stop her.

"Don't even think about it unless you want me to beat your ass. Now fuck off. I'm going to take Lathan inside now and rock his world." I sway a little in case she is in on the drugging plan. I'm not entirely sure if this is one big town conspiracy, or if there are a couple of games in play. Michelle and Lucy live with Sophie's family. Supposedly, they are exchange students. Lathan is doing some digging into both of their backgrounds but hasn't gotten anything yet.

Pushing her hard, I grab Lathan and weave our way into the ranger's house. When we get just inside the door, I pull him toward me, and he crowds me against the wall and kisses me hard. I'm so distracted by how good his mouth and roaming hands feel, I almost forget to scope out the crowded living area, but when I look over his shoulder, I just about choke on his tongue in surprise. There is a rousing game of strip poker going on at a big dining table. It looks like everyone is having a bad day, because a majority of the people are mostly naked. At a little coffee table in front of some battered sofa are lines of coke, and people are handing cash over to a guy to sit and snort a line. In the corner of the room, I can see a guy getting a blow job from not just one girl, but two, while making out with another one standing next to him.

"Oh my fucking god. This is a high school party?" I blink at Lathan, and he chuckles.

"Yeah, ecstasy was given out as a party favor to the first hundred that turned up." He fishes around in his pocket and pulls out a little bag with a small pill in it. "Not many people say no."

Billy and his cronies walk in from the back of the house. What's surprising is that Bishop isn't with them. The crowd looks up, and all the dudes cheer, and some of the half naked chicks from the poker game stand up and wave them over to seats. The football players join the poker game, hauling the naked girls into their laps, but Billy leans against the wall. He doesn't hide the fact that he's staring at us.

"Okay, showtime," I tell Lathan.

He grabs my hand and leads me back toward where I assume a bedroom is. The thought of lying on one of those beds when I know exactly what goes on in this house is repulsive, but we need to sell the show. We pass Billy, and I giggle and stumble slightly. With lightning quick reflexes, he reaches out and steadies me.

"Hey there, you look like you've had too much to drink," he says.

"Nope, I've only had one," I slur, and he frowns.

"One?" He looks at Lathan. "Hey, man, that's not cool. She must have been drugged or something. Maybe I should take her home." Wow, now that was not the angle I thought he'd take. He'd almost seem decent if I hadn't watched the video.

"Fuck off," Lathan tells Billy. "She's fine. Don't be a cockblocker, man."

We push past him, and when I turn back to look, Billy's glaring after us and pulling his phone out of his pocket. Lathan and I stumble into the room, but I can't help dropping the act for a moment as I look around. There's a bed in the middle of the room, but hanging above it is a damn stuffed deer head with its giant antlers hanging out over the bed.

I giggle and jump up onto it. "Look at this. Do you think people use it to hang on to?" I grab hold of the antlers and turn back to look at Lathan, who smiles indulgently at me, when I hear a click and the antlers move. The bed shudders and slides to the side, exposing a stairway that leads under the building.

I'm speechless, but thankfully Lathan reacts quickly. He closes the bedroom door and takes out his phone.

"Mac and I found a secret passage under the house. We're going to check it out." He pauses as he listens to whoever he's talking to. "We don't have time to wait. Billy is already being too nosy. We don't want anyone to come searching for us and not find us in here."

He holds out a hand to help me down, and then we take the steps.

"Okay, fine, but you'll have to catch up," is the last thing he says before he hangs up. "Where do you think this goes?" he asks me, turning on the flashlight on his phone, which gives us a little bit of light. He also reaches behind him and pulls out a gun, offering it to me.

"Wow, I didn't even notice that was there," I tell him as I take it, and he grins.

"We were a little busy playing tonsil hockey."

I playfully pout. "Yeah, and I was hoping we would at least get to third base before we were interrupted."

He stops and yanks me toward him. "Raincheck?" he asks, looking very serious, and it's all I can do not to melt into his arms like an idiot.

"Absolutely," I promise before we continue on our way.

The tunnel has clearly been down here for a while. It's well-built and well-traveled if the state of the ground has anything to say, but it's musty and dank, and I wrinkle my nose in distaste.

"What do you think this is for?" I ask.

"I bet it has nothing to do with the ranger, that's for sure," Lathan replies.

I'm not sure how far we've gone, Lathan's gun held

out in front of me just in case, but we've probably been walking for fifteen minutes. Just when I think it's most likely an old access tunnel from prohibition times or something, the tunnel opens out into a large space. It continues on the opposite side, but we stop so Lathan can aim his light around. The two of us stare at what's in front of us.

"Nope, definitely can't see the ranger needing cells like this, can you?" he says dryly, and I shake my head, stepping forward to get a better look. I don't get very far before I stumble over something. I right myself as Lathan shines his light at my feet so we can see what I tripped on.

"Oh fuck," I mutter as noises come down the tunnel we just left.

Lathan and I spin to face what's coming, my gun held at the ready, when Ryland and Miller appear. Miller has a high-powered flashlight, and Ryland is holding his own weapon. Miller shines his light around, both of them looking as surprised as I was, before finding the same thing I tripped over.

"What the fuck, Mac?" Miller barks as the four of us stare down at the wide open, clearly lifeless eyes of Bishop.

"Hey, she didn't do it." Lathan jumps to my defense, as does Ryland.

"We didn't hear a gunshot, you idiot." He drops his own gun and looks down at his teammate with sadness. "Well, I guess that solves one problem at least."

"Yeah, but now we have another." I sigh, looking down the tunnel that we haven't been down yet. "We saw no one, so who did this and why? Did he blow his cover, or was he just in the wrong place at the wrong time?"

AFTERWORD

Thank you all for reading Spies Like Me I can't tell you how much it means to me. I hope you enjoyed the book. It would be super awesome if you could leave a review wherever you bought it, because I love to hear what you thought of the story.

I'll get back to the MITHOS world later in the year. I've got a couple of other series to wrap up first. Keep an eye on my Facebook group for all things Lexie.

In the mean time why don't you check out one of my other series. You can find everything on my website at www.lexiewinston.com

ACKNOWLEDGMENTS

To my cover designer Natasha of Dazed Designs. Once again she nailed my vision perfectly.

Thank you to Jess at Elemental Editing for being the flexible wonderful person that you are. My book is pretty and readable thanks to you

Thank you to Chloe Campbell, Belinda Jamieson, Caroline Mallika and Lindsey Morgan for your name suggestions so many months ago. You have no idea how helpful it was.

Kerry Keller. You are my rock of ages. Thank you without you I could not have finished this book. You helped me over every hump and hurdle I had when I got stuck with the storyline. You are the bestest alpha a girl could want.

And lastly to you guys the readers. I love what I do, and probably would do it regardless if anyone read them or not, but you guys make it that much sweeter so thank you.

MITHOS goes on the back burner for the next couple of months while I wrap up a couple of other series but I can't wait to dive back in. I hope you hang around to find out what happens to Kenzie and the guys.

Until next time, happy reading!

Lexie